GRANDFATHER GHOST

ANTHONY W. EICHENLAUB

ISBN: 978-1-950542-21-5

oakleafbooks.com

Cover Art by: Anthony W. Eichenlaub

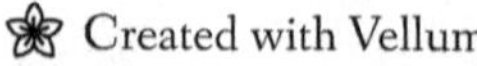 Created with Vellum

To those who strive to leave this world a little bit better for the next generation.

CHAPTER ONE

As FAR AS Ajay Andersen could tell, the three most secure computer systems in the state of Minnesota were the communications systems that connected the governor's residence to the National Guard, the Mall of America food court after the hamburger incident, and the internal network of the new Paul Bunyan Middle School in Bemidji, where he was now headed.

Ajay walked his lazy bloodhound Garrison, cursing the perfectly seasonable cool December weather. Fat, wet flakes fell, making an uneven hazard of crumbling sidewalks. He placed his cane carefully on the packed snow, knowing that a wrong step might land him on his ass or possibly in a hospital. It was the least of the many concerns that plagued his retirement.

It amazed Ajay how sometimes technology stepped backward in the name of progress. Before the Internet, networks were strange, isolated things. They shuttled information quickly through a local campus or top-secret facility but denied access to the outside world. Networks were tools used to command screaming dot-matrix printers or to send opaque memos to a thousand employees in the blink of an eye.

Isolated networks were before Ajay Andersen's time, despite his advanced years. Once someone had the idea to connect networks together into one worldwide monstrosity, humanity thought it would never go back. In a way, it didn't, but worldwide networks weren't secure. The Age of Honesty saw quantum computing break all encryption. Connected systems were compromised systems.

This morose line of thinking occupied Ajay as he snipped the links of the fence outside the middle school campus, hours after dark in the middle of the annoyingly productive snowstorm.

"This is a ridiculous amount of security for a middle school," he whispered to Garrison. The place's security was part of the reason Ajay felt comfortable sending his granddaughter Kylie there, even though she resented the very idea of non-virtual classes.

He felt it was better for her development to have real interactions with human beings. Maybe one day she would forgive him for his old-fashioned ways.

"People stink," she always said.

It took him a while to realize that she meant it literally. Kylie grew up in a lab, where all of her associations had been virtual, except for her sister. Maybe that was why she didn't know how to make friends. It might also be that the computer half of her brain was slowly damaging the tissue around it.

After clipping one last link, Ajay removed his glove and activated the dim glow of his fidget computer. The device was a new model, but one he had selected for performance rather than glamor. Loops of metal fit over the fingers of his left hand and displayed a flickering diagram over the back of his liver-spotted flesh. Augmented data appeared in the slim half-moon glasses perched on the bridge of his nose. He needed his cheaters to read, but they also helped him interact with the fidget.

On his screen, he tracked the chatter of a dozen moving signals. "Drones," he cursed. He had expected they would be shut down due to the snowstorm. They weren't. This was a problem.

Garrison gave no response, which Ajay took as grudging acceptance of the absolutely ridiculous level of Paul Bunyan Middle School's security protocols. Ajay needed proximity to initiate his hack on the isolated network.

This was a matter of life and death.

Kylie wasn't any ordinary twelve-year-old kid. She and her sister Isabelle were the oldest and strongest result of a program that enhanced the brains of children. Through new-fangled biotech, wild neuroscience, and an utter lack of ethics, the Haveraptics Corporation had developed a number of enhanced children able to connect to and control wireless computers with a thought. Kylie and Isabelle could also alter their own brain chemistry and shut down or change parts of their minds. It was terrifying tech to put in a developing child, and Ajay still sought a way to mitigate it and give her a normal life.

His best hope was Silas Cardoso, an old colleague with connections in biotech. Ajay had given the old man the scans and instructed him to find a fix, but that had been months ago, and he hadn't heard anything. Every time he thought about it, Ajay doubted he had done the right thing.

For now, he only needed to make sure nobody found Kylie.

That was why, under the snow-white glow of a Minnesota winter, Ajay had taken Garrison for a walk so that he had an excuse to be close to the school. The alerts he had installed on her records during the last parent-teacher conference had fired, showing that someone had accessed Kylie's records.

He needed to find out who.

The drones schooled like fish. A swarm of them could maintain uniform spacing, covering an optimal amount of ground with their sensors. Fortunately, with the bad weather, their sensor coverage was sporadic. They were stretched too thin.

Ajay tied Garrison to the fence and pocketed the wire cutters. His coat caught as he squeezed through the hole, but he tore it free. "Stay here, Gare," he said to his dog.

His heart thrummed in his chest. The glory of a good hack vibrated his old bones. There was something thrilling about being somewhere forbidden. Ajay had worked for the government during his long career, hacking whatever the NSA told him to hack. The thrill may have been muted back then—with only the occasional excitement of taking down a foreign national or even retaliating for the digital intrusions of a non-governmental group. He'd been a digital hitman, a clever solution to a problem many didn't take seri-ously until it was too late.

Now, in retirement, he was a free agent. The NSA had fallen, broken apart, and been absorbed into other agencies. He'd left his government work behind, bitter at the way he'd been used, and swore to only use his skills for good.

Mostly.

Ajay checked his fidget again. Its blue light flickered across his cheaters and danced across the falling snow.

He ran a hand through his white hair. Natural camou-flage, unlike his light brown skin. That skin made him stand out far more than he wanted in this northern climate, though not as much as it had when he was young. The influx of scientists and migrant workers in the area brought a wide variety of colors and shapes. Perfect for hiding in plain sight.

Perfect for fleeing the corporations who would harm his granddaughters.

Ajay pressed himself under the left front leg of an enor-mous blue ox statue. With a gesture of his left hand, he ran the same protocol he'd used once before to mimic a teacher's work device, hoping that the real device wasn't present already on the system.

It wasn't.

Connected.

Ajay took a moment to check his traps.

His hearing aid clicked with an incoming call. He ignored it.

Hacking wasn't a digital battle of wills. Not exactly. A good hack was won with preparation as much as ingenuity.

He'd programmed his routines for weeks before making his first attempt. Months, even. Once he had placed his payload on the system, it sat invisible for weeks before testing the merest tweak of surveillance. He couldn't afford to get caught. That would defeat the purpose of living in this frozen wasteland of northern Minnesota.

One routine checked a single row in a single database every day. This, on its own, would not be enough. Every read of the database was registered in an encrypted vault. That vault was locked with powerful obfuscation measures in addition to its encryption. Quantum computing destroyed all illusions of rock-solid computer privacy, but things could still be hidden in plain sight. In this case, the obfuscation came in the form of labeling the database Lunch Menu Experiments.

Why did a middle school need such privacy?

Ajay appreciated it nonetheless. If he hadn't been able to keep Kylie's data private, he would have had to go through more drastic means to keep her hidden. Her father's company still searched for Ajay's granddaughters, even after their parents died tragically last year.

No, Haveraptics only really searched for Isabelle. They'd experimented on the older sister with their neurotech, only catching Kylie when their viral delivery survived longer than it should have.

His earpiece clicked again. He ignored it.

Ajay initiated a procedure to penetrate the next line of defense. He was in the public layer already, masquerading as Ms. Barret, Kylie's least pleasant teacher. There was plenty to see in the public layer, especially as a teacher, but what he needed was login data from much deeper in the admin network.

He ran the routine as a gust of wind blew wet snow down the back of his coat.

Alarm subsystems flared. He swiped them away by directing their output into a bit bucket. When more arose, he executed a quick program to do the same. His routine hummed, touching each file in the enormous middle school network. American History flew past in his screen, along with early lessons of algebra mixed with strangely politicized versions of reproductive health.

A second wave of alerts flared, but they wouldn't die so easily. Ajay rerouted them to the Phys Ed server, where the slow processing would buy him more time. Working on his tiny glasses strained his old eyes, but he squinted through it. Access opened, and he took it.

Operator.

As operator, Ajay could make changes to the curriculum. He could change schedules and erase merits. There were so many merits to erase. Ajay resisted the urge to glance at Kylie's record. Had she stood out too much? He had told her to be normal, but she wasn't normal.

She wasn't the sort of kid to stay unnoticed, which was part of his problem.

Ajay used his new operator status to swim through seas of data, executing algorithms that burned the trail behind him. It removed Ms. Barret's identity from his public access and made changes to the Lunch Menu entries that recorded his previous access. This wasn't hard, but even these manual changes were logged in another obfuscated and encrypted database.

Ajay set his sights on the Hallway Poster Approval Database, which contained the next level of tracking.

The system burned with alerts, from the base code at the root of the system all the way up to the user-level interface. If any teachers huddled in their cold classrooms on this Thursday night, working late to grade assignments, they might notice the whole network slowing to a crawl from the sheer number of messages flying into Ajay's nets. He caught them all, then redirected, rewrote, and reconfigured each through procedural masking. If even one of them got loose, it would fire a message to the system admin, revealing the attack and uncovering both Kylie and himself.

But Ajay was too good to let that happen.

A bead of sweat formed on his brow. With a swipe of two fingers, he slashed the alerts out of the way. The running procedures would handle those, and he needed to concentrate.

His hearing aid clicked again, but this time he answered it. "Eh?"

"Papa?" It was a girl's voice. Not Kylie.

Sashi? He almost asked it, but his daughter was dead. Gone forever in a destructive scan meant to help her daughters recover from the changes in their brains. He had watched her die, but this... The display hovering over his left hand quavered. "Who is this?"

But as soon as he asked it, he knew the answer.

"Papa, you have to leave," said Isabelle. She sounded so old.

"How do you know where I am?" he asked. Maybe it had been her in the middle school's network. He'd done everything he could to hide Kylie, but that was nothing against Isabelle's command of the computing networks. If she was trying to find them, she could do it.

He hadn't known she was trying, and the idea of it brought a lump to the back of his throat.

His display flared red, flashing a dozen warnings at once. In a panic, he cleared them all, escalated the attack, and fired a barrage of counter procedures. "Isabelle," he said when air returned to his lungs. "How have you been?"

"There's going to be too much activity in Bemidji," Isabelle said. "You have to leave town tonight. And never come back."

Ajay scrambled to recover access, but his operator level authority was faltering. Something in the system was shutting him out piece by piece. "Your sister needs stability. She has friends here."

"Friends never did me any good."

"You never had friends," Ajay snapped. He was right, but far crueler than he had any right to be. Something about her hard voice set him on edge. She was seventeen, but her words tripped over gravel like an aging rocker.

"I had my sister," she said.

Ajay was silent for a long time. He regained his operator access by sending a coded message to the root authority. Then he spliced the admin password file into the encryption engine. Would they have reused the same encryption they used for the obfuscated databases?

The systems opened, and he had everything.

"I'll keep her safe," he promised Isabelle.

"I know you'll try."

There wasn't a hint of accusation in the tone of her voice, but Ajay heard it anyway. He had once promised to keep all of them safe, including Sashi. She was dead, Isabelle was untraceable, and Kylie was in hiding. He could make an argument that two of those were something like safe, but Sashi was still dead.

He scrubbed his presence from the databases. All records of his intrusion would disappear when he was gone. Then, he scanned the tools he'd buried deep within the system, coiled into the machine code. Who had touched Kylie's records? He had to check, even though he now knew it was likely Isabelle.

But it wasn't Isabelle. A lone record sat unscrubbed, revealing the identity of the person who had cracked admin access in the middle school database, changed a single grade in a single file, then erased almost every sign of intrusion.

"You won't like what you find," Isabelle said.

"I don't like it already." He stared at the text on his screen. Kylie's name flashed in dull green. She had been the one to hack her own records.

"You better get home before Kylie."

Why did Isabelle sound so old? She sounded at least thirty. Ajay closed out his connections, verifying again that his intrusion would leave no trace. He erased Kylie's involvement, too, just to be safe. He needed to talk with her about this, but he was not looking forward to it.

"What am I going to find?" he asked Isabelle.

The line clicked, and she was gone.

Ajay ghosted his way past the drones, fetched Garrison, and made his way home through the heavy snow.

Isabelle had been right. He did not like one bit what he found there.

Drunken footprints led up to the doorway of his house, faded into dimples by the blowing wind. A crater graced the side of the sidewalk where someone had fallen—a struggle, maybe. The trail led up to Ajay's door, which stood wide open to the cold wind.

Inside, a man's lifeless corpse sat in Ajay's favorite chair.

"Silas Cardoso," Ajay muttered, recognizing the body. "You son of a bitch."

Kylie Andersen didn't much like in-person events.

In virtual school, she could be whoever she wanted. People didn't see her darker-than-Swedish skin and assume she was Ojibwa or Lakota. In virtual school, she didn't have to worry about whether the slight curl in the end of her shoulder-length dark hair was in fashion or a terrible mistake.

Everything she did in the real world was always a terrible mistake, especially going to the Liam Thompson presentation at the Bemidji State campus for extra credit. He was presenting in the new Thompson Hall, which Kylie thought probably helped boost his already overinflated ego.

"I always knew I would return to Minnesota," said the slender man in the steel gray suit on stage in front of a packed auditorium. Mr. Thompson radiated confidence, and his bright blond hair made him look young, even though Kylie could see the makeup caked on his face to cover the wrinkles in the corners of his eyes. "Even when I was cleaning up the Gulf of Mexico's worst ever oil spill, I had dreams of these great pine forests and crystal-clear lakes."

She needed the extra credit, even though she knew how to change her grades. Grades were much harder in in-person school, and not only because the teachers remembered their students. Virtual school was easy. Every lesson was automatically tailored to the students' skills, so they always learned fast and succeeded. In in-person school, ninety percent of the material was way too easy, and the rest was impossibly hard.

"*People* magazine called me the greatest environmentalist in human history," Mr. Thompson said, "and I owe every bit of that to the Minnesota that made me, from our fabulous boundary waters where I spent countless summers to the old growth forests and even the wetlands."

Papa had told her that making friends was easy. All she had to do was talk to people and they would instantly like her. This was the exact opposite of her experience, but she had to try again or risk hearing the same dull lecture about the importance of integrating into society. As if her very grumpy grandpa ever did anything like that.

To her left was a woman with grayish-blonde hair wearing the drabbest gray cardigan Kylie had ever seen over a flower print dress. Kylie opened her mouth to say something witty about Mr. Thompson's enormous ego, but the lady reminded her of Olivia. Olivia Bjornson had died in front of Kylie over a year ago, but Kylie still heard the old woman's voice in her dreams. It had been a bad time for

Kylie's family. Her mother had murdered her father, then killed herself in a bid to save her daughters. Kylie's sister Isabelle had left, maybe forever.

Her mother's sacrifice had amounted to nothing, which probably just made it a regular suicide. That thought lingered in Kylie's brain, spiraling ever downward and ever darker. It had all been a waste. All that death. Now she lived with Papa in a small town and sat through dreadfully boring lectures by exceptionally pompous white men.

"This guy's full of it," whispered the boy to her right. He had dark skin except for a white patch on his chin, and his black hair was in messy cornrows. He still wore his heavy orange winter coat despite the warmth of the packed auditorium.

Kylie was unprepared for conversation. She had seen the boy in her classes before, but she didn't remember his name. Any communication with him would be awkward because of that, and she couldn't stand it.

Mr. Thompson paced across the wide stage. Behind him, images of felled rainforests scrolled across a gigantic screen. "In the beginning of this millennium, millions of our world's precious forests were being clear-cut for the sake of paper and profit, but we knew there must be a better way."

"I mean, look at him," whispered the boy, "he's got to be what, a hundred years old? He probably caused all those environmental disasters when he invented gasoline automobiles."

Kylie cast the boy a wary look. She couldn't tell if he

was joking. She could never tell if *anyone* was joking. Maybe that's why she didn't have any friends.

On the screens, the ruined forests were replaced with rows upon rows of planted trees. Those faded to be replaced with larger trees with snow-white leaves, interspersed with clusters of human and wildlife habitats. As the trees grew, they became part of a sprawling land where villages lived and worked in conjunction with nature. Kylie couldn't see the exact moment where the video switched from real footage to computer animation, but toward the end, it was definitely fake.

"That's not real, is it?" she whispered to the boy, whose name she still didn't remember.

The woman to her left shushed her, and a chill ran up Kylie's spine. It sounded like the kind of shush she would have gotten from Olivia.

"He's probably making all of this up," said the boy, earning a glare from the woman. "I mean, this guy's uber-rich. Where's the profit in planting trees?"

"Maybe he makes people pay taxes or something," Kylie said, turning to shut out the woman on her left.

"He's not the government."

"My goal was to save the environment from climate change," said Mr. Thompson, "but I brought justice and peace to Brazil as a side effect." The smile that crinkled the corners of the man's eyes made him look like he thought he was very clever. "I suppose everything we do has unintended side effects."

"Like oppressing the native populations," whispered the boy.

Kylie wondered if he had said it for her benefit. Her lineage, if she traced it back far enough, was from India. Not Native American at all. Still, as she watched the video, she noticed a lot of white settler faces in the forest homes. What happened to the native peoples of Brazil?

On the screen, the video faded, replaced by drone footage that Kylie recognized as Chernobyl. The wild had reclaimed both the nuclear power plant and the city, absorbing the man-made structures and making a creepy, surreal world of post-humanity.

"The last centuries have been hard on this world in a number of ways," said Mr. Thompson. "Climate change, mass extinctions, and even nuclear disasters. I've spent the years of my career fighting against this travesty, which is why I led the effort to clean up the world's worst nuclear disaster."

The video faded again, and glass towers rose from the ruins of Chernobyl.

"With my patented techniques, the world's waste sites have been restored to glory." Again, that quirky smile. "Something Russia was eager to pay handsomely for. No longer is Chernobyl humanity's greatest defeat. It's now Russia's crowning achievement."

"I hear their hockey mascot is the two-headed stag," whispered the boy.

Kylie snickered at that. She *had* to figure out what this boy's name was. Concentrating on the hidden part of her brain, she reached out to the fidget attached to the boy's hand.

The man on stage droned on, his voice growing flat and

gray. Beside her, the boy whispered in a staccato rhythm with words that blurred at their edges and faded into the background noise of a hundred pattering signals. Kylie knew better than to push too hard on her abilities. She didn't want to end up like her sister, who had lost herself in the white noise of the wireless world.

Maybe it was better there, where nothing could hurt and everything made sense. It sounded a lot nicer than trying to have a stilted conversation with a nameless boy.

Austin. Austin Giles. She found his name in his device's wide-open registry data calling out to the world from his fidget. The green glow of the device flickered as she gave it a little nudge of appreciation.

She remembered Austin now that she saw his address and birth certificate. He lived only two doors down from Grandpa, and he walked past her house every day on the way to school. Why had he been so hard to recognize? Were her abilities causing localized brain damage, or was she just this bad with people? Thinking about it made her palms sweat with anxiety.

Kylie started to withdraw from his device when a flurry of images washed past. Austin was active in a dozen clubs, including scouting and basketball. He had a big family, with three sisters and two brothers, all older. Last week, he had gone sledding with one of his brothers and saw someone there. It was a boy in the grade above them, and Austin...

"Jason Smit," Kylie whispered.

"What?"

Kylie knew there was emotion in Austin's voice. Was it

anger or delight or exasperation? She couldn't tell. She withdrew from his device, shutting all of the doors behind her.

Swallowing the lump in the back of her throat, she said, "Do you like Jason Smit?"

He pressed his lips together nightly into a line. He turned back to the stage and watched Liam Thompson emote about the amazing experience of being Liam Thompson.

"My dream is to one day build the City of the Future, right here in Minnesota." Another quirky smile brightened the old man's eyes. "All I need to do is find somewhere to do it."

Behind him, an animation showed a vast city rising up from an old growth oak forest. Kylie thought it looked like someplace that would be inhabited by elves, if elves owned flying drone cars and drank mai tais in the comfort of their treetop swimming pools. How would that even work? The demonstration was hazy on details, but the people in the animation looked comfortable enough.

"Does anyone else think Minnesota would be a good place for the most advanced city in the world?"

The crowd erupted in applause.

Lights on the stage faded while Liam Thompson took his bow. The animation played in the background to a standing ovation. Only Kylie and Austin didn't stand until the auditorium lights turned on and people started filing away.

Austin caught up to Kylie as she stepped outside into

the swirling snow. "How did you know about Jason?" he asked once they were reasonably far away from others.

Perfect. Kylie had snooped in his device to avoid the awkward situation of asking his name and ended up with the awkward situation of explaining how she knew so much about him.

"I haven't talked to anyone about it," Austin said. "Is it some sort of girl intuition?"

Kylie kept walking at a brisk pace, despite the slippery sidewalk. "There's no such thing as girl intuition. It's just regular intuition."

"Well—"

"I guessed," she snapped. "But you're too good for him. Jason Smit is a jerk."

"Can I walk home with you?"

Thick snow swallowed the world, leaving Kylie alone with Austin in what could have been the trackless wilds of Minnesota. "You can come over and have hot chocolate," she said, making a tremendous, for her, effort at friendship. "But we can't talk about Jason anymore."

"Deal." He sounded relieved.

They walked side by side, and Kylie wondered if she had finally made a friend or if it was the blowing wind that kept them in companionable silence. Grandpa only lived a mile from the college, so despite the low visibility, the walk wasn't a difficult one. When they needed to cross the last street, they had to wait for a long time as the traffic cleared. There was still a steady stream of people leaving Thompson Hall in their tiny two-person vehicles. Their headlights made the whole world glow. Kylie's head hurt from using her tech during the presentation, and every light she saw had a sharp halo. She'd have a migraine soon, and she wasn't looking forward to it.

Austin followed as she tromped up the steps to her house and pushed through the unlocked door.

Inside, she hung up her coat and motioned for Austin to do the same. "Grandpa doesn't like snow in his house."

After a slight hesitation that Kylie didn't understand, Austin let the coat drop from his shoulders. He was much skinnier than she had guessed. He was taller, too, and once his boots were off, he slouched over to the sofa and sat.

Kylie sat in Grandpa's favorite chair, but nothing felt right. The cushions were configured strangely, and there was a wet spot near the armrest. When she poked at it with a finger, a tiny data key dropped from the armchair's fluffy folds. It must have been Grandpa's, so she tucked it in her pocket so she could give it to him later.

She closed her eyes and drew a deep breath. Her headache thumped in the back of her skull. "That guy sure was full of shit, right?"

"You probably mean to say he was the environmental hero of the twenty-first century," Austin said. "And we're *so* glad he's graced us with his presence here in Minnesota." Even Kylie could detect his sarcasm.

Kylie snorted. "That's what you'll say when you write your paper."

"Well, yeah."

"Not me. I'm going to tell it like it is."

Austin waved that off. "Homework's not about the truth. It's about barfing up what the teacher wants to read."

The back screen door slammed, and Kylie heard Papa Ajay coming in. Garrison, the big bloodhound, plodded through the house with snowy feet and rested his wet jowls on Austin's leg. The boy looked terrified.

Kylie was about to tell him that Garrison was harmless when Papa stepped around the corner with such a look of horror it made her heart hammer in her chest. He waved her up and out of his chair, which was totally unfair.

"Go," choked Papa. He spotted Austin on the sofa and flashed a phony smile. "It's nice to meet you, but please leave."

Kylie finally gathered herself enough to show outrage, but it didn't matter. Papa shuffled Austin out of the room, tromped snow all over the house from his own boots—something she would definitely give him a hard time about later —and then hurried back out into the backyard.

"Bye, then," Kylie said to Austin as he left. So much for making friends.

Liam Thompson loved Minnesota. He really did. Minnesota forged him into what he was: a legend in the environmental movement. His years growing up on the iron range showed him what passion for the environment could do. Passion moved mountains and boiled oceans. He had leveraged that power to build his empire.

He loved Minnesota, but he hated everything about it.

The accents, for one.

"Did I sound like an idiot up there?" he asked as he pulled on his suit coat.

"Frontier doesn't pay me to have an opinion on that, sir," said Tenen Lang, Liam's chief bodyguard. Liam thought he paid Frontier Arms enough to have all the opinions he wanted. Tenen was tall and dark-skinned, with only enough handsome in his rugged features to not stand out among the masses.

"I worked hard to abolish that accent, and now I can

taste it on my tongue every time I speak," said Liam. "It was difficult to stand up there and cultivate it again. I sounded like a damn Canadian."

Tenen's only answer was a quick flash of a smile in the corner of his lips.

Then there was Minnesota's weather. Liam had always hated the cold.

He shrugged on a black wool coat lined with the best winter technology from the most rugged corners of the world. He could have worn the coat and nothing else in the depths of Siberia and been perfectly comfortable, but the current style was to leave the front hanging open, so that's what he did. He, Tenen, and half a dozen other thugs from the Frontier Arms mercenary team made their way out of the auditorium into the driving snow. The wind cut through the open front of Liam's coat and sank deep into his bones.

"You shouldn't fly in this weather, sir," said Tenen.

Liam would fly if he wanted. "I didn't invest billions in drone tech to drive on poorly maintained roads." He stalked across the lot to his snow-covered vehicle. It seated only one, but Liam didn't need his bodyguard while he was in the air. His retinue would follow him to his estate by the roads.

"I need you to look into something for me," he said to Tenen. He flicked his sleeve and sent a digital instruction packet to the bodyguard. "As soon as possible."

"The roads outside of town are impassible," said the big man. His accent marked him as a native of Mississippi, and he clearly did not know an impassable road when he saw it. "Can it wait until tomorrow?"

"Our timeline is tight, Tenen."

"Yes, sir."

Liam climbed into his vehicle. The oversized drone made a whump as the doors closed and the world disappeared. The display flashed to life, showing a single red dot in the vast, lake-filled landscape.

Liam released a long breath, and with it, all the poise he carried with him every waking moment of every day. He could almost feel the cancer coursing through his veins, sapping his strength. For a brief moment, he let himself wallow in the bone-deep exhaustion of the day as it mixed with the exhilaration of public speaking.

Because that speech was the first step in his plan. He knew he was the hero Minnesota wanted. They would flock to his city, if only they had a reason.

With a few swipes on the screen, Liam brought up the map. Copper-nickel mining had never been as popular as iron, and it had never done quite as much for the economy as it had promised.

It *had* brought the potential for devastating environmental disaster. For that, Liam was grateful. Copper-nickel mining would be the enemy. It would be the lynchpin for a plan that would solidify Liam's legacy.

Because legacy was all he had anymore.

He pressed a few buttons on his display, and the drone lifted into the pure white sky.

Then, of course, there were the people of Minnesota.

Those people would need to mobilize in order to bring him what he wanted. Those stoic, understated, passive-aggressive people would need to finally find the passion to move the world.

He hated them most of all.

CHAPTER FOUR

AJAY never much liked Silas Cardoso, but he hadn't expected to one day need to dispose of his body.

Silas had been an NSA hacker like Ajay, but worse in every way. He'd been a thick-headed sloth of a programmer, lazy, ineffective, and extraordinarily hairy. He'd been disreputable and backstabbing. The few times Ajay worked directly with the man, he'd seen Silas steal someone else's lunch from the office fridge, leave leftover fish in the office garbage over a long weekend, and blame an intern for the catastrophic crashing of the O'Hare aircraft controller servers.

All this, but when Ajay needed someone to dig up information, Silas Cardoso had been the only man for the job.

The best thing Ajay could say about the old man now was that he was light. Not light enough for Ajay to carry outright, but light enough that he didn't have too much trouble dragging the frail body across the gathering snow to the shed. Garrison followed, positive that something exciting was about to happen. Ajay certainly hoped not.

He couldn't call the police. Police would bring an investigation, even if it turned out poor Silas had simply succumbed to congenital heart failure, which Ajay found highly doubtful. An investigation would uncover Ajay's big hack—the hack that scrubbed his identity every night. It was an enormous plague of viruses he had put in place before leaving the NSA. It kept him anonymous and safe by severing any connections formed by the automatic processes that kept the civilized world functioning. Ownership, financials, legal problems, and even his birthday were all reset.

It worked perfectly, as long as nobody looked too closely.

He'd have to figure out how Silas had died later. For now, it would be enough to hide him in the shed. Kylie never went into the shed. She said it smelled like dead grass and motor oil. She wasn't wrong.

Ajay's own heart nearly failed when he returned to the house. Kylie sat in the dead man's chair, chatting like a normal kid after a normal day. One of the obnoxious neighbor kids sat on the sofa.

"Come back tomorrow," Ajay said to the kid.

"But—"

"Tomorrow." Ajay made his best snarl. "You can build a snowman."

"Well, I—"

Ajay cut him off with a wave of his hand.

"Papa," protested Kylie, "we were just—"

"Bzzt." Ajay snapped his forefinger and thumb together. "Tomorrow."

Kylie showed him one of the meanest scowls he had ever seen, and it was like an ice pick stabbed into his heart. He'd seen that look before. With her brown hair and darker features, Kylie resembled her mother so much it hurt. Ajay regretted coming down so hard on her, but she sat where a dead man had been not ten minutes prior.

"Okay, I'll see you later," said the boy as if it wasn't a big deal.

When he was sure the boy was gone, Ajay shuffled back outside to lock the deadbolt on the shed. Last thing he needed was someone snooping around and finding the frozen corpse of Silas Cardoso.

Crap. It was going to be frozen. He hoped he'd still be able to move it. Where did anyone dispose of bodies in this part of the world, anyway? Ajay chose not to search for the information online. That was the kind of search that landed a person on the kind of lists Silas Cardoso used to ineptly compile.

Ajay washed his hands. Then he washed them again. He started the oven.

"Frozen pizza all right with you?" he called into the other room.

Kylie didn't answer, which Ajay took as an affirmative. She had already disappeared into the sanctuary of her room.

It felt like the middle of a long, dreadful night, but it was only a little after eight. Late for a Midwestern supper, but both he and Kylie had been busy, and even though the discovery of a body in his living room didn't do much for his hunger, he knew they ought to eat. If things went bad, he would need the strength that only low-grade mozzarella on a cardboard crust could provide.

Ajay peered out into the backyard, but the falling snow had already softened his tracks to the shed.

"How was the speech?" he asked once he'd lured her out of hiding with molten grease.

"Good." Monosyllabic speech was not a good sign.

The pizza between them drowned in pools of pepperoni grease, but it was the only kind Ajay could get her to eat, and he didn't want a fight. It sat on the folding table where they ate most of their evening meals, in a room decorated with kitsch. The flower pattern on the ancient linoleum floor was slick with melted snow, which bothered Ajay enough that he kept his shoes on and allowed Kylie to do the same.

All the better if they needed to leave without warning.

"I remember reading about that Thompson guy years ago," Ajay said. "He was on the cover of *People*."

"He's just an environmentalist," Kylie said in a flat voice.

Ajay wondered if she had been using the tech in her head again. Her mood always flattened when she did. Or, rather, her expression of her mood flattened. He suspected her emotions roiled around all the same; they just came out in strange ways. Ajay hated this. Wondering whether or not she was hurting herself was the worst part of parenting.

Before he could stop himself, he asked, "Did you change your grades?"

She froze with a slice of pizza halfway to her mouth. The key to good parenting was timing. Knowing when the child is ready to accept a hard lesson or negotiate on rewards. Timing meant the difference between allies discussing how to form the best results and enemies facing off across the battlefield. Even when discussing a broken rule, the timing of the discussion meant more than the actual words.

Ajay had a knack for picking the worst times. "I know some subjects are hard," Ajay continued, "But it's not okay to break into their servers."

She set her slice down and jutted her jaw out. "I can't do phys ed. It's not fair. I don't know the games."

"You weren't failing."

"I had a C!" she shouted. Her flat tone had snapped all the way back. "That's the same as failing."

Ajay reached out a hand to comfort his granddaughter, but she pulled away.

"It's. Not. Good. Enough." Her sudden thunderclap of rage shook her whole body.

"For who?" Ajay snapped. He knew he shouldn't have asked as soon as the words slipped past his lips.

Because the answer was obvious. Mediocre grades weren't good enough for Kylie's mother. The same mother who had slipped into insanity and tried to kill Isabelle. That wasn't a conversational path Ajay was prepared to wander down. Not in the current state of things, anyway.

"I don't want you cheating anymore," he said, forcing his voice to calm again.

"You're a hacker. You always cheat."

Ajay fought the annoyance bristling across the back of his neck. He bit back the words that would have told her not to be anything like him. She didn't need to hear that. "There's a difference between finding a clever solution to a difficult problem and cheating the system."

She didn't look convinced. "Whatever. Why do you care?"

"I have a responsibility to check up on you," Ajay hissed.

Kylie crossed her arms. "Where's my right to privacy?"

"There's no such thing as privacy."

Ajay glanced out the window. A car's headlights made shadows across the empty backyard.

It must have been the wind, howling through the trees. His footprints were all but gone in the heavy snow, and there was no sign of anything else moving in their tiny postage stamp of a yard. Forcing himself to remain calm, he picked up a slice of terrible pizza and took a bite.

He tried a change in topic. "You made a friend?"

"Austin's not a friend."

"He's the boy from a couple doors down."

She narrowed her eyes. Worry still ate at the edge of her expression, but she softened a little. "Are we going to have to leave?"

Yes. Ajay knew the answer but couldn't bring himself to say it. Because, of course, they were going to need to leave. He had just found a body in his house. If Silas was murdered, Ajay and his granddaughter were probably in danger. If he wasn't, then how had he found Ajay? Silas couldn't possibly have penetrated the layers of deception

Ajay had built like castle walls around his and Kylie's Minnesota lives. Was that knowledge in the clear out in the world somewhere? Silas might have been the first to knock on his door, but he definitely wouldn't be the last.

"Not yet," Ajay said after too long a pause. "Not at all if I can help it, but we might need to go somewhere to be safe for a little while."

He could see the thoughts dancing through her head because they were the logical thoughts that he considered every time he moved. What was the point of forming serious relationships if they were just going to leave? Why bother working hard if the end result was going to be a forged transcript and a new falsified identity?

"Listen," Ajay said. "We're going to stay with this life as long as we can. If things go well, that'll be long after you've left high school. I promise you we'll do our best."

"What if our best isn't good enough?"

"Then we'll make another life somewhere else, and nobody will find you." He swallowed another bite of cardboard pizza. "I promise you they won't ever take you away."

She pushed her plate away, her pizza only half-eaten. Her eyes darted to the window.

Following her gaze, Ajay saw only snow. "Did you see something out there?"

"No." Kylie didn't sound convinced.

Ajay didn't stop looking in the backyard for a long time, even after Kylie cleared her plate and locked herself in her room. He saw nothing out there but snow, piling higher against the shed and the wooden fence. Nobody could know there was a body in that shed. Why would anyone try sneaking in that way? Why did that not comfort him at all?

His hand shook as he dumped the remains of the pizza in the garbage where it belonged. He knew he should eat more, but he couldn't do it.

Ajay needed answers.

CHAPTER FIVE

A SLOW TSUNAMI of paranoia rumbled through Ajay's whole body. Cold sweat ran down his back as he checked his security systems. His palms went greasy slick as he verified his local sensors. Alerts reported full functionality, even though they had obviously been circumvented. His mouth went dry as he saw how all his recording equipment had failed. Silas must have taken them down when he broke into the house. How had he broken into the house?

How had he even *found* the house?

The lock had been picked. Ajay could picture the old turd desperately working the physical lock with frozen tools, his knobby knuckles shivering against the cold. It was what Ajay would have done. Disable the cameras, hop the sensors, and enter the house. That way, no recordings would exist as proof, and since the sensors still functioned, they wouldn't report a failure on their next self-evaluation.

Ajay chewed his lip. He would need to rethink that system if it was really so easy to circumvent. A dozen layers of self-checking was supposed to alert him of any tampering, but if a sloth like Silas had found a way past it, there was something fundamentally wrong.

Then, of course, there were the maps. Ajay spent an hour checking each of the most common mapping services. He had long since hacked each, placing code in their core systems that would alert him if anyone ever searched for his address. His changes were all in place, and he verified that they all still worked. So, if Silas had searched for his address, he hadn't used those services. Would he have used a paper map? Ajay hadn't seen one on the corpse, nor did he see a car parked nearby.

Ajay *had* to know how he had been found.

He searched his favorite chair where he had found the corpse. Silas's pockets had been empty. The old man hadn't even been carrying a wallet.

A quick pat-down of the cushions didn't reveal anything. He tipped the chair up and searched among cracker crumbs and stale popcorn.

Nothing.

Garrison helped by hoovering up the popcorn.

"Thanks, Gare," Ajay said.

Ajay had meant his promise to Kylie, as foolish as he knew it was. He would hold onto this life as long as he possibly could. That meant no cops. No criminals. No corpses discovered on the property by authorities who might want to delve deeper into the backgrounds of the people living there.

It didn't make sense that Silas came with nothing. Not when Ajay had trusted his former colleague to use his connections to gather information about Kylie's condition. Silas's murderers must have taken whatever he brought.

"Stop thinking of ways this could be worse," he mumbled to himself. It didn't help.

It occurred to him that Kylie could have taken it, and that worried him even more. She wasn't ready for that information. Not for a while, anyway.

Ajay used a flashlight to prod the inner workings of his reclining chair. On its back, the black aluminum inner workings were exposed. Grime and dust-covered levers and gears. If Silas had brought anything, he could have easily hidden it there before he passed, but again, Ajay found nothing.

Ajay couldn't trust his house's sensors, so he dug around the cluttered workspace of his garage until he found a pair of motion sensors. He rigged one to send him an alert if any movement was detected and buried outside his front door where newly fallen snow had already hidden Silas's drunken tracks. The snow might muddy its sensory range, but it would detect anyone within a few feet of his sidewalk. It would be good enough.

He pulled on his white coat, gloves, and boots. Ajay didn't bother with a hat. His ears had grown tough and senseless over the years, and he didn't like the idea of muffling his hearing, despite the exceptional quality of his hearing aid.

The world was smothered by a quiet that only comes at the end of a big snow. A few lazy flakes still fell from the slate gray sky to pile atop the eight inches balanced atop Ajay's wooden fence. He appreciated the extra privacy but regretted the need to set new tracks in the sticky stuff, which had completely covered his tracks from earlier in the night. If he stepped into the backyard, there would be no covering the fact that he ventured to his shed again.

But what else could he do? He needed to search the body for anything that might tell him why or how Silas had tracked him. There was nothing in the chair. He needed a better search of the body.

A ping fired in his earpiece as he took his first step into the snow. He removed his left glove, pulled up his holographic screen in the cool night air, and scanned his array of paranoia for answers.

An address search for his home. Someone was coming.

His heart pounded in his throat. Which mapping service was it? There were military solutions, maps used by the old NSA agents like Silas or Ajay, or half a dozen consumer-facing solutions.

He stepped inside as he scanned the data. His address had come up in a search of a little-known European mapping network. It wasn't one he had ever used, and he didn't know who the system's primary client base was. Not the cops. Not military.

Bringing up the front-facing site, he perused the system. No, it wasn't military. Not really. It was customer-facing, consumer-grade stuff, but with a false patina of military aesthetic meant to make it feel like a military solution. Everything was rendered in various shades of tactical black with a big metal logo.

His hearing aid pinged again, and his hand twitched. Could they be here already?

No, it was another voice call. "Two in one day," he muttered to himself. "Must be a record." The call came from an unknown number, but he answered anyway. "Speak."

The voice that came through the other end was a man's voice, but high and shaky, with a hint of a Russian accent. "They are not the police."

"A lot of people aren't the police," Ajay said.

"The men on their way to your house. They are not the police, and you should stream your encounter with them."

"Sure," said Ajay. "Sounds like a big help for someone trying to solve my murder."

There was a long pause on the line. "It will help."

"Care to let me know who I'm talking to?"

"It's been a long time, Mr. Andersen," said the Russian. "But if you do not remember me, then it's best we keep my name out of this." Then, with a click, the line went dead. Ajay was beginning to suspect that his location wasn't as secret as he had hoped.

The new sensor in front of Ajay's house pinged with detected movement. They had arrived. In the seconds before they got to the door, Ajay had to make a decision.

He could run. Kylie was likely still awake. If he grabbed her and ran through one of his pre-planned escape routes, they might be able to ditch whoever was at the door. They weren't cops. That's all Ajay knew. If they weren't cops, then who were they? He brought up the video surveillance of the front stoop.

They were cops. He could see that much. Their faces were blurry in the image, but their badges shone with reflected light from his front window. All of his lights were on. All of his drapes were drawn. One of the officers stepped off of the sidewalk and peered in the front window. If Silas's body had still been in the living room, he would have been looking right at it through the crack between drapes.

Ajay couldn't pretend not to be there. Any other day, if Kylie hadn't been around, he might have pretended not to hear the doorbell.

The doorbell rang, loud and clear throughout the house.

If he didn't answer, they would ring again. Eventually, Kylie might answer out of pure annoyance, and that was a situation Ajay knew he wanted to avoid.

It was too late to run. The Russian had said to stream the encounter, but Ajay wasn't comfortable with the false safety that offered. Anyone willing to dress up as a police officer and visit someone late at night would also potentially be able to scrub his video before it reached the wider network. Not that he didn't have ways to avoid that scrub, but it would be difficult to execute proper routines if he was a corpse cooling under fresh snow.

The doorbell rang again. In the video feed, the men tensed, as if they were starting to expect trouble.

They expected trouble, so Ajay figured he'd give it to them.

He opened the door. "Can I help you fine gentlemen?" Ajay said, keeping almost all of the sarcasm out of his voice.

The cops pushed past him as if wasn't there. Taken aback, Ajay opted to pretend everything was normal and not a terrible violation of his rights. He motioned for the men to sit on the sofa and uprighted his recliner so that he could settle himself into it.

"A bit late for a social visit, don't you think?" he asked.

The first officer, the one who had looked in his window, stood several heads taller than Ajay. He declined the offer of a seat and didn't take his piercing gaze off Ajay. The other officer stood a step back in deference to his boss. Tattoos peeked out from under the officer's dark blue turtleneck, and his eyes flashed an unnatural green.

The big officer said, "We're after a fugitive." He gestured with his left hand, and his fidget displayed an outdated image of a young Silas Cardoso with the perfectly crisp detail of an image rendered on a device far above a police officer's paygrade. The old man in the image wore a Hawaiian shirt and a goofy grin. That was the Silas Ajay remembered, and even though he didn't think the man did good work, he still felt a pang of regret at his death.

"Never seen him," said Ajay.

The second officer rested a hand on his sidearm and stepped toward the hallway.

"Witnesses indicate he came this way," said the big officer.

"Witnesses?" Ajay followed the second officer. "In this storm?"

The second officer moved through the kitchen like he suspected someone would jump out at him. He brushed the blinds aside and peered into the backyard. Ajay was thankful the snow had covered his tracks to the shed but tried not to show his relief.

"Drone coverage was still adequate," said the big officer.

It was a lie, as far as Ajay knew. A storm like that would interfere with even the best drone surveillance, and one of the reasons he had picked northern Minnesota was because the drones weren't up to date. They still used decade-old technology, even for the worst cases. The only people running tech powerful enough to cut through a snowstorm were the environmentalists, who liked to keep an eye on mining corporations even in horrible conditions.

And even those drones would struggle with this wet snow.

"Do you live alone?" asked the big man.

From the kitchen, the green-eyed officer found the stairs to the basement. Ajay tried to remember if he had anything dangerous sitting out down there, but he had gotten better at concealing his tech. Not that he even had anything really dangerous. His diamond-optic quantum computer was disassembled, and he had stowed the parts under the workbench in the garage.

Ajay followed the second officer down into the unfinished basement. The space contained his washer and dryer, an old cot, and piles of empty luggage. Nothing incriminating at all.

He noticed that the second officer's gun was now nestled comfortably in one hand. In the dim light of the basement, Ajay couldn't see if the safety was off yet. He figured it probably was.

"It's been quiet around here, except for that Liam Thompson speech tonight," Ajay said. "Bunch of folks walked past when that was done. Maybe your old man was part of that group."

The second officer tapped on the cinder block walls of the foundation. "Who said it was an old man?"

Ajay struggled to keep his heart from hammering loud enough to give him away. He had made a mistake, and the officers knew it. He turned to leave the basement, only to find the big officer blocking the way.

"We're looking for a dangerous criminal," he said. "He stole something very valuable."

Ajay met the big man's steely gaze, not flinching when the other officer stepped up behind him. In the cool damp of the unfinished basement, Ajay could imagine the kinds of things these men might do to get the answers they wanted. He had never been trained to deal with situations like this. His work in the NSA had been behind a bank of computer screens a thousand miles from any kind of action. Even if Garrison decided to come down and help, he didn't think he'd stand a chance against these men.

Worse, actually. All they needed to do was threaten his dog and he'd cave. But what did they want? Why did they want Silas Cardoso, a moderately competent hacker whose skills were decades out of date? Ajay's mind raced.

"Papa?"

Ajay looked past the big officer to see Kylie standing at the top of the stairs. Kylie, who needed to stay hidden from unsavory sorts. Kylie, whose head was full of the kind of technology that could make or break whole governments. Who was supposed to be concealed and quiet in her room, not interfering with Ajay's insufficient attempts to keep them both safe?

The big guy turned to fire a scathing look at the girl.

"Oh," Kylie said. Her face was silhouetted by the kitchen light behind her head. "You have police over." She seemed to consider this for a second and brought up the blue display of her fidget. "It looks like you didn't start the recorders. I'll switch those on for you." Her smile seeped into her voice.

Without another word, she disappeared back through the house.

Ajay drew a deep breath. "You were just saying something about leaving to go get a warrant?"

"I don't think he's here," said the big guy. "It was a bad tip." He made his way up the stairs, and the other officer followed.

Ajay stood in the doorway for several minutes, breathing the damp, cool air. They weren't officers, but who were they? Smart enough to know that being recorded would give away too much information.

Not smart enough to know that Ajay's house didn't have internal recording.

Ajay closed and locked the door once they left. He reset the motion detectors and double-checked the alerts for mapping services. He checked his back window to make sure nobody had tried to sneak into the yard. Still no footprints.

Good.

His adrenaline crashed, and he suddenly felt very ill. Despite the wave of exhaustion and nausea, there was one more thing he wanted to do before the bed swallowed him whole.

He delved into the routing information for the call he had received before the officers had arrived. It was obfuscated, of course, routed through a dozen bounces through encrypted channels. It took him an hour to crack the origin number, but when he did, he dialed it without hesitation.

"I don't know what you're talking about," said the Russian accented voice.

"Let's meet tomorrow," said Ajay. "You have some explaining to do."

CHAPTER SIX

THE OLD RUSSIAN, Olexie Sokolov, was built like bloc housing with all the decorative flair of a concrete slab, with a solid square jaw, rectangular gray hair, and tightly corded muscle under faded tattoos. He peered at Ajay through tiny wire glasses.

They sat in a crowded coffee house on the lake side of the freshly plowed Paul Bunyan Drive. The decor was strictly pseudo pine Minnesota kitsch with framed artwork for sale on the walls.

"I've never met you in my life," Ajay said.

"People don't usually bring their children to meetings like this," the Russian said, casting a glance at a nearby table where Kylie and Austin nursed their hot chocolate.

"I prefer if they stay close."

"Sometimes close is more dangerous," Olexie said. "Your kids would be safer at home."

"Somehow I don't feel like home is all that safe right now," Ajay said. The image of Silas Cardoso's lifeless body flashed before him. "And I would very much like to know what you know about that."

"Do your kids know what you did for a living?"

"I'm retired."

Olexie raised one well-trimmed eyebrow.

"It doesn't matter what I did for a living. Once you retire, it's sunshine and roses." Ajay leaned forward. "Then you die."

"Your kids—"

"The boy in the orange coat isn't mine."

Olexie crossed his beefy arms. "You said your granddaughter scared the officers away? She doesn't look very intimidating."

"There's nothing more intimidating than a middle school girl, Olexie," growled Ajay. He watched as Kylie destroyed Austin with a frown. Poor kid. "I'm not here to talk about the kids."

Olexie clicked his tongue. "You want to know why those men visited you."

"The two officers aren't the visitors I'm most curious about," said Ajay.

Olexie's expression grew somber. "Silas was a good friend and solid ally."

"Silas Cardoso was nobody's solid ally. He was a talentless script kiddie and an artless hack."

A waitress in a green blouse brought Ajay his black coffee and set a flowery cappuccino in front of Olexie.

Olexie raised the cup to his nose and breathed in its aroma. "Are you sure you don't want something fancier? You're missing out."

"I'm allergic to fluff." Ajay wrapped his hands around his coffee cup but didn't drink. The cup was almost hot enough to scald his tough palms. "All I want is black coffee and answers."

"Have you heard of the Counter Capitalist Society?" Olexie mumbled into his cup.

"Countercapitalists?" Ajay gripped his cup tighter. "Borderline terrorist group, right? Eat the rich sorts? Seems like a funny conversation to have while sipping cappuccinos in a trendy cafe."

A hint of a smile crossed Olexie's thin lips. "Good coffee fairly sourced is not the kind of capitalism anyone has a problem with." He took a sip. "Plus, a person doesn't need to swear off all purchases just to acknowledge that there is corruption all the way at the top of an unjust system."

"What does that have to do with Silas?" Ajay asked.

Olexie didn't respond, but Ajay saw answers behind the tall man's flat eyes.

"I hear Liam Thompson is in town." Ajay took a tentative sip of his coffee. It was burnt and bitter, just how he liked it. "You're after the world's richest environmentalist?"

"Any industry can become corrupt," said Olexie after a long pause. "Silas was investigating him when he died."

"What does that have to do with me?"

"Nothing, as far as I know. You were close."

"We were never close," Ajay said.

"He must have been desperate."

Ajay took another too-hot sip of his coffee. "Why go after Liam Thompson? You're old enough to remember how things used to be. Used to be only bleeding hearts would help save the planet, and then only if it was convenient. Liam made doing the right thing profitable. That change really made a difference."

"The man who made Chernobyl habitable," growled Olexie. "Yes, I'm aware of how that man made profits."

The mention of Chernobyl left a sour taste in Ajay's mouth. According to public knowledge, Chernobyl had been the world's worst nuclear disaster, and cleaning it had been Russia's greatest triumph. Nothing could be that simple when geopolitics were involved.

Kylie laughed at something Austin said, and it sent a flutter of joy through Ajay's heart. She was making a friend at last, and here he was making more enemies.

"They deserve better," said Olexie. "When we're gone."

"Grandparents have been saying that for hundreds of years, but nothing ever gets better. Not really."

"My grandchildren..." His eyes looked sad behind his thin glasses. "We do what we can. I haven't always been on the right side of things, but Thompson is trouble."

Ajay took a big gulp of his coffee. It was still too hot, but he liked how it burned on its way down. "What happened with Silas?"

"I don't know."

"You're lying."

Olexie stared into his floofy drink. "CCS is a loose organization, so I didn't work with him much. He worked with Maja, and she told me what information I needed to collect. It's been months since I saw Silas in person. That was when he gave me your number."

"He told you to contact me?"

"Not as much." Olexie raised his cup but didn't take a drink. Ajay got the impression of the tall Russian hiding behind a cinnamon and nutmeg atrocity. "He told me if everything went south, you could probably manage."

"That doesn't sound like Silas."

Olexie sipped his drink. "He may have referred to you as a 'crotchety old bunghole' once or twice, but he also called you passably competent."

That sounded more like the old bastard. Silas had never minced words, and even though he hadn't known good script from bad ASCII art, he'd always been overconfident. "Yeah," Ajay conceded. "Who is Maja?"

"She is a pain in my ass," Olexie said. "Silas sent me a ping yesterday, but by the time I got to town, those mercenaries were already on the move. Everything's in high gear around here now, and my gut tells me it all revolves around Thompson."

"The only thing Thompson cares about is fixing the damn environment."

Olexie barked out a laugh. "People change, old man."

Ajay waved the words off. "Not that I've ever seen."

"He's up to no good," Olexie said. "I don't care if he used to be the Pope. He's corrupt, and his people killed Silas. I'm sure if it."

"Prove it."

Olexie leaned in close. "You really don't remember me, do you?"

Ajay peered at the other man. The face didn't raise any flags at all, even when he looked into the Russian's blue eyes. "The only Russians I've ever known were on the other end of a computer screen."

The corner of Olexie's left eye twitched. "If you wait for me to finish my drink, I will walk with you and show you what you need to see."

"Very mysterious." Ajay took a big gulp of his coffee. "Let's go."

Olexie took a sip. "There is no mystery," he said. He peered down into his cappuccino. "The little foam flower they make on the top is part of the experience. If I poured it into a to-go cup, it would be ruined."

Ajay stood and clicked his tongue.

Kylie shot him an annoyed look. "We're staying here."

Ajay tensed, ready for the fight. But then he thought better of it. "Meet us on the corner in ten minutes."

The girl pretended that Ajay didn't exist, which he took for an affirmative.

Olexie led Ajay along the partially cleared sidewalk. It was the day after the big storm, and while everyone had done their duty to clear a path, nobody had bothered yet to make it look nice. For a while, they walked single file while the cars in the street crunched over frozen slush. The low morning sun danced across the partially frozen lake and glared off the fresh snow, blinding Ajay as several large vehicles passed. He made his way cautiously after Olexie, cane gripped tight in his gloved hand.

"When did you defect?" Ajay asked when they were able to walk side-by-side again.

"What makes you think I defected?" asked Olexie.

"Tattoos."

A sad smile flashed across Olexie's face. He didn't bring a hand to the tattoo peeking out from under his coat, but Ajay could sense the man's attention on it. The tattoo depicted the Russian flag with its hammer and sickle, superseded by an American flag with its stars and stripes. The American flag was much newer and not very artfully done. The effect was a little on the nose.

"Sometimes our own people don't see how valuable we are when things go badly." Olexie stopped at the corner to allow a sleek car with black tinted windows cruise through the intersection. "I gave up a few years before encryption broke and our industry changed." He elbowed Ajay. "Cyberspying isn't what it used to be, is it, old buddy?"

"We're not buddies."

"Would you rather I say comrade?" He laid the Russian accent on thick with the last word, then took a big sip of his floofy coffee from his cardboard cup.

"You left Russia and decided to come over here and punch capitalism in the face alongside a bunch of counter-capitalist terrorists?"

"I decided to come over here," said Olexie. He gestured at the building in front of them. "And your government welcomed me when I agreed to divulge Russian state secrets."

"Made some enemies?"

"Not as many as I've made in the time since."

"The terrorist thing."

"They are not terrorists!" Olexie roared. He looked

sheepishly around until the few pedestrians lost interest in him. Quieter, he said, "It is very complicated."

Ajay rested both hands on his cane. "You'd better start talking, or pretty soon you'll make me your enemy."

A wide grin spread across Olexie's face. "This is the opposite of that, Ajay Andersen." He slapped Ajay on the back. "This is a very different thing indeed, Grandfather Anonymous."

Ajay did his best not to react. The fact that Olexie knew the handle was bad. How much had Silas told him? How much had Silas *known?*

"We have *always* been enemies," said Olexie Sokolov. He gestured at the building across the street. "Today, when you see what is on the paper files in this government building? Then, maybe, we will be friends."

CHAPTER SEVEN

"Your grandpa's weird," said Austin. The boy walked on the piled-up snow while Kylie kept her boots clean walking along the shoveled path. He wore a bright orange shirt under his bright orange coat, which was so bright it was hard to look at. Kylie wore a gray sweater and a brown coat, the same neutral pallet as everyone else on the street.

"He's not weird."

"Is it true he was a hitman for the government?"

"He wasn't a hitman."

Kylie hadn't meant to bring Austin along, but he had appeared at her house right before Papa wanted to leave for the coffee shop. She had offered a trip to the cafe instead of building a snowman, certain he would turn down.

He hadn't. She still wasn't sure why. So, now he sat in front of her with his orange puffy winter coat opened to show his bright orange shirt. Apparently, he had a favorite color and didn't mind sticking out in a crowd. Kylie wasn't sure if that was brave or annoying. Maybe both?

"I was pretty sure he was going to murder me last night."

"There's nothing weird about my grandpa," Kylie said, sounding a little more defensive than she intended. "All grandpas are pretty much like him."

"I have three grandpas," said Austin. "They all like fishing and sitting in front of the big screen all the time."

Kylie didn't know if Papa liked fishing. She figured he probably did, but they never got around to it. "He has hobbies."

"Like having secret meetings with strange Russian guys."

"This is obviously not a secret." Kylie regretted telling him about this meeting at all. Maybe it should have been a secret.

"And he gets mysterious visits from shady people dressed up as cops."

She *definitely* regretted telling Austin about the visitors, even though she'd been awake all night worrying about who they were.

A row of heavy vehicles thundered past, cutting through the frozen slush like a herd of elephants through grass. Kylie squinted to get a better look at them, but the white winter sun made it hard to make out anything.

"Maybe they were undercover FBI agents," Austin said, hopping from one heap of snow to the next.

"Undercover as police officers?" Kylie raised an eyebrow. "Why would they even do that?"

She stopped at the corner where a slow vehicle skidded around the corner, barely in control on the frozen street.

This was where she was supposed to meet Papa, but it had been fifteen minutes and he still wasn't there.

"Your grandpa didn't tell you who those guys were?" asked Austin.

"He said they were police."

"But they weren't."

"No."

Kylie watched a single-passenger vehicle glide through an intersection. It pulled up close to them and parked at the snowy curb.

Austin rushed over to Kylie and whispered, "Is that Liam Thompson?"

Kylie peered at the tinted windows but couldn't make out anything inside other than the shadow of movement.

"It's a BMW 16i with the custom sports package."

"So?"

He waved his arms in barely controlled excitement. "I've *never* seen a car like this in Bemidji. Not even during tourist season when people drive up from The Cities."

Kylie gave him a skeptical look, but she could see where he was going.

Austin pulled her down the street a little further, to a place where they could get a better look at the vehicle. "It's a drone car," he whispered. "Fully automated single-seater vehicle with foldable rotors that can be used for short-distance flights. It's really fast, all-electric, and ultra light."

"That—doesn't sound safe," Kylie said, now peering closer at the car. She spotted the folded rotor arms, which she supposed must emerge when the town's superstar trillionaire wanted to fly home. "Doesn't sound safe at all."

"It's totally *not*," Austin said as if it were the coolest thing in the world. "Not even a little."

"How fast is it?"

"All the way fast," said Austin, not taking his eyes from the car.

"What does it cost?"

"*Way* too much."

"Why isn't he getting out?"

Austin opened his mouth as if to respond, but no words came out, so he clapped it shut again. He stood in the ankle-deep snow and stared at the sleek lines of the exquisitely crafted vehicle.

"Maybe he's just taking a break," Kylie said. She crossed her arms and leaned against the brick building behind her. It was a bakery of some sort, and when the wind turned just right, a breeze from the lake blew the scent of sugary bliss to her. "We should—"

Kylie stopped. Austin stared at her, leaning forward in anticipation of her next words.

It was the big officer, but he was no longer dressed as a cop. The man wore a long trench coat, sleek, streamlined sunglasses, and a cowboy hat. Three others followed him, a man and two women, all dressed similarly. When they reached the top of the stone steps, he turned her direction, removed his hat, and winked.

"That was the guy," Kylie gasped.

"Who?"

"The cop. One of them, anyway."

Austin's eyes got wide.

"Papa's in trouble."

Austin stared at her. Stared at the guy. Stared back at her. "What do we do?"

Kylie flashed through her fidget's controls, but the wireless signal faded to static. She couldn't call. She pressed her lips into a line. Papa would want her to leave. He'd expect to meet her back home or in one of several safe locations around town. They had planned for something like this, and her grandfather had always told her to escape at all costs.

She took Austin's hand and pulled him across the street toward the government center. "We need to find him," she said. "Something bad is about to happen."

CHAPTER EIGHT

The Beltrami County Courthouse was a majestic Beaux-Arts style building of red brick and sandstone nestled in the center of the drab brick of cheap government expansion. It stood just beyond a small treeless park, now buried for the winter in the snow. The jailhouse on the far corner of the government block stood with all the decorative glory of an all-gray Rubik's Cube, frosted by new snow which was somehow already filthy. On an adjacent corner stood the equally drab clerk's court, which was open but mostly empty due to the storm.

Ajay stood at the data kiosk in the clerk court library on the second floor. His shoes dripped on threadbare carpet. The shaky green display showed maps of Beltrami and nearby counties, their population centers, and an in-depth soil analysis. "This doesn't tell me much of anything."

"Not on the surface, no." Olexie cast a glance at the scrawny clerk, who peered at papers through thick glasses that made his blue eyes look tiny. "But we're not really surface people, are we?"

"When it comes to soil, yes. I am definitely a surface kind of person."

"I mean the computer."

Ajay brought up his fidget and clicked it to connect to the kiosk's data center. "I'm not your hacker, Russian. You're not going to trick me into cracking a government database just so you can steal whatever you need."

"The thought hadn't occurred to me," Olexie said in an amused tone that implied the exact opposite. "But the information here is all public access. Maja told me where to look, but it will take some digging."

The clerk stood, stretched, and moved to a bookshelf across the room. He selected a number of dusty tomes from a large selection and proceeded to page through them.

"What do they do here, anyway?" Ajay asked.

Olexie frowned. "I imagine it is very exciting."

Ajay swiped through some of his most basic procedures, looking for a way into the database. Getting in wasn't much of a challenge for a database like this. After all, things weren't exactly private in a largely transparent government. Not soil surveys, anyway.

His fidget clicked with an incoming message, but the signal was hazy, probably due to the density of the stone walls. This building really was isolated in several ways. The call came from Kylie, but instead of a voice or video stream, she sent only one image as her message.

"Dammit," muttered Ajay.

"What?"

The clerk shushed them both.

Ajay held up the image for Olexie to see. It showed a big man in a cowboy hat and sleek sunglasses. His long coat bulged in a way that was likely a poorly concealed weapon. "This is the cop who came to visit yesterday."

"I told you he wasn't police."

"I figured that out on my own," said Ajay. "What's he doing here?"

"Soil research?" deadpanned Olexie. He glanced out into the hallway.

Ajay cut his connection and asked the clerk, "Is there a back room we can use?"

The clerk looked up at Ajay through his thick glasses. The fidget on his left hand flashed a government blue. "I'm not supposed to let anyone back there."

Olexie flashed some papers in front of the clerk. "Excuse me, sir," he said with a Texas drawl, "we've come up here on orders from the governor. Is there someplace we can use for our operations this week?"

The clerk furrowed his brow. "You're soil conservationists?"

"On emergency orders," said Olexie. A hint of Russian slipped back into his accent.

"For soil," Ajay added.

Olexie showed his crooked teeth in a smile. "Seems the sandy loam might be showing problems with its infiltration rates in the lower regions of glacial till."

"I see." The clerk sighed but led them through the door

into a short hallway. Off of that, they found a small confer-ence room with a flickering light and shockingly gray walls. "You can have this room if you want, but if you stay for very long, you might have to share."

"With who?"

"I'm just the assistant."

As soon as the clerk left, Ajay cracked the local network. "You'd better start talking, Olexie," Ajay said as he worked. "Who is that guy and why's he following me?"

"He's not following you. You have too much ego."

"He was at my house in the middle of the night. Now he's here. What's the story?"

"That's Tenen Lang," said Olexie, "and one of the women with him is Chay Quinn. They're both dangerous, and they work for Frontier Arms."

"Never heard of 'em."

"Frontier is a new mercenary organization. They've grown fast. Maybe too fast."

"Mercenaries? What are they doing here?"

"They have a strong presence in the Midwest. I figured a guy like you would keep up on stuff like this."

"I'm retired."

Olexie raised an eyebrow at Ajay's quick fingers as they danced over the controls of his machine. "Do you have a hobby?"

"I golf."

"It's winter." When Ajay didn't respond, Olexie said, "What can you see?"

"I can't do much from here," said Ajay as data streamed

over his cheaters, "but I should be able to get access to surveillance. At least we can figure out what they want." He looked up at the Russian. "Unless you'd care to enlighten me?"

Olexie said, "We suspect they work for Liam Thompson."

"You really have it in for him, huh?"

"We have no idea what they do for him. Most benign guess is they're just bodyguards, but why send four bodyguards into the government center on the day after a big storm?"

"Research," said Ajay.

"Yeah." Olexie's Russian accent was back full force. "For the soil."

"He *is* an environmentalist."

Ajay spliced his feed into the local network's surveillance using an old buffer overflow script he'd written half a decade ago. Once he had access, he pitched the video of the records room to one of the big screens on the wall. The clerk worked in the library, rearranging a series of paper documents.

A woman walked into the records room. The smile on her face twisted the scar on her nose, and her hair was pulled back into a tight bun.

"That's Quinn," said Olexie. "She's a mean one, and second to Tenen Lang in their wing of the organization."

When Chay Quinn spoke, her voice came through the surveillance system garbled and strange.

"Privacy filter," said Olexie. "The government scrambles all of its feeds whenever it spies on itself."

"I'm aware." Ajay scrambled through his encryption crackers for the right tool. He tried several, but they didn't work.

"I thought you were good at this," Olexie said.

"So did I." Ajay wrote a script that tried the cracks in sequence, unscrambling a snippet of voice for each attempt.

The voices still came out garbled or strange, and on the screen, the conversation continued. The clerk twitched nervously, then moved to a rack filled with large sheets of paper. He drew out one giant roll and spread it out over the large desktop. Ajay couldn't understand what he said, but the tone of his voice came through. He was explaining something, but he was nervous.

"Where are the others?" Ajay asked Olexie.

Olexie interacted with the big screen to split the video feed. He scrolled through a menu and found streams for hallways and office spaces. He finally found Tenen and the two other thugs walking down the marble hallways of the adjacent courthouse.

"What are they looking for?"

Ajay didn't respond and instead listened to Quinn's filtered words as they played over and over again through his collection of decryption tools.

"—If you want to live," said Quinn in his recording.

"Got it!" Ajay hissed. He snapped the tool in place to process the live feed.

"You're sure about this?" asked Quinn. She leaned over the broad sheet of paper. Ajay tried focusing on the image, but all he could see was the yellow sheet of a detailed soil survey. "The survey is complete?"

"It is," said the clerk. "We had some funding problems, so it's taken a decade, but last year we had a big donation and things finally moved forward. We're very excited to see this kind of data for one of Minnesota's oldest forests."

"He's a talker," said Olexie.

Ajay shot him a questioning look.

"He talks a lot when he's nervous." Olexie pointed at the screen. Quinn had her hand concealed under her coat. "She has a weapon pointed at him."

"I guess that's one way to do research."

"Most librarians frown upon it."

On the other image, the giant Tenen and his two goons split to search different parts of the courthouse. The video followed the big guy as he shattered the lock on a judge's private office.

"What are these guys here for?" muttered Ajay.

"Don't ask that," Olexie said, pointing at another window that had just popped up. "Instead, why don't you ask what *they* are doing here?"

On the screen, Kylie and Austin crept through the side entrance of the Beltrami County Courthouse, gently closing the door so it wouldn't send a resounding boom through the entire building.

Which was good, because they were only twenty feet and around a corner from one of Tenen's thugs.

The triple thump of a silenced pistol shattered the silence of the records room. Chay Quinn eased the dead clerk to the floor and kicked his broken glasses away.

"Thank you for your help," she said with a hint of amusement in her voice.

"What the hell did you get us into?" Ajay whispered.

But Olexie said nothing, his jaw slightly open in stunned silence.

CHAPTER NINE

OLEXIE CUT the lights and killed power to the screens. He pulled Ajay against the wall with the door and held up a finger to keep him quiet. His breath smelled like nutmeg.

Ajay tuned his hearing aid to pick up the faint sounds of movement. Quinn opened the door to their hallway and strolled through, taking time to glance in through the door of their conference room.

"I've got the surveys," she said in a quiet voice. "Cleanup has started." After a brief pause, she hissed, "Of course I work fast, Lang. I'm a professional."

Then she moved away. Ajay touched his fidget and sent a message to Kylie. *Hide.* Text only. Everything else was still a wall of static.

Olexie brought up the screen least likely to be seen from the hallway and retrieved a map of the government center. "Memorize this." He tossed a small piece of plastic to Ajay. "Put this in your ear."

Ajay frowned at the comm unit. Instead of pushing it

into an ear, he paired it with his hearing aid so that he could splice the line in with the rest of the noise. "Got it," he said. It made his voice sound funny. He peered at the hallway map of the government buildings and where they attached to the courthouse.

"Tenen's people are here, here, and here," whispered Olexie. Ajay heard his voice doubled through his earpiece. "Your granddaughter was here when we saw her last."

"Is this comm encrypted?" asked Ajay.

"Rolling encryption every thirty seconds, so even if they crack our feed, it won't last."

"A decent quantum computer will break that in two seconds."

Olexie gave a thin smile. "If they have easy access to powerful quantum computing, then we're screwed anyway, aren't we?"

"Once they break in, they can just grab the new keys."

"What?"

"This is basically no protection at all. Plus, what if our clocks aren't synced?" Ajay couldn't stop imagining the problems they might run into with such a simple problem. Best case, the clocks of all their devices were tuned to a single source, like the GPS system, which could keep them close enough. It was really only a problem if the rolling encryption keys ran on a tighter schedule, but this could still result in lost information. "This is the dumbest system I've ever seen."

Olexie muttered something that sounded suspiciously like, "Op sec asshole," but the comm didn't pick it up so Ajay couldn't be sure.

With the map memorized and an idea of where everyone was, Ajay crept into the short hall. The lights were off, so he had to navigate by the dim glow coming from the records room. He used his cane carefully, depending on the corroded rubber tip to not make much noise on the thin carpet. He pushed the records room open and found chaos. Papers were strewn everywhere, and the kiosk he had used before was throwing sparks.

"Quinn has a funny idea about what cleanup is," he said.

"Your granddaughter moved upstairs in the courthouse," said Olexie. "Move quickly."

Ajay crossed the room to where a shelf had been emptied over the poor corpse of the clerk. With his cane, he pushed the papers aside so that he could look at the man. Definitely dead. Two bullets in the chest and a third piercing the man's cheekbone. Ajay's stomach twisted.

"I'm not trained for this," he said deliberately.

"Yes, yes," said the Russian. "You are a behind-the-screen kind of guy, but now you need to be a ghost." Amusement danced at the edges of the man's voice. "Or you will be a ghost."

"It's not me I'm worried about."

Ajay was a terrible ghost. His muscles ached from tension, and his breathing sounded like the rasp of dry paper against his throat. He rubbed his sweaty palms on his shirt as he edged his way down the wide hall toward the nearest stairs. He had to trust Olexie to guide him, and the dependence grated on his nerves.

"Hurry," said Olexie. "One of the goons is looping back your way."

Ajay stepped faster, but his patent leather shoes weren't made for stealth. He pushed through the door, flinching as it squeaked.

"He heard you," said Olexie.

A message from Kylie pinged, *I think we're clear.*

Ajay wrote back, *Stay where you are.*

"Your kids need to move," said Olexie.

Ajay swore and relayed the message as he climbed to the second story. His breath was short, and his hip ached something fierce. After a brief interchange with Olexie, he wrote, *Go through to the connected room. I'll meet you there. This text is not secure.* Even though Ajay always kept the messages on a secure channel, he couldn't be sure. An organization like Frontier Arms would have all the basic cracks covered. Even a simple message like this was too much risk. He needed to talk to her directly.

"There are police less than a block away," whispered Ajay. "Can't you raise the alarm?"

"I'm cut off," said Olexie. "You'll need to get free of the building to get a line out."

"Don't you have a team?"

"It's complicated."

"What good is CCS if they can't back you up?"

"They are very busy."

Ajay sighed.

"Quiet," said Olexie, more urgent now. "Be very still."

Ajay froze, his hand on the second-floor doorway. Below, he heard the same squeak of the stairwell door. For the eternity of a few seconds, Ajay didn't know if someone was coming up the stairs.

The door creaked again and thumped closed.

"Move," said Olexie.

Ajay, more carefully this time, opened the door and slipped through. The hallway he entered had a marble floor that was impossible to stay silent on, so instead, he settled for fast.

At the end of the hall, he found an office door already open. Inside, the papers were ransacked and the furniture overturned. The blinds were pulled and the windows frosted from the recent snow. He pushed the blinds aside and unlocked the window. With some effort, he managed to open a narrow crack.

Across a span of fewer than ten feet, he saw Kylie and Austin in the adjacent courthouse. They frantically pushed their own window open.

"Can you get out?" Ajay asked in a loud whisper. If anyone came back through his hall he didn't want them hearing him.

Kylie whispered, "The fake cops are here."

Thanks. Ajay bit back the bitter sarcasm that had no place in a supportive parental relationship. "There are four of them, and Olexie is watching them on surveillance." He glanced out the door. "Olexie, can the kids get out yet?"

"Tenen is just down the hall, and there is someone guarding the staircase they used to get to where they are."

"That's not helpful."

"If the kids go left, then to the end of the hall, they can take the stairs to the back entrance. It is unguarded."

Ajay relayed the instructions. "Kylie, these men are dangerous. If they see you, they're going to chase. Do you understand?" Ajay hated scaring her, but she had to know to run as fast as she could. Whenever Ajay closed his eyes he saw the dead clerk, efficiently slain through no fault but the fact that he was present. "Your only goal is to get out. Get Austin to safety."

The boy's eyes were so wide Ajay could see their whites, even through the cold glass.

"Don't worry about us," said Kylie in a whisper. "We can handle it."

"Get out," said Ajay. "And when you do, you should be able to connect to the area network. Drop an anonymous emergency call to the police like I showed you. Do you remember that?" He hadn't taught her everything about hacking, but anonymous messaging was basic stuff.

"Got it," Kylie whispered. She turned to leave, but then reconsidered. "Papa?"

"Yes, dear?"

"You need to stay safe, too."

"I will," Ajay promised. "I'll get out as soon as I can."

With that, Kylie and Austin disappeared from their open window into the dark confines of the courthouse.

CHAPTER TEN

"My family all thinks that my aunt was a spy," Austin whispered as they hurried down the marble-floored hall in their socks so that they wouldn't make any noise. Austin carried both of their pairs of boots so that Kylie could open doors quickly and quietly. "It was a long time ago."

"How do you know?"

"She lived in northern Montana," said Austin. "There was a militia there."

"Is that different from southern Montana?"

"It's pretty much all the same."

"Huh."

"She disappeared right after the FBI raided the militia's compound. They were a bunch of white supremacists."

"The FBI were white supremacists?"

"I—I don't know."

Kylie thought she and Austin were making a pretty good team. "Did she die?" whispered Kylie.

Austin furrowed his brow. "We prefer to think she got

into witness protection. Could you imagine having to start over and hide the rest of your life?"

"Not really." Yes, absolutely.

They padded toward the back stairwell without being spotted, though they heard the echoing voices of the bad people arguing in one of the offices.

Kylie wondered what they were looking for. She pressed a finger to her lips to signal silence from Austin.

"What? Oh, yeah, okay." He eventually understood.

She peeked in the window of the office where she heard the voices. The big man stood there—the false cop who had been in her house the previous night. He had a man with him, also dressed in black. They were silent as she watched, but when the big guy paced across the room, she saw who they were talking to.

It was the woman she had sat next to during the Liam Thompson propaganda fest. Kylie recognized her drab cardigan and grayish-blonde hair. Thick strips of duct tape bound the woman to her chair, and tears flowed from her red, puffy eyes. Heart hammering in her chest, Kylie moved on down the hall.

Kylie froze at the door to the stairwell and listened as hard as she could. The thugs' words echoed in the empty hall.

"Come on," whispered Austin, holding her elbow.

Kylie looked him in the eyes. A spot behind her chest itched uncomfortably with the eye contact, but she held his gaze for several seconds. "You should run," she whispered.

He pushed the door to the stairwell open very carefully and drew her through it. "We both have to run. I'm not letting you stand out there alone with those thugs wandering around."

Austin might have been talking about running away, but Kylie thought he sounded very brave. Was this what having a friend felt like?

"Look," he said, "we need to get somewhere safe."

Kylie blinked. "Right," she said. "We need to know what these people want." What if it was important? Why would Papa's friend bring them here if he wasn't involved? And, if Papa's friend was involved, then Papa was involved.

"That's not what I said," whispered Austin.

"If Papa is involved, then I'm involved." She turned to open the door.

"No," Austin said, blocking her. "We have to run."

Rage bubbled in Kylie's chest. Tension ached in her fists.

His voice faltered. "I mean—"

"No," she interrupted. "You're right." She had a better idea.

They descended the stairs, padding softly with their socked feet. The building around them felt cold and strong and empty, as if there wasn't anything strange happening in all the world. She stepped in a wet spot but ignored the ice as it soaked into her socks.

When they reached the ground floor, Kylie turned to Austin. "I have to do something."

"What are you going to do?" asked Austin, following her like a lost puppy. "You can't fight those guys."

Kylie bit her lower lip. Austin didn't know what she

could do. He didn't know how she could touch computers and make them give her what she wanted.

But what good was that? Nothing she had would let her fight those men. Austin was right about that. Maybe she could still do some good.

The staircase continued past the exit to the basement, and Kylie smiled when she saw how it was locked. She touched the digital display where a worker would scan their keycard. Closing her eyes, she reached out to the complex electromagnetic signal surrounding the device. The lock functioned on several levels, scanning and listening to the different flows of the binary datastream. But what was it looking for?

The answer, when she found it, was simple. It sought a sequence of a hundred digits following a certain encryption pattern. The encryption pattern would normally have been difficult to guess, maybe even requiring a quantum computer to crack, but Kylie had more tools at her disposal than the typical hacker. She listened deep in the device, and it told her what its pattern was. It practically shouted it. She sent the expected pulse, and the door clicked open.

"How did you do that?" Austin asked.

"Wishful thinking."

They slipped their boots back on.

The lights didn't activate when Kylie and Austin descended into the basement. As they passed the old fallout shelter sign and down into the depths of gray stone, the air cooled and turned dry. Another door led them to a dusty passageway surrounded by clear walls, behind which stood the glowing facades of a dozen computer racks.

Kylie pressed through a glass door into a room with a single desk with five monitors. The keyboard sat askew at the desk, cast aside as if it hadn't been used in years. She straightened it, sat, and wiggled the old-style mouse.

The monitors flared to life, each hazier and blurrier than the last.

"Ugh," she said. "I probably should have expected low-quality poor resolution screens for a government server."

"I don't think this is a good idea," said Austin.

"It's not." Kylie clicked through some menu options and brought up the surveillance program. She found Papa without any trouble.

On the screen, the old man crept through a library on the third floor, among shelves stacked to the ceiling with paperwork. In the same room, another of the goons crept along the adjacent aisle. Kylie's heart hammered at the thought of Papa getting caught. She checked her fidget. No signal. Not even a direct text line to Papa. She couldn't warn him, except for maybe something through the government center's systems. What could she do?

Lights?

She had control over the lights, but anything she did would be noticed by the thug, too.

Except.

Papa touched his ear and changed his course. He no longer headed toward the goon, but he stayed in the room.

"Dad thinks my aunt got caught," whispered Austin. "He thinks she's in a shallow grave somewhere, but I don't believe it."

"We have to help," Kylie said, ignoring him. Her voice

sounded flat even to her own ears. She had used her tech too much and now she struggled to feel anything at all, even the life-threatening danger that seemed to bother Austin so much. She took one of his hands in hers. "We're safe here."

Austin's shoulders slumped and he squinted at the screen. "Yeah, you're right." A grin spread across his face, almost as if he was starting to enjoy the idea of being spies. "They won't come down here, and with access to this system, we have all the power."

Kylie pushed a button and brought up video and audio of the room where the thugs had tied up the woman. She wanted to hear what they were saying, or at least get a hint of what the bad people were looking for.

The big fake cop raised a black pistol and shot the woman in the face.

CHAPTER ELEVEN

"I HAVE TO MOVE," said Olexie. "Quinn is headed back over here."

"Coffee and a newspaper," muttered Ajay.

"Excuse me?"

Ajay subvocalized into his comm, "Every morning until you showed up. Coffee. Newspaper. Maybe a mid-morning nap." He padded across the thin carpeted library, listening carefully for the movements of the thug in the room. Olexie's instructions had kept him safe, but if Olexie had to move, then Ajay might not be able to follow up on whatever the thug was doing. "It was nice."

"I got a message out. My people are on their way," said Olexie.

"Your CCS terrorists?" Ajay wasn't sure if that was a good thing.

"Give them five minutes and they'll extract us."

"The police are literally next door," whispered Ajay. Ajay expected the police to come seconds after the kids dialed in the anonymous 911 call, but there hadn't been any sign, and that worried him. When movement on the first floor forced him farther upstairs, he had thought it a temporary measure. Now he was trapped again.

"It would be best if the police were not involved until after we left," said Olexie.

"That might have been nice to know earlier."

"It was implied."

Ajay ducked into the next aisle as the thug moved on. Slowly, carefully, Ajay approached the place where the woman had been rifling through papers. Land management reports from the early nineties. Not useful for anyone, as far as Ajay could tell. He crept down to the end of the aisle to listen.

Then he saw the device. A thick cylinder sat nestled behind the rows of manila folders. Ajay used his fidget to cast a haze of green light across it and read the letters etched in the side. A serial number and a letter designation. He snapped a picture.

His mouth tasted of bitter stress, and he didn't like it. A quick search recognized that device. It was a high temperature flare. There was no good reason to have that here in the building.

No reason at all except for one.

So, they were planning on burning the records. Torch all evidence of their exploits here and better conceal whatever it is they're taking. Ajay bristled at the idea. He had always had respect for libraries, even these boring old archives of paper records.

Footsteps.

Ajay froze, clutching his cane. The bronze head felt heavy in his grip.

He was halfway down his aisle. No chance to sneak away. If the thug decided to circle back, she would see him. He heard her walking briskly down the adjacent aisle.

She walked past the end of his aisle, file folder in one hand. The tails of her black coat fluttered behind her.

Then, she stopped.

There was a sound of metal sliding across leather. The light snick as the mechanics of death clicked into place. Ajay had no time to react.

Run.

But he didn't run. He stepped lightly forward. Fast and quiet. He clutched his cane in two hands.

She stepped around the corner with her gun raised. She had him dead to rights, grim determination plastered on her pale face. Pistol leveled straight at his chest.

Their eyes met, and Ajay thought he saw an apology there.

Then, the lights died. The library fell to pitch black. Ajay stepped to one side as the blinding flash of the pistol fired once. Twice.

He swung the cane, aiming just behind the flash. The bronze head cracked against bone. The woman cried out.

The lights returned as the pistol skittered across the thin carpet.

Ajay swung his cane again, but she was ready. She stepped inside, blocking with the meat of her forearm. The cane thunked into flesh and would probably leave a hell of a bruise, but she didn't slow. She brought her other fist up without dropping the papers and slammed Ajay in the neck.

He stumbled backward, gasping.

The thug swung again. Papers scattered as she smashed a fist into Ajay's stomach. Cursing, she swept up her papers.

Ajay spotted the gun a long putt away. He hooked her foot as she lunged for the weapon, and she fell hard. He swung at her head.

Missed. She rolled to the side and came up with a hard kick to his thigh. Ajay growled in pain, but the damage was done. He stumbled backward as she scrambled toward the gun. He couldn't stop her now.

Instead, he grabbed a paper that she'd dropped and ran the other way down the long aisle, ignoring the pain in his hip and thigh. There would be time to worry about that later.

The lights fell black again. From memory, he felt his way to the end of the aisle and ducked around the shelf.

Another flash of muffled gunfire, but he was around the corner. The door was halfway between him and the thug, with the long aisles in between. He could run for it, but she'd likely shoot him as soon as he let in light from the hallway.

More gunshots, this time louder, sharper, and farther away. Outside? Maybe it was Olexie's team or the police.

The thug hadn't made any sound for several seconds, and it made Ajay nervous. He crept farther from the door rather than closer, figuring she'd want to escape. At this point, he was perfectly happy letting her do that.

His eyes adjusted slowly to the dark, but the dim display on his cheaters showed him the shapes of the shelves. He listened carefully as he crept away, hoping to get some idea of where the goon was. She could just as easily be working her way around to meet him.

"I'm on my way," she said, way too close. Not even a long putt away. She had been sneaking up on him.

Not anymore. She made her way to the room's exit and pushed her way through. Gone.

Ajay folded the paper he'd taken from her and stuffed it in his coat pocket.

The lights returned.

"Thanks, Kylie," he said, and he made his way to the exit.

He smelled a sharp, bitter odor as he stepped out of the room, and as he walked down the hallway, a blinding flash exploded from the library. The thug had set off her flares.

Everything was going to burn.

CHAPTER TWELVE

"I wonder if Aunt Candice ever did anything like this," whispered Austin.

"How did she infiltrate a white supremacist group?"

"I don't know," Austin mused. "She had *very* dark skin. I've seen pictures. She was one of the blackest people in my whole family."

Kylie furrowed her brow but didn't say anything else. She couldn't think of any pleasant way for that to work.

Half of the screens in the server room were whited out by blinding light. Records rooms and libraries throughout the courthouse had simultaneously burst into flames. Offices all along the upper levels had similarly ignited, and the hallways were filling with smoke.

Austin tugged on Kylie's sleeve. "We need to leave."

"Okay, okay," Kylie said without moving. She had saved Papa. She was sure of it. Cutting the lights at the right moment had kept the person from shooting him, but now she couldn't find him on the surveillance system.

"Come on."

Kylie swiped across the controls and locked down the entire computing grid.

Was she imagining the smell of smoke? The air in the server room was carefully filtered, but her nose tickled with the aroma of campfires.

Now coughing, they made their way out of the glass-enclosed chamber. Outside the enclosure, the air was a ghostly haze, with thick smoke gathering in the corners of the dingy hallway. Her eyes watered and her head hurt.

Austin pulled her down, where the smoke wasn't so thick. He led her to the exit and up the stairs where they could see a hint of the blinding light of day. Still hacking smoke from their lungs, they stumbled forward into the entryway.

"Goddamnit," said a voice from above.

Kylie squinted up the stairs and saw a man in a black coat.

He had a gun in his hand, and he pointed it at Austin.

"Lang," he said, "I found a couple of kids."

There was a brief pause as he listened to his comm. Kylie stared in horror into the man's half-lidded eyes and tried to interpret the emotions there. She couldn't. Her head throbbed. She focused on his gun, a black finger of death pointed right at her. He wore a ring on his gun hand that said Frontier in a shape that resembled a police badge, but he wasn't police.

"This wasn't the deal," said the thug. "They're just kids. What could the boss possibly want with the girl?"

Again, he waited for an answer. Kylie pressed Austin behind her and tried to back farther into the corner. Maybe the man wouldn't shoot her if she just ran away. He didn't seem to *want* to shoot her. Austin choked on a sob behind her.

If the thug decided to shoot, there was basically no chance of him missing. He'd kill both of them in half a second. Kylie took Austin's cold hand in her own, giving it a squeeze to comfort him. He didn't deserve to die this way. He was just a kid.

She was just a kid.

"What would Aunt Candice do?" Austin whispered.

Kylie didn't think Candice would have any good options.

"I'd better get a damn bonus for this," said the thug. He raised the gun.

The gunshots weren't muffled like Kylie had heard before. They were claps of thunder that shattered the air in the tiny space of the side entrance stairwell. The shots broke the outside door's window and smashed into the stone wall, throwing glass and chips of rock everywhere.

The shots came from outside.

When Kylie forced open her eyes—she hadn't even realized she was pinching them shut—she saw the man in black scrambling backward up the stairs, trailing spatters of bright blood.

"Under fire," he shouted as he ran. "Under fire in the southwest stairwell."

Then, he was gone.

The tall Russian guy, Olexie, slammed the broken door open and said, "You need to run." In his hand, he held a big pistol, but he didn't point it at them.

Kylie stared at the Russian, not fully understanding his words.

"What would Candice do, what would Candice do?" whispered Austin over and over.

"Run fast," Olexie said. He pointed across the snowy space. "To that van."

A white van stood across the street from the courthouse. Beside it, two men in white coats pointed rifles at another location that Kylie couldn't see. Gunshots rang from far away, and each crack of thunder sent chills down her spine.

"We can do this," Austin said. He still held her hand. "We're going to run for that van and then we'll be safe." He turned to Olexie. "Right?"

Olexie shrugged. "Pretty much."

"Pretty much?" squeaked Austin.

Olexie stole a glance at the scene outside and raised his gun. "There will be shooting."

"Where's my grandpa?" asked Kylie. She knew better than to get in a van with strangers, even if they were rescuing her from other strangers.

Olexie fired two thundering shots. He swore and ducked back. "You need to go." He touched his ear. "I have them, Ajay. Get to the van."

Then, everything broke into chaos and noise. A rattle of cover fire from the van roared across the snow. Why was Austin wearing so much orange? Olexie crouched behind a snowbank ten feet from the door. He fired several wild shots, waving for Kylie and Austin to run.

Their boots pounded through the deep snow, and they ducked low so they wouldn't draw as much attention. Olexie fired several more shots, the report of his big gun echoing off the old brick buildings.

To their right, Kylie saw movement from the other building. Papa. The old man rushed as fast as he could with his cane, moving straight toward the street.

Something hissed through the snow at Kylie's feet, and she did her best not to think about what it was. Then she thought about it too much, and the weight of it all stopped her in her tracks.

"What would Candice do?" Austin cried, panic dripping from his voice. He gripped Kylie's arm.

"She would fucking move!" roared Olexie. He ran up behind them and bowled them forward across the street.

The three tumbled into the van and he slammed the door shut. On the other side of the vehicle, Ajay wrenched the door open and piled in.

Two others in the back of the van peppered the courthouse with bullets, and the driver and passenger climbed in. With a hissing skid of tires against packed snow, the van launched forward.

Kylie lay on the floor of the van, staring at the light coming through what she presumed were seven bullet holes. Three in the top, four in the side.

"Well," said Olexie. "That was certainly more exciting than coffee, a newspaper, and a nap."

"I." Papa gasped for breath. "Never." Another gasp. "Saw your proof."

CHAPTER THIRTEEN

AJAY RAN his fingers through hair that he was sure would be even grayer the next time he looked in the mirror. He sat on a bench along the side of the white van as it sped down the Minnesota highway. They'd escaped. The children had escaped.

That didn't mean he was happy.

"Peace and quiet," he muttered. "That's what retirement's supposed to be."

"Sounds dreadful," said the tall Russian.

"You need to drop us off," Ajay said. "We'll make our own way home."

Olexie furrowed his brow. "I don't think that's a good idea."

He was probably right, but Ajay didn't like it. "We can take Austin home. He doesn't need to be part of this."

"My parents won't notice if I'm gone," whispered Austin.

"Hold on," said the woman driving. Her gray-blonde

hair drifted over more freckles than Ajay could count, and her blue eyes sparkled with the sunlight off the newly fallen snow. She wore light gray fatigues and a trio of grenade-sized drones clipped to her belt. "You can't go back."

"This is Maja Berg," Olexie said by way of introduction. "I told you she was a pain in the ass."

"Ajay Andersen," Ajay said. "We at least need to take Austin home. Kylie and I will disappear."

"What?" snapped Kylie, clearly upset. "But you said—"

"Things have changed."

Kylie's expression was a mask of hurt and anger.

"We'll talk about it later," growled Ajay. He didn't know if they would need to leave, but he needed to assess the damage. It wasn't looking good.

The other passengers in the van dutifully avoided eye contact and shifted uncomfortably.

"One of the Frontier mercenaries got a good look at the boy." Olexie glanced at Kylie. "Her, too."

"We don't usually bring our children on missions," said Maja.

"I tried to tell him," Olexie muttered.

Ajay opened his mouth to protest, but the quirky smile on Maja's face stopped him. He redoubled his efforts to stay calm. "What the hell are you getting me tangled up in, and how are you getting us out?"

"I told you," gasped Olexie. He favored one side and leaned against the back of the van like he might require it for support. "Countercapitalism."

"Capitalism has been pretty kind to me, thank you very much."

"Has it?"

Austin whispered something to Kylie.

"Something to share?" Olexie fixed the boy with a hard gaze.

Austin shook his head, his eyes wide with fear.

"We're not terrorists," Olexie grumbled.

"Fine. Austin can stay with Kylie," said Ajay. "Austin, text your parents and tell them that you'd like to spend the night at a friend's house."

At first, Ajay thought the boy wasn't going to speak, but eventually, he gave a quick nod. "I don't really have any friends, but yeah."

"Well, you made some friends today," Ajay said as he fired a message to his next-door neighbor, telling him he was in the hospital. They had an agreement that Ms. Overly would watch Garrison and water the plants for him in case of emergency.

"Olexie's right," said the woman with the freckles. She watched Ajay from the driver's seat for several seconds longer than was comfortable. "We're not terrorists. We're fighting for what's right."

"Is she *driving?*" asked Austin.

Kylie whispered, "People up north drive their own cars a lot. They don't like safety."

"We're protesters and we're activists. We sometimes defend ourselves from violent counterprotests, but that doesn't make us violent."

"Is that what happened to Silas Cardoso?" asked Ajay. "A violent counterprotest got him?"

The van rumbled along in silence for several tense breaths.

"We don't know," said Olexie.

Ajay gripped his cane. "I want you to clean up your mess." He would have liked to get a better look at Silas to learn more about his death, but these terrorists had to know a good way to dispose of a corpse. Better than Ajay having to do it himself.

"Silas was more than a mess," snapped Maja. Quieter, she said, "He was a friend."

Olexie shrugged as if he didn't quite agree. "He was an asset, anyway."

Ajay peered at the old Russian, trying once again to figure out the man's story. "He's a body in my shed, and I want you to take care of him. Those mercenaries were looking for him. Or at least they wanted something he had."

"Those guys?" asked Maja.

"Yeah. One of them came by dressed like a cop. They had a picture of Silas."

At this, Kylie looked up. Ajay met her gaze and gave a little shake of his head. She knew something, but he didn't want her to talk about it yet.

"What did he have?" Maja asked. "When you found him?"

"Nothing," Ajay said.

"Olexie tells me he was working for you when he died."

After a pause, Maja said, "He was looking into something Liam Thompson is planning."

"What did he find out?"

"That's what I'd like to know," said Maja. "All we know is that Thompson is dying of cancer. Silas was going to dig into the organization Thompson is setting up to run the project after he's gone. Bad enough that the guy hoards wealth while he's alive, but now he's planning something that'll keep consolidating power." She let out a sigh. "He must have gotten too close. Figured something out."

They rode in silence for a while longer. The benches on either side of the van were hard, unpadded things that made Ajay's tailbone ache. Austin and Kylie sat on one side, whispering to each other. He stole glances at his granddaughter from time to time, feeling a flutter of satisfaction that she seemed to be making a friend. After over a year trying to get her to fit in, she finally managed to make a connection.

It just happened to be in the middle of a crisis.

"If anyone finds us," said Ajay, "I'll tell them you kidnapped us."

"They won't find us," said Olexie. He sat straighter and no longer favored his ribs, though his breathing was shallow and his skin a shade pale. "Our hideout is very good."

"So you're not terrorists," said Ajay. "You're activists with a secret hideout?"

"That's right."

Kylie said, "I saw you shoot someone."

Olexie's expression grew grim. "It would have been better for you if I had killed him. Then your friend could go home."

Austin looked up from his fidget. The display's text

blinked above his hand. "My mom says I can spend the night. She expects me home tomorrow, though."

"Great." Ajay placed a hand on the boy's shoulder. That would at least give them a little time to figure out the mess they'd been dealt. He turned to Olexie. "Where is this hideout of yours?"

"You'll see."

Ajay's jaw ached, and he realized he had been grinding his teeth. He didn't like this. Not being shot at. Not trusting Olexie. Not disappearing into an unknown hideout some-where deep in northern Minnesota.

"I'll tell you when we arrive," said Olexie. "Unless you remember where you know me from."

Ajay looked at the man in the shadows across from him. He still had no recollection of this man or any hint that he had ever seen his face. Then again, Ajay didn't exactly meet a lot of people face to face. If he knew Olexie, it would have been online.

Olexie was a Russian and slightly younger than Ajay. He was a hacker, or at least something similar. A memory clicked in the back of Ajay's brain. Something cold and muddied from years ago.

The van bumped and hitched over a poorly cleared gravel road, rumbling over the patchy ice. Ajay held tight to the bench to keep from sliding around too much.

As the van pulled to a stop under the dark cover of a large shed, Ajay fixed Olexie's gaze and leveled his accusa-tion. "You were the Ghost of Lenin."

The Ghost of Lenin had driven a stake in the heart of America. This man, Olexie Sokolov, had been a thorn in

Ajay's side for the first decades of his career. Ajay had scrambled to stabilize his country while people like Olexie worked for the opposite. The Ghost of Lenin supported politicians who sowed chaos. They stoked fires under the opposition to the point where civil war seemed a realistic concern. Behind it all was one hacker. One clever young leader who was known only by his frightening moniker.

A smile spread across Olexie's lips even as sadness deepened in his eyes. "It was a long time ago." He opened the van's back door and stepped out into the cold wind. "Welcome to the Soudan Mine, repurposed as the hideout of the CCS."

Ajay said, "You're not terrorists, but you have a hideout in an abandoned mine?"

Three men with assault rifles stood outside the ancient tin-roofed building that enclosed a single elevator. Ajay squinted against the blinding light of the snowy world, taking in the small ramshackle buildings, the decrepit sheds, and the footprints. There were so many tracks in the fresh snow. A lot of people had been here recently.

"Looking for a ride down?" asked a man with a mop of steel-gray hair poking up from under a thick parka.

"New recruits, Walt," said Maja.

Walt sized them up, a little taken aback by the children. "Younger every year."

"Walt is the elevator operator," said Olexie. The scrape of metal on metal signaled the elevator's operation. "There's an override inside the elevator, but the system works better if someone runs it from up here."

Ajay said, "I've always wanted to feel trapped under a million tons of iron ore."

Olexie slapped him on the back. "Always the positive thinker, Ajay Andersen."

It was too late to turn back. He knew that the second he stepped out of the van. Too late for protest, and the dead signal on his fidget told him it was too late to message anyone about his location.

"Come on, kids," Ajay said, putting as much confidence he could toward the decision. "It's time to see what this countercapitalism thing is all about."

Kylie took his hand as they crossed the slippery packed snow. He thought at first it was so that she could support him, but then he felt what she pressed into his palm.

A data chip.

He gave her a reassuring squeeze as they stepped into the ancient elevator.

CHAPTER FOURTEEN

THE SOUDAN MINE was one of many abandoned holes in the rocky crust of the Iron Range of northern Minnesota. It had once been the center of wealth nestled at the edge of the coniferous wilds of the north, but when its high-oxygen iron fell out of favor, the mine was shut down. The machinery of excavation still loomed in the dark, rusted monsters of an ancient civilization. They lay at rest in the cool air of the abandoned tunnels far beneath the earth, rusting into the walls, one day to become part of the ancient underground.

The mine didn't end when the Iron Range's profitability dried up. The area became a hotbed of scientific inquiry, testing anything from dark matter to the capture of neutrinos produced from a super collider in Chicago. The mine had supported tourism back when Minnesota's Iron Range was a quaint artifact of Americana. Eventually, the mine had fallen into the hands of private owners.

"This is the old science wing," Olexie said once they

had settled in around a wide table across from a woman who worked quietly on a rectangle of unrecognizable food. The room's drop ceiling gave it the air of a fifty-year-old cheap office building. The Russian waved a hand at the decor. "They caught particles and got very excited about physics that do not matter one bit."

Kylie said, "They don't do that here anymore?"

"The place is abandoned," Olexie said. "The owner uses some of the levels above for storage, but otherwise there is nothing here."

"What owner?" asked Ajay.

"I'm told it doesn't matter," said Olexie, glancing at Maja.

"But there's a lot of history here," said Kylie, ever curious. Ajay watched the girl closely. She wasn't showing any signs of the fear she ought to be feeling in the situation. Not like Austin. That kid was terrified behind his brave mask. Kylie showed nothing, and Ajay wondered if she was suppressing it all.

"We should introduce our friend to the others," sighed Maja. She looked older in the light of the lab than she had in the bright light of day. Harsh LED lighting sank her eyes into pits and highlighted cruel wrinkles at the corners of her eyes. She gestured to the woman who was quietly trying to ignore them. "Starting with our head of security."

"They don't need to know everyone," said Olexie, glancing at the others in the room. He leaned forward with a whisper, "I don't even remember the names of the hired help."

"But it might be good for Shannon to know them," said Maja.

The head of security looked up at them, seeming to notice the newcomers for the first time. Some head of security. She raised an eyebrow.

"I'm Ajay Andersen," Ajay said.

"Retired computer scientist," Maja droned, looking at a screen in her palm. "Golfer, grandfather, no outstanding parking tickets." She looked up at him, and Ajay expected her to wish him a happy birthday. The unique worm he had programmed to constantly rewrite his background always made today his birthday. She didn't mention it. Instead, she said, "How is your retirement, Mr. Andersen?"

"You know how retirement goes," he said. "Sunshine and roses, then you die. I'm clearly in the sunshine and roses part."

"Shannon Fox," said Olexie, gesturing to the woman at the table. "Computer engineer and weapons specialist. She will help you with whatever you need here. Shannon, these are our new guests. Do not shoot them."

Ajay scowled at the woman. "You're hired help, then?"

"Something like that," said Shannon. Her chestnut hair was pulled back into a neat ponytail, revealing an angry scar along her jawline. A crease along the bridge of her nose hinted at glasses, but she wasn't wearing any. To Kylie and Austin, she said, "Olexie doesn't think my people are necessary around here." The amusement in her voice was a shade more sour than Ajay would have liked.

Maja tapped her screen. "Many of the people here are

believers in our cause. Others are hired to fill skill gaps. Shannon helps keep things smooth."

"This seems like an odd way to run a countercapitalist organization."

Olexie barked a sharp laugh. "That is what I said."

"And yet you're not willing to do the heavy lifting," Maja said, ice on the tip of her tongue.

"I am old," Olexie said.

Maja flashed a sweet smile at Ajay. "He's old when it's time to do hard work. Young when it comes to deciding who has to sit out the cushy missions."

"The Bemidji government center was not cushy," protested Olexie.

Ajay plastered a polite grin on his face. "I'm not a true believer or hired help." To Shannon, he said, "We'll be out of your hair as soon as it's safe."

Shannon leaned back in her chair. "I'm paid either way."

"A wonderful attitude," muttered Olexie.

"And this is Nick Hampton," said Maja as a shorter man in black fatigues entered the room. The man flashed a charming smile, then poured himself a cup of coffee. "Shannon and Nick are both team leads here. They manage the defensive wing of this activist group and keep the rest of us out of trouble."

"A defensive wing," deadpanned Ajay.

"In case of counterprotests," said Olexie.

"Is that what happened today?"

"They extracted you as quickly as they could," said Maja, her voice so carefully calm as to be infuriating.

Ajay slammed an open palm on the table. "You put my granddaughter at risk."

Maja leaned forward. "We had nothing to do with that attack."

"Bullshit."

Maja raised an eyebrow at Olexie, who waved her off. He said, "Ajay, we didn't want you involved in all this."

"But Silas did, didn't he?"

Again, some unspoken communication passed among the members of the counter capitalist group. Olexie said, "Do you know how he found you?"

"We should send the kids out," Maja murmured.

Ajay ignored her. "How *did* you find me?" This was something he *had* to know. If he'd left an opening that Silas could follow, then anyone could find him.

"I have a theory," said Olexie.

Ajay's hands clenched into fists. "Explain."

Olexie cast a look at Kylie, who sat close to Austin. "He was helping you find a cure."

Ajay had been looking for a cure for Kylie since her mother had died obtaining the scan that might lead to it. His search had scoured the globe and drawn the wrong kinds of attention, but he had been careful not to lead that attention back to himself. Hadn't he? "How?"

"I think someone else has been looking for that same cure," said Olexie. "Someone working for Frontier Arms. Silas managed to swipe the data from them, and they also had your location. He was going to bring that information to you, but Frontier Arms must have had him poisoned."

"Poisoned?" Ajay's hands shook. He remembered the

drunken footprints in front of his house. Someone else was looking for the cure. Someone else had his address. "How? How did they get to him?"

"Are we going to have to move?" Kylie asked.

Ajay patted her hand but couldn't give an answer. Not one that would make her feel any better.

"I thought so," Kylie said. He saw that dangerous rage flash across her face.

"This all sounds like an exceptionally convenient lie," Ajay said after absorbing the new information. "You want to make me interested in hacking Frontier Arms because then you can get inside and hurt that rich guy who hired them."

"Nobody's suggesting you hack Frontier," said Shannon.

"Thompson's up to something," said Maya.

"I don't get what Liam Thompson has to do with this," said Kylie.

"Frontier Arms works for him as bodyguards," explained Ajay. "They happen to have my information. Very convenient."

"Nobody needs that many bodyguards," said Maja. "And bodyguards don't ransack and burn government buildings in small town Minnesota."

"Everybody needs a hobby," said Ajay.

"Is this about Mr. Thompson's city of the future?" asked Kylie. "Because that didn't sound very evil."

Maja rolled her eyes.

Olexie said, "Unchecked capitalism gives some people

far too much power. It doesn't matter how they use it because it is fundamentally corrupt."

"But Mr. Thompson's city is going to be environmentally neutral. It's going to have housing for everyone and no energy footprint. It's going to be all green space, and the entire center of the city will be designed for pedestrians, not cars." Kylie glanced at Austin, who nodded grimly. "It's going to be amazing, and he's going to put it in northern Minnesota where it can revitalize an economically depressed part of the country."

Olexie said, "Where exactly?"

Kylie furrowed her brow. "What do you mean?"

"Where in northern Minnesota? Here, on the mine? Which forest will he cut to make room for his buildings? Where will he buy agricultural land to support it? What wetlands will he fill?"

"None." Kylie stood and her chair flew back and toppled to the floor. "He's an environmentalist, and he cares about the forests and wetlands. That's why he wants to build this new city."

Ajay reached out to touch her hand, but she pulled away. In the middle of her temper, he wasn't sure if he could stop her from doing whatever she was going to do. "It's fine," he said to her.

She scowled at Ajay, gestured to Austin, and then stormed out of the room. Austin looked lost for several seconds, then followed her.

"That boy doesn't know what he's getting into," said Olexie.

"Do any of us?" Ajay asked.

"They don't need to hear this." Maja motioned with her chin, and Shannon followed the kids. "Ajay, I didn't want to bring you here."

Ajay leaned back in his chair and placed two hands on the head of his cane. "And yet."

Olexie said, "Silas thought a guy like you might be able to hack Thompson's systems."

"I didn't agree," said Maja.

"Yet, here we are," said Olexie. "And now we no longer have Silas."

Ajay met the old Russian's emotionless gaze for a long time before offering his calculated response. "Go to hell, Ghost of Lenin."

"That was a long time ago," growled Olexie.

"A long time ago and thousands of lives. Hundreds of thousands."

Olexie's fists clenched into iron hammers, but he kept them on the table. "I did what I had to do for what I believed was right."

"Your social media barrage sowed chaos where there was peace. You convinced millions to hate their own health and despise their fellow countrymen. You spread pestilence during a pandemic and discord during some of the tensest moments of American history."

Maja shifted uncomfortably but didn't respond.

"For that," Ajay said, "I will never trust you."

Olexie stood, his rage finally boiling over. When he spoke, his accent twisted the words. "You were far worse, Ajay Andersen. Your hacks brought nuclear reactors to the brink of meltdown. You shattered Russian companies on the stock exchange and are personally responsible for millions starving during the harsh winters in the late twenties." He jabbed a finger at Ajay. "You will *not* judge me, old man. I chose to defect, and I chose to *forgive*." His voice cracked on that last word. "I will not be preached to by the likes of you."

With that, Olexie stomped out of the room. Maja gestured again, and Nick followed. Ajay was left with a racing heart, sweaty palms, and a hard-eyed woman.

Maja shrugged. "Olexie has always hated seeing what the ultra-rich do to this world. He hated it when he worked for the Russian oligarchs, and he hated it when he defected and retired to the United States. That's why his retirement didn't last."

"You pulled him out of retirement for this?"

She leaned back and folded her hands over her stomach. "Some people don't like the idea of wasting their final years. They want to make a difference."

"I tried to make a difference once," Ajay said. "It didn't work out."

"You don't want to try to do better?"

"I'll settle for a few more years of golf."

Maja sighed. "You think of us as a terrorist group, so think of this as a cell. We have our purpose. Our goal right now is to watch Liam Thompson and stop him if he decides to do something horrible."

"Silas thought something bad was going to happen. I'm surprised he came up with that much."

"He wasn't bad at what he did. Silas had one of the best mentors in the world."

"I might have been one of the best hackers in my day," said Ajay, "but I was not anywhere near a decent mentor."

"The wealthy are never great at hiding the existence of their plots, are they? Details, maybe, but what fun is being ultrarich if you can't brag a little?"

"The city of the future. You think it's a front for something."

Maja leaned forward, her elbows on the table. "No, Mr. Andersen. I think it's exactly what he says it is, and if he succeeds, it'll affect the futures of those kids."

"I just want them to *have* a future."

"Then you're going to want to help."

CHAPTER FIFTEEN

"Why is it so cold in here?" asked Kylie. They stood on a metal walkway high above the stone floor, where a dozen men and women worked on screens. Along the far wall, across a vast, open space, stood a several-stories-tall metal octagon, its panels like petals of a flower. The place made Kylie uncomfortable, but it wasn't just the temperature.

"It's always cold underground," said Austin. "It's the average of the year's outside temperature."

Kylie hugged her black coat close to her body. Austin was too smart for his own good. "How do you know that?"

"My grandma used to take me on a lot of trips. We went to a place called Mystery Cave." He wiggled his fingers when he said the name, as if a hole in the ground might actually be mysterious. "It's amazing and full of bats. We learned all about cave systems."

Kylie thought Mystery Cave sounded like an awful vacation but decided not to mention that. Bats were pretty cool, though. "She doesn't take you anymore?"

Austin was silent for a few breaths. He stared at the huge metal plates. "She was really old," he finally said.

Kylie glanced back the way they had come. Papa was old, too, but she didn't really have an idea of *how* old. He never would admit to an actual birthday, as if he'd spawned from the earth all gray-haired and grumpy.

Shannon—the intense woman from the other room—lingered in the doorway, watching Kylie and Austin with narrow eyes.

"Come on," Kylie whispered. "Let's explore."

They descended some metal stairs—the kind that a person could see through, which made Kylie way more nervous than she was willing to admit. Every step rattled the ancient stairs. Austin didn't seem to have a problem with either the walkway or the stairs. Maybe his brain was still numb from having a gun pointed at him.

With stone under their feet again, Kylie felt a little more confident, but the edge of discomfort still itched at her brain. The rows of desks where people worked were still twenty feet away, and the huge metal octagon loomed over them.

"It's part of a physics experiment," said Austin. "They used it to catch neutrinos."

"What do they do with them?"

Austin didn't have an answer to that one. They made their way past the people working at the desks and back behind an array of old machinery. Shannon followed them, but every time they turned a corner, they had a few seconds without her.

"What do you think these people are doing down here?" Kylie whispered.

"I don't know. Terrorist stuff?"

Kylie poked her head around the corner and watched the people working at the computers. "They don't look like terrorists."

"What do terrorists look like?"

"I don't know." Austin's eyes sparkled. "All crazy and fanatical in the eyes, I guess. These people look like they're here to do a job."

"Like mercenaries."

"Sure."

"Maybe they're hired assassins."

Kylie snorted. She was starting to feel comfortable around Austin. "Like Star Blade Princess," she said before her better judgment could stop her. No way did Austin know anything about an obscure anime about spacefaring assassin princesses.

Shannon rounded the corner and acted all surprised to see them there. "Hey, kids," she said. "Can I give you a tour?"

"We're fine on our own, thanks," Kylie said. She took Austin's hand and ran as fast as she deemed polite, which was extremely fast.

"She gives me the creeps," Austin said when they rounded a corner.

"Me, too."

Her fidget didn't connect to anything when she tried, and neither did Austin's. That made sense, since they were about a million miles under iron-rich ore. The people at the computers seemed to have a connection, though, and it wasn't a raised floor, so Kylie could see where the cords went. They snaked back the direction they had come and were joined by a variety of power and data cables.

"I want to know more about these people," Kylie whispered as they turned a bend around the huge metal plates. The plate went back farther than she had thought, and they followed layer after layer deep into the stone. "But we can't learn anything without a connection to the outside world."

Austin froze, his eyes wide. Kylie recognized the fear on his face and placed a hopefully comforting hand on his. "What is it?"

"They won't want anyone to discover their location," he said.

"True. So what?"

"So, they're not going to let us connect to anything. They're not going to let us call home." He swallowed. "They're not going to let us leave, either."

Shannon rounded the corner and watched them with a raised eyebrow. She leaned against the stone wall with her pistol jutting from her hip.

"I know," whispered Kylie. "That's why it's a good thing I'm a hacker."

CHAPTER SIXTEEN

AJAY SPREAD the paper he'd taken from the thug in Bemidji on the table. He sat alone with Maja. She folded her arms and watched him as he did his best to figure out which direction was north on the map. He felt the weight of her eyes on him, which compounded his uncertainty at helping her.

Maja leaned forward, a flat look in her eyes. "You weren't going to show us this?"

Ajay did his best not to think about Silas's data chip, which he wouldn't share until he had a chance to take a look at it. "This is one of the papers they were trying to steal."

Maja picked up a corner of it and poked a pinky finger through a hole. "Bullet hole?"

"Maybe." Ajay tried not to think about it.

"Olexie said you were never a field agent. How come you're so cool under pressure that you managed to steal one of the papers while under close small arms fire?"

"I didn't feel very cool under pressure. It felt a lot more like sheer panic."

"Great, isn't it?" Maja's eyes sparkled. "You and Olexie had all the fun."

Ajay drew a long breath as the day's events finally started to catch up to him. It had all happened so fast, and he was still trying to make sense of everything. The adrenaline that had sustained him through the events of the morning now dragged like a nasty hangover on his old brain, amplifying the aches in his knuckles and the persistent pain in his hip and thigh. It wasn't great, he decided. It was not great at all.

He finally decided to ask a question that had been bothering him. "Why does Olexie do all this?" At Maja's questioning expression, he continued, "The countercapitalism thing. He's from a pretty broken time in Russia's long history of broken times. Why does he care about America enough to want to fix things?"

"You don't think he's trustworthy."

"True."

Maja met his gaze for a long time. He read compassion there as if she understood everything he was going through. "I've worked for America a long time, and I can tell you what we do here has nothing to do with love of the country. This goes against the fundamental ideals of the American dream."

"The dream that says anyone could become ultra-wealthy?"

"It isn't power that breeds corruption," Maja said. "It's the opposite. Corruption is a precursor to power. A requirement. Olexie saw naked corruption in his home country, and when he came here, he thought he'd escaped it."

"You're saying he's an idiot. That doesn't really make me trust him anymore."

"You can't really trust anyone, because everyone has secret desires," Maja purred.

"What is it you want?" Ajay asked, unsure if she was flirting with him and doubly unsure if he was flirting back. He decided she wasn't flirting, but she was friendly. Everything she did made it easier to treat her like an old friend.

She gestured at the crumpled paper on the table. "I want to know what this is all about."

Ajay flattened the map again. "It's a soil chart."

"Wonderful."

"This Thompson guy is an environmentalist. He can probably read these charts without any trouble. I'd look up a guide for it, but you've cut off all network access."

Maja consulted the codes that dotted sections of the sheet and copied them into her fidget. "I'll look up how to read them later."

Ajay peered at the paper. The key was missing, but he could guess at some of the notation. "This is a slope here," he said, pointing to the topographical lines. "And these numbers indicate infiltration rates." He considered the lines of the graph. "This might be depth of soil. A lot of this is really thin, though. It would be only a few inches before you hit bedrock."

Olexie's gruff voice came from behind Ajay. "Infiltration rates?"

"It's the rate water is absorbed into the soil," Ajay said without looking up.

"You've decided to help," said the Russian dubiously, sitting at the table.

"Do you really think knowing infiltration rates is helpful?"

"No."

The puzzle of it itched at Ajay. "This map represents one nine-acre block in the middle of a vast forest. Once you figure out where this block is, you still won't have any idea what the plan is for this city of the future. Do you think Liam fucking Thompson, hero environmentalist to the people, is going to clear-cut the forest to build this city? Doesn't seem very likely."

Olexie crossed the room and sat quietly at the end of the table.

"Is this all we have?" said Maja. "Did we get anything from the librarian?"

"Didn't have time," Olexie grumbled. "They came soon after we got there."

Ajay cocked his head. "What exactly were you looking for?"

"Ownership documents. It's all online, but Silas's last message mentioned irregularities in the digital records all across the region." Olexie leaned forward and peered at the paper. "We never thought to look at the soil survey reports."

"No," said Ajay. "Who would? It's soil." His curiosity was piqued. "There's nothing here that's very damning. Nothing about toxic chemicals or anything. Nothing more than the regular 3M-anointed petrochemicals found in every lake around the world. And, even so, the rates of those are relatively low. There's no hint of runoff from the copper-nickel mines, and there isn't even evidence of damage from old iron mining. This is the soil we would expect to see in virgin or near-virgin forest."

Maja brought a holographic projector from another room and set it so they could all see. "One of the analysts was able to locate the GPS coordinates of this report, and you're right. It's in the middle of a north woods with nothing around it for miles. The nearest mine is copper-nickel, but it's miles away. The only sign of human activity in the area is a single snowmobile trail."

Ajay peered at the satellite view of the area. It was a forest of skeletal trees clouded with clumps of white snow. The single path that ran through didn't look well traveled and was barely visible except for the few places where fallen trees had been removed from the trail.

Olexie made a grunt of frustration. "I *know* he's up to something."

"You don't have proof," Ajay said.

"He's doing something."

"You don't even have evidence."

Olexie clenched his fists. "He is a snake."

"Just because he's rich—"

"Liam Thompson needs to die!" Olexie roared. He stood with enough force to send his chair tumbling across the room.

"What this is about, Olexie?"

Olexie's nostrils flared. "It is about doing the right thing."

"Murder's the right thing?"

"If need be."

Ajay fought to keep his voice calm and almost succeeded. "Without evidence?"

"There is evidence," Olexie growled.

"None that I've seen," said Ajay.

Olexie kicked the fallen chair, and it cracked against the wall.

"If Thompson is doing something illegal, you can get the police involved," Ajay said.

"He is beyond the law," grumbled Olexie. He set the chair back on its feet and sat. The back leaned to one side where he had cracked the plastic, but it still held his tall frame. "Rich people aren't like us mere mortals."

After several long, slow breaths, Ajay said, "I'm not helping. I'm consulting." He clutched his cane tighter. "But only if you promise not to murder anyone."

Olexie let out a single, harsh laugh. "You will change your mind."

"Thompson's forest city isn't going to make me want to kill him. Even if you have evidence."

"It's not the city that's the problem," growled Olexie. "It's the lies."

Ajay forced himself to draw several slow breaths before responding. The truth was that he *did* know better than anyone, but the Ghost of Lenin's exploits had been horrible for the world. Olexie had been so good at his job, he'd cratered American ingenuity for decades. Ajay had never been able to fight the kinds of attacks the Russian used because Ajay always worked in the shadows. Olexie had been a hundred faces in the crowd speaking in unison. He had been a bot swarm tangling public opinion as easily as a fisherman ties knots. He had bought into Russian lies, and the world burned because of it.

"Lies don't bother me," said Ajay. "Murder does."

Maja smiled. "See, Olexie. I told you he was my kind of guy."

Olexie said, "She only lies."

Maja shot him a sour look.

"I'm not anyone's kind of guy," said Ajay. "All I want is for my granddaughter and her friend to return home tomorrow morning without anything hanging over their heads. Your enemies aren't my enemies, and I don't give one good goddamn whether or not Liam Thompson burns down the entire north woods." Not true, but it made a point.

"You care," whispered Maja.

"I *just* said I didn't mind lies. If we have to tear down a rich man's project to keep those kids safe, then I'll do it, but I won't kill anyone."

Olexie ran his fingers through the bristles of his square hair. To Maja, he said, "Can we make it safe for the children? Can we get them out of this?"

Maja panned on her holographic projection for a time, taking notes as he scrolled through pages of aerial drone images. Ajay wondered how recent those images were. Was she working with today's drone footage, or archive footage from an official record somewhere? Either way, there were bound to be inaccuracies. Live drone footage would show a terrain covered in snow, concealing even activity from the previous week. Then again, Ajay could see the snowmobile tracks in the images that she followed. If that was new footage, then those tracks had been traveled in the previous twenty-four hours.

Finally, she looked up, grim triumph on her face. She spun the image so that Ajay and Olexie could get a better look. The image showed a sprawling building nestled into the deep woods and surrounded by Douglas fir.

"Liam Thompson's wolf lodge," said Olexie.

"Wolf lodge?" asked Ajay. "Are there wolves?"

"Plenty," said Maja, "but that's not the point. Thompson owns dozens of properties around the area. Whole lakes, actually. This lodge is east of Ely, right at the edge of the Boundary Waters."

The Boundary Waters Canoe Area was Minnesota's greatest natural treasure. It made sense that a rabid environmentalist like Liam Thompson would be a fan of it enough to build property right on the edge. Something about being rich often made people want to have national treasures in their backyards.

Ajay peered at the enormous lodge. "Why are there snowmobile tracks? Where is he sending patrols?"

"Up into the BWCA itself," said Maja, "but there's nothing there, and motorized vehicles normally aren't allowed. Some of the water is still open, but most of it's frozen already. He can get pretty far on a tank of gas, but there's really nothing out there but some decent ice fishing and a whole lot of forest." She zoomed out on the image.

"Maybe he's enjoying his retirement," deadpanned

Ajay. "Some people do that." He exchanged flat looks with Maja and Olexie. "Or so I've heard."

"Battery," Olexie said.

Maja furrowed her brow at him. "Excuse me?"

"Modern snowmobiles don't use gas. They run silent, and they use lithium iron phosphate batteries that perform well in cold."

She gave him several slow blinks before continuing, "It's just forests and lakes up there. Our drones have made a sweep of the area, but if he has a major operation up there, it's invisible to us."

"We need to know what he's planning," Olexie said to Ajay.

Ajay thought about it. Curiosity was almost enough to convince him to help, but there was more. If Liam's body-guards collected info about Kylie and Austin, he could purge that data if he could get into their system.

"You said yourself he's venturing into the BWCA here. There's no way this is where he plans on building his city of the future. No Minnesotan would allow anyone to touch that land."

Maja tapped the map Ajay had brought. "This is in the BWCA."

Ajay stared at the map and then at the image of the wolf lodge. "There would be riots if he even mentioned building there."

Maja shrugged. "They almost allowed mining up there a decade ago."

Ajay waved it off. "That was different. Lawyers fighting lawyers. That kind of thing happens all the time, and nobody ever sunk a pick into the rocks that close to the border."

Olexie furrowed his brow. "That isn't how modern mining works."

"The picks are bigger," Ajay said, "but it's basically the same."

"There *were* riots," said Maja. "Violent ones."

"True," said Ajay.

The three sat in silence for a while, and Ajay considered his situation. He didn't trust Maja or Olexie, but Liam Thompson was up to something. He had to be. Nobody launches an assault on the government center of a small town and murders two people without some nefarious plans in place. The charts they found involved land north of Thompson's wolf lodge, a sprawling estate on the edge of the BWCA. Ajay might put up a good front about not caring what the man was up to, but this bothered him. Those mercenaries had killed innocent people in cold blood.

"How do I know Liam was behind the attack at the government center?" Ajay asked.

Maja shot him a wary look. "He was there. Didn't you see his BMW parked on the block?"

"There are a lot of those, I'm sure," Ajay conjectured.

"They're expensive," Maja said. "If it wasn't him, then it was at least a drone from his fleet."

"He has more than one?"

"Of course," said Maja. "Why own only one prohibitively expensive vehicle?"

Ajay drew a long breath. Olexie was right. He needed

to get close to the lodge so that he could see what these people knew about Kylie and Austin. At the very least he needed information that he could use to barter with Liam to force his mercenaries to leave the kids alone. If there was any chance of returning to their quiet life, this was it.

"I'm not helping you kill anyone," Ajay said.

"We don't expect you to," said Maja.

"And I expect you to solve this without violence if at all possible. Even after I'm gone."

"Of course." The slight hesitation in Maja's response rendered it all the more believable.

"We go tonight," Ajay said. "We'll hack the lodge's network and figure out what this guy is planning. I'll do what I need to do to keep the kids safe, and then I'm done."

A big grin spread across Olexie's face.

Ajay thumped his cane on the floor and pulled his weary bones to his feet. The bronze head of his cane felt like a weapon in his hand, but he felt like it wouldn't be enough. Picking it up, he hefted the cane and asked, "Did you say you have a workshop down here somewhere?"

CHAPTER SEVENTEEN

Liam Thompson almost wished he had dedicated his life and his wealth to solving the problems of medical science rather than the environment. Sure, the environment would serve generations of humanity. The future of the human race owed its existence to his innovations and investments.

But medical science—maybe he could have done away with the toxic chemo he currently endured. It might extend his life by months, but it extended his misery by a hundred lifetimes.

Liam sat behind his monolithic oak desk, shivering in the fireplace's warmth in the elegant study of his wolf lodge. The IV stand next to him dripped poison into a vein in his left arm. The room was done in earthy wood tones, in the style of an old wolf lodge, but the technology integrated into his mansion was all modern. He had the best in network security, including a direct laser uplink to a satellite in geosynchronous orbit specifically for his own use. His home's integrated accessibility features would handle all of his needs until he could no longer exist on this planet. The lodge provided every creature comfort he could want in his final days, even if the warm fire that crackled in the fireplace couldn't warm his bones. Everything here was perfect.

He was not ready to give up. Not when he was so close.

Before him, in a heavy oak chair covered in velvet plush, sat the accountant. His unkempt gray mop of hair failed to cover the mottled bruise marring the left side of his pale face. The way the man's shattered glasses hung at a crooked angle irritated Liam.

Liam glanced at the objects on his desk, letting his eyes dance from the yellow papers to the Sig Sauer pistol that acted as a paperweight. "Mr. Lang tells me you have something to say, Mr. Gilbert."

The accountant gave a small, dry cough.

Poison continued to pulse through Liam's veins. "There's a certain point at the end of a man's life when he thinks not of himself but of his legacy. What will your legacy be?"

"I—I don't know," Gilbert whispered. A rime of blood brightened his lips.

"Perhaps it will be a legacy of truth," said Liam. "That's what being an accountant is all about, isn't it? There is a certain elegant truth in numbers. Numbers do not lie. It is as you said, the numbers show that the mining started. Numbers show that profits were made. Anyone could take a careful look at those books and see where those numbers converge, showing clear misdeeds on the parts of those companies making exploratory ventures into the BWCA wilderness. Is that what you will have, Mr. Gilbert? A legacy of truth?"

Gilbert swallowed, and pain crinkled the corners of his eyes. "I have a family."

"Yes, yes. A family. Many men see family as their legacy. Your children live on and tell stories of their wonderful father who worked all day and night. The father whose passion for numbers drove him to seek the environmental justice that saved Minnesota's landscape. Maybe that will be your legacy."

"I just want to go home," Gilbert sobbed. His snot and tears and blood mixed, and it disgusted Liam.

"I have very few employees, you know. Tenen Lang," Liam gestured at Mr. Gilbert's bruises, "with whom you are well acquainted, is my primary contact with Frontier Arms. He learns my plans before they are executed, but almost everyone else in that organization is in the dark. Do you think I should stop trusting Mr. Lang?"

The accountant glared at Liam through eyes hooded with rage. Who knew a numbers man could get so angry?

"No, you're right," said Liam. "Tenen is trustworthy. The terrorists had someone in the courthouse before we even got there, but Frontier Arms couldn't have tipped them off. They didn't know. Someone shot one of our people and stole some of the papers that you said would poison my legacy." At this, Liam let his gaze linger on the IV standing next to his desk. "I know how to handle poison, you know. I've made something of a career of it."

"I didn't tell anyone," whispered the accountant. "I

swear." A log in the fireplace popped, and the accountant jumped.

Liam drew a long breath. His whole body ached, and the nausea started to settle in. This would be a difficult chemo session, but he couldn't put it off anymore, not even for the few days it would take to get his project started.

"We ran into men like you in the oil industry, you know," Liam said. "Numbers men. Accountants. You were always the ones who could balance the sheets and tell everyone that of course their gasoline cars weren't destroying the planet because something else was much worse. You were the kind of people who told executives that there was one clear way to run a business, and that was the pursuit of short-term profit. Always. Forever."

"That's not how it works," said the accountant.

"Isn't it?" Liam raised an eyebrow in mock question. "Didn't you tell me that you worked for Cable Sawyer Mining? Was it not you who told me that they balanced their sheets and discovered that the profits of starting their operation before the permits were in place would lead to more income than the fines could possibly dent? Didn't you tell me they made a fortune before abandoning the project because permits never came through?"

"The permits were never going to be approved," Gilbert said. "It was a legal house of mirrors meant to cover their operation within the borders of the BWCA."

"And now a wastewater reservoir sits where nobody will find it in one of America's most treasured wildernesses."

"Which is why I came to you. You are renowned for cleaning up messes like this."

Liam wasn't sure if his sneer of disgust was from the man's words or from the wave of nausea that threatened to overtake him. "I am renowned for cleaning messes far greater than this, Mr. Gilbert. Far greater."

"Of course."

"Legacy is a continuation of reputation. I have a reputation for fixing the greatest environmental disasters the world has created. My legacy isn't going to be my city of the future. Do you know that? My legacy will be saving the BWCA from the greatest environmental disaster it has ever faced. A disaster that you and Cable Sawyer will be known for perpetrating upon the altar of profit."

"The site is contained," said Mr. Gilbert. "That was critical for our calculations."

Liam drummed his fingernails on the oak table next to his pistol. He didn't take his eyes from the accountant. "Yes, that's true today, but eventually all those heavy metals will leak."

The accountant smiled through bloody teeth. "Long after we're dead, Mr. Thompson."

"Right," said Liam. "And that's the problem, isn't it?"

The mining company had crunched their numbers. Liam saw how they worked. He had seen it all before. They weighed their risks, assuming that they would be long gone —at least the entity called Cable Sawyer would be disbanded before their poison was discovered. If not, the executives would be long gone and dissociated from the ramifications of their illegal activity. All they would have to show for it would be record profits and a vacation home somewhere without extradition. Liam had made a career of sucking such corporations dry and using the money for cleanup, but he rarely saw the executives pay for their crimes.

Even less often did he see accountants pay for theirs.

"Right," Liam repeated, eying the IV in his pale arm. "Yes, we'll both be long gone before anyone really pays for any of this."

In one smooth movement, he picked up the pistol and shot the accountant three times.

"But there are ways to expedite timelines," he said, "and I have a strong feeling that the world will learn of your crimes sooner rather than later."

Liam Thompson set his pistol down, turned to the side, and dry heaved in the general direction of his wastebasket. When his stomach settled, he rang for Tenen Lang to dispose of the body. It gave him great comfort to have at least one employee he could trust.

"WHAT ABOUT A MACHINE GUN CANE?" asked Austin. "And a razor blade top hat." His chin rested on folded fingers as he watched Kylie in the hideout's workshop. A metal lathe whirred behind him, and all around, power tools hummed. The air smelled of woodsmoke and iron. "Or a sword cane."

This was as close as she could get to the computer lines, and Kylie still couldn't get a signal from one of the connected systems. It had taken a half hour of begging and cajoling just to be allowed to help Papa in the workshop. Shannon had finally relented with an exasperated, "Fine, cut your fucking fingers off."

Kylie was really starting to dislike Shannon.

Then Papa had left them alone to work while he toured the rest of the facility. Kylie thought he was probably snooping around, but probably he was just looking for a bathroom. He did that a lot.

Kylie raised an eyebrow at Austin. "First of all, how

would a machine gun cane even work? There's no room. He would just be carrying around a gun, and he doesn't like guns."

"What about the top hat?"

Kylie scrunched up her nose. "Some old people have bleeding disorders."

"Fair enough." Austin picked up a heavy metal piece that Kylie was sure must be an important component of a gun. He pointed the wrong end at the wall and made shooting noises, earning a dirty look from Shannon. "No sharp clothing. No guns. Got it."

"And I can't make a sword cane without first making a sword. Do you know how to make a sword? I'm sure they have the equipment for it here, but I didn't exactly take that elective in sixth grade."

Austin made a pouty face.

"Have you tried a taser cane?" asked a man at the next workbench. He had dark skin and an infectious smile. "If you're looking for ways to be dangerous and stylish at the same time."

Austin shrank into his big orange coat.

"I'm Samuel," said the man. He flipped a cylinder the size of his pinky in the air and caught it. "Can I help you attach this to your cane?"

Samuel showed Kylie how to set up the drill press, and she drilled a three-quarter-inch hole in the tip of Papa's cane. The rubber tip shredded away, but she didn't care. "A taser cane is going to be pretty cool," she admitted.

"Definitely," said Samuel.

"What if we added a poison gas canister?" asked Austin.

Kylie glanced at Samuel, who shook his head.

"Bees?" Austin tried.

Kylie stopped her work and glared at the boy. "How would that even work, Austin?"

He shrugged. "Maybe if your grandpa had psychic control over Hymenoptera."

"He's not a supervillain." Kylie wrenched the cane from the press brackets and carried it to another workbench.

"He kind of is, though, isn't he?" When Kylie glared at him, Austin raised his hands in surrender. "I won't tell anyone, I promise, but we're in a terrorist base camp deep underground building secret hidden weapons for him. That sounds pretty villainous to me."

Kylie inserted the taser cylinder into the end of the cane and cinched it in place with an iron ring. "He's a hero. Not a superhero. Just a hero. If he has to work with these people, then it's something good and not evil."

Austin didn't say anything for a long time. Samuel went back to his own work, painting a stack of assault rifles white with gray splotches. It looked boring, but probably made them better for the winter.

"I feel three pounds lighter," said Papa as he shuffled past the ever-present Shannon, whose only response was a disgusted sneer. He placed a warm hand on Kylie's shoulder and said, "How is arts and crafts time coming?"

"I made you this," Kylie said, holding up the cane.

When Papa frowned at it, Austin explained, "It's a taser cane."

"You trigger it with your fidget," Kylie said and showed him how to connect to the wireless taser attachment. "Jab and zap."

Papa chuckled. "Not a sword cane?"

Kylie scowled at him.

"Well, hopefully, it won't come to all that." He thumped the cane on the floor, and it made an odd clack. "The tip's broken."

"It had to go."

"That's the part that keeps it from slipping." He flashed a quirky grin. "Your added feature has compromised the cane's primary function."

Kylie furrowed her brow. "You're really breaking into a rich guy's well-guarded mansion?"

"No, of course not." Papa gestured for them to follow and walked from the workroom. Kylie hoped the modifications she made to his cane hadn't ruined it. He rarely leaned on his cane, so it would probably be fine. Maybe it was more style than an actual necessity for the old man. Maybe she *would* make him a razor blade top hat for Christmas.

"If we're not breaking in, then what are we doing?" asked Kylie.

"First of all," said Papa, "*We* aren't doing anything. *You* stay here where it's safe."

"But I can guess encryption keys better than you."

He gave a sharp wave of his cane to cut off her protest. "What have I told you about hacking?"

"Guess the hashed version used internally instead because it's shorter?"

Papa scowled. "I shouldn't have shown you how to hack anything."

"I want to help."

"It's dangerous!" he snapped. "*I* am going to move a par three's distance from a rich man's lodge so I can hack its network, remove any mention of you kids, and maybe steal some information for these kind countercapitalists."

Austin whispered, "Supervillain."

Kylie whispered back, "Regular villain."

Papa chewed on his next words before speaking them. "These people might be doing the right thing, or they might be terrorists. I don't really know. When you saw Liam Thompson, what you saw was his public persona. A sort of version of himself built up for our benefit." He sucked on his teeth. "I think these people are right that he's hiding something. It's not a bad thing to see what that is."

"Right," said Kylie. "Stealing is okay."

"It's not stealing," Papa snapped. "It's just an invasion of privacy."

"I thought people had a right to privacy," said Kylie.

Papa sputtered, and Kylie couldn't stop the big grin that spread across her face. Nothing in the world quite compared to the feeling of getting Papa into this state.

"We could use some privacy right now, now that you mention it," Papa said, waving Austin away. Once the boy had moved to the other end of the hall, Papa leaned down and whispered to Kylie, "Did you look at that thing you gave me?"

Kylie furrowed her brow. Why was he telling her about it? She had given it to him so that he kept it safe. It had nothing to do with her. "It was just a bunch of spreadsheets."

"Someday I'll teach you how to hide a secret partition on any data storage device. It's not hard."

"Huh." Kylie hadn't known that was possible.

"I think it's the developments regarding your mother's scan. There's a new procedure." The next words stuck in the old man's throat.

"What?" Kylie couldn't bear the anticipation.

"There's a procedure to make you normal."

Normal? Kylie blinked at that. Anger. She was feeling anger. Normal? "Should I do it?" Her voice sounded flat, even to her, but it was a result of her anger, not because she was stomping down her own emotions.

Papa sucked on his teeth for a little while before answering. "Don't use your abilities, hon. Even if it seems like a good idea."

She couldn't tear her eyes from the sliver of metal and plastic. Normal. What did that even mean?

"Every time you use that tech in your head, it does something to your brain. I can see it in your eyes and in how you talk. If you use it to change yourself too much, it may cause permanent brain damage." Papa clutched the top of his cane. "We might be able to fix this, Kylie."

Kylie wrenched herself away from her grandpa. "I'm not *broken*."

"I didn't mean—"

Kylie held out her hand. "I want the chip."

"I think I should hold onto it, dear," said Papa in a deeply condescending voice. "To keep it safe."

A hot well of seething rage bubbled in Kylie's belly. Papa didn't want her to use her power to stomp out her feelings? Fine. She'd bubble with anger all day long and point it all at him. She never should have given the data chip back to him.

"Are you almost done?" called Austin from down the hall. "I'm getting really hungry."

"You're always hungry." Kylie stalked away from Papa. "Let's go back to that cafeteria. I think we're going to be here a while."

She left without looking back at her grandfather.

She'd never be normal.

CHAPTER NINETEEN

The electric Polaris snowmobiles whispered through the snow under a fat silver moon. Cold chilled Ajay to his bones even through his puffy white coat as they sped through the frigid night. Wind pulled at his elbows and rattled the top of his helmet. He clung to Olexie, who drove at the front of their small pack. Behind them, Maja and four other snowmobiles zipped quietly through the night.

Olexie had suggested the approach, and Maja had insisted on bringing their most loyal countercapitalists, leaving Nick and Shannon back at the base to watch over the kids and the rest of the hired help.

"The best of the true believers," Maya claimed when they stopped to regroup a few miles from the lodge. "Alvin, Tabitha, Powell, and Yates." They were the same four Ajay recognized from the van earlier.

Olexie hadn't responded, but Ajay could see the irritation on the tall man's face.

Maja put a hand on Ajay's shoulder. "This operation is all about you, Ajay. Let us know what you need."

"All I need is a data connection," said Ajay. "For that, I just need to get close enough to access his private network."

"I brought drones, too," Olexie said. "If we need to get closer."

"Good." Ajay should have thought of that. He wasn't thinking clearly. "That'll be a good backup."

"They'll be safe," Olexie said to Ajay through the comm as they sped through the snowy night.

Ajay wondered how the Russian knew what he was thinking. "I don't like letting them out of my sight. Especially not with those mercenaries." This was the same feeling he got every time Kylie left for school, and he knew it was something he had to ignore. He'd suffered it every time his daughter had left, too, but he hadn't handled it well back then. There had to be a better way.

"Nick is a decent guy," Olexie said. "He remembers people's birthdays."

"I thought Shannon was looking after the kids."

Ajay felt Olexie's shrug through the layers of padded coat. "Nick will look after Shannon, probably." The last word was spoken so quietly, the comm almost didn't pick it up.

Ajay didn't like being away, but it couldn't be helped. Even if he had sent a competent team to plant a relay, he would have needed to get close. There simply wasn't a good way to hack a high-security system like this without being in the vicinity. He wasn't sure there was a good way to hack it at all. Not if his skills and tools were too outdated.

If there was one thing Ajay never wanted to be, it was outdated.

Olexie stopped their snowmobile on a short rise overlooking a frozen lake. Across the lake, glowing with rich, golden light, was Liam's wolf lodge. It looked just as it had in the surveillance footage, with a facade of timber covering a sprawling building. Looking through a spyglass, Ajay saw Liam's security personnel loitering on the snowy paths in front of a huge garage set in the hillside under the building.

"Maja should have let me use my distraction," grumbled Olexie.

"You couldn't possibly organize a protest quickly enough," said Ajay. He glanced at the Russian. "And this works much better if they don't notice anything wrong at all."

Olexie waved the others by, and Maja led her group into position around the lodge. "How close do you need to be?" he asked Ajay.

Ajay checked the readout on his fidget. A weak signal permeated the frozen air, but it wasn't enough to skim data. "A lot closer," he said.

"Follow me."

They removed their helmets in exchange for white ski masks. Along with their white coats, boots, and gloves, they were well camouflaged for the Minnesota winter landscape. Even the wide expanse of the lake might keep them concealed, but they didn't risk it. The forest along the shore ran right up to the edge of the water.

Creeping slowly, they made their way to the lodge. "I have a hundred protesters with a thousand allies each," whispered Olexie through the earpiece. "They will be anywhere I tell them to be. They could be right here protesting illegal fisheries if that's what I post on social media."

"After all this time, you're still twisting people's minds on social media." Ajay rapped the ice with his knuckles. "There's no illegal fishing happening here."

"Oh, Ajay," said Olexie, his voice dripping with mock pity. "Have you not learned that internet outrage need not be connected to reality?"

"I'd hate to see you burn such a resource on a mission like this."

"Burn it? That's not how it works at all." Olexie held out an open palm, and the two men crouched very still behind a fallen pine half frozen into the lake. "People become more passionate the more worthless their protests are. It's pathological."

"You're a monster," said Ajay.

"I am a monster with whom you are working. What does that make you?"

A flicker of signal flashed over Ajay's display. This wasn't right. It should be stronger. "We still need to get closer."

Olexie sighed and crept forward. Even with the bright light of the silver moon reflecting off of the clean white snow, the Russian disappeared when he moved more than ten feet ahead. Ajay struggled to keep up, their movement through the shallow snow at the edge of the windswept lake enough to keep his heart thundering in his chest. Twenty feet passed, then thirty. Ajay could see figures moving inside the lodge. Dark shapes of security guards and, at one point, the slender form of a man in a dressing robe.

Liam Thompson.

"He's here," whispered Ajay.

"Of course, he's here," Olexie said. "If you were about to execute an evil plan, wouldn't you want to be close?"

"I would want to distance myself."

"That, my friend, is why you are not a trillionaire."

"Fair enough." He checked his signal again. "No good. We're going to need that drone."

Olexie fished a tiny drone from his pocket and set it on a clear patch of ice. After calibrating the controls, he programmed a route for the device and set it on its way. Ajay picked up a signal from it.

"It will extend the range of any signal it locates. It beams it straight to us, so there shouldn't be much chance that it is discovered."

Ajay scraped the signal for a video feed, which showed the lodge from a perspective ten feet above the highest corner of its roof.

"Five guards outside," said Maja through the earpiece. "We've spotted at least five more indoors."

"So, they outnumber us," said Olexie.

"Won't matter," Ajay muttered. "They don't even need to know we're here."

The drone circled the lodge, taking loop after loop in the airspace above, beaming its signal back to Ajay.

Nothing.

"Maybe this is where he goes to disconnect from his hectic life," said Ajay. "Maybe there's no evil plot at all."

"People like him do not disconnect," Olexie said. "They can't afford to."

"Are you kidding? A man that rich can afford dry-clean-only solid gold socks."

Olexie sounded genuinely sad when he said, "All that wealth costs them their independence. Even a moment away could be the moment that ruins them. They live in absolute fear."

"I wonder what that's like."

This got a snort of a laugh from Olexie. "Try defecting to your enemy."

"Try working next to a Russian bot farmer."

The drone took another circle around the lodge but didn't turn up any new information. Olexie had it running an ever-tightening spiral, narrowing its orbit until it hovered directly above the lodge roof.

"There," Ajay said, peering at the video feed. "He's using a laser uplink. Park your drone over that."

Olexie grunted.

"Well?" whispered Ajay.

"Can't," said Olexie. "Once it's in flight, I don't control it."

A remote-control drone would send up too much signal in all directions. They would be transmitting their presence everywhere. It was bad enough that the drone constantly sent a beam back to their location. A sensitive enough security system might pick that up on the bounce and deduce their position, no matter how carefully they aimed the laser.

Olexie reached into his pack, consulted their records, and launched a second drone. It flew to the laser uplink, parked there, and scraped the laser signal. The whole operation took ten minutes, and the cold sank into Ajay's bones.

But they had their data. Or at least, they had a datastream to skim from.

"ETA?" Maja asked over the comm.

"I can't influence the stream," Ajay said. "Not yet anyway. We can capture the digital noise coming through their direct satellite uplink, but it's going to take some work to decipher any of it."

"How much work?" Olexie asked.

"A lot."

Olexie peered at the lodge. "You sound like Silas."

"We're seeing some activity over here," said Maja. "You might need to move in."

"Silas was a slug of a programmer." Ajay watched as the readout flickered across the holographic images on the back of his hand. With a flick of his controls, he ran a series of decryption routines and found something he could use.

"I always considered you a worthy adversary," said Olexie.

Ajay flicked a map file over to Olexie's fidget. "I always considered you an asshole," he muttered.

"More maps," grunted the Russian, nodding approvingly. "Could be useful."

The whine of a motor pierced the night, its hum echoing across the open lake before fading to the muffled silence of a powerful electric motor. Under the lodge, the hillside split, and an enormous set of garage doors opened. The opening was only a good five iron away, and Ajay could clearly see the rows of snowmobiles inside.

"The patrol," said Olexie.

"We're on it," replied Maja. "But you need to speed things up."

Three snowmobiles emerged from the doorway to blast across the open lake. They sped through the night, kicking fresh powder up behind them.

Olexie planted a recording unit in the snow. "This will scrape your data," he said. "Let's move."

"What?"

"We're going inside." He gestured at the garage doors, which were slowly closing. "To get you more control."

Maja's voice came over the line. "Quickly."

Olexie crept forward through the snow, breaking into a crouching run.

"This wasn't the deal," Ajay hissed.

The Russian said, "The patrol will run its loop and find our tracks. They'll find us in an hour, easy."

"You knew this would happen," Ajay said, but he followed through the snow. By the time they were halfway to the door, both Olexie and Ajay were gasping for breath.

"Stop," said Maja.

Olexie froze. He and Ajay dropped down into the snow and went still. The frozen wind rushed through the icy landscape under the silver moon. Ajay did his best not to shiver from the bitter cold.

"Go," Maja said. "They rounded the corner."

Olexie moved, and Ajay struggled to keep up. He held tight to his cane but couldn't use it on the snow-covered earth. His pack jostled uncomfortably against his back.

The door was almost closed when they reached it.

Olexie darted inside. Ajay did the same, barely squeezing under as the door thumped shut, leaving them in total blackness.

"Can you work in here?" Olexie asked.

Ajay summoned the hologram display on his fidget. It showed a weak wireless signal, secured by several layers of obfuscation and a series of standard off-the-shelf encryption mechanisms. "I can crack it."

Olexie clapped him on the back. "See, you are just like Silas."

"I'm nothing like him."

The whole world dropped away when Ajay dove into the hack. It didn't matter that he was breaking laws and surrounded by enemies. It didn't matter that he didn't trust his allies. He ignored the smells of oil and ice lingering in the pitch-dark garage and silent stutters of the lodge above. He almost even forgot about Kylie hiding somewhere far away.

The only thing that mattered was the hack.

It started with the gentle nudge on unknown tokens. He probed the edges of the wireless interface, testing avenues of attack that would least likely trigger response. He probed with a token and was greeted with half of a key. He, of course, didn't know the other half.

So, he spoofed the wireless router. The next device to connect sent a token.

He offered back the half of the key he'd found.

And the device gave him the second half. With both halves, he made the handshake and was in. The list of other devices on the network appeared. Five minutes had passed.

Sweat dripped under his heavy coat, so he shrugged it off and left it in a heap.

"It's all about trust," he told the Russian.

"That's what I say in my business, too."

Ajay started several exploratory programs, searching the network for devices with weak security. He found a lamp that shifted color tones which was left completely insecure. The heating and cooling systems were behind weak encryption, probably something over a decade old from when encryption still meant something. One of the thugs carried a phone that didn't have the latest security patches, but it kept moving in and out of range. That was the device Ajay was spoofing to get access to the network. It wouldn't be able to properly connect until he left.

Then, there was the surveillance system. It sat like a brick atop the entire network, its walls impregnable from Ajay's position on the network. He would need heightened authority to even touch that.

But where best to find it?

A single personal computer sat on the network, but directly accessing it proved difficult with Ajay's current set of tools. He frowned at his screen for a full minute trying to think of his angle.

The bang on the door was their only warning that someone was coming. Olexie yanked Ajay back behind the workbench just as the lights flared to life.

Lights.

Ajay took control of the color-changing light and made it flicker.

A man entered the garage and set a wrench down on

the workbench, barely a short putt away. With the lights on, Ajay saw his coat in a heap on the floor. Two steps and the man would see it.

But Ajay didn't care. He was caught in the hack. That surveillance system danced dangerously outside his grasp—a puzzle that needed to be solved. He flickered the color-changing light again.

The man whistled as he straightened the contents of the workbench. Metal scraped against metal, and he rearranged tools, putting some away and taking others out. He took a step toward the corner where Ajay's coat lay.

Ajay flickered the light again.

Jackpot! The computer opened a direct connection to the light. Using that erroneously trusted connection, Ajay gained a foothold to Liam Thompson's personal computer.

Then, he had it all. Access to every system on the network, including surveillance. It was all he could do to keep himself from shouting in triumph. He fed the video streams through his fidget, grabbed the audio through his earpiece, and started a file download from the computer. He had it all.

"We're good," he whispered into his comm. "Ten more seconds and we can move out."

Just then, the alarm sounded, and everything locked down hard.

CHAPTER TWENTY

Kylie felt the signals of every tiny machine in the entry to the mine. The controllers for the elevator were too far away, but she felt the locks in the doors and the sensors embedded in the panels. The cameras spoke to her in their weird visual way. Everything twitched when she told it to twitch. This was a world she controlled, and she didn't give a damn if Papa thought it was normal.

"Kylie," whispered Austin through the thick fog coating Kylie's brain, "why are you acting strange?"

The cold fist of logic clamped around her skull and shut out the furious irrationality of emotion. Kylie could finally process their situation. It all made logical sense in a way that she could arrange and rearrange like the pieces of a giant puzzle. Papa didn't want her to use her skills, but his request didn't make any sense. She could learn more this way. She could *be* more.

Austin tugged on her sleeve.

"I act strange because I am strange," she said. Her voice

sounded flat, even to her. She thought of ways she might get Austin to stop bothering her. She could hurt him.

"Okay," said Austin. "Let's stop messing around."

The woman who had been following them—Shannon—had disappeared shortly after Papa had left for the surface. Kylie had wanted to know what the woman was doing, but the cameras only trailed her as far as the exit. Austin said he hadn't heard the elevator run again, so where could she have gone?

Kylie asked all of the machines, but none of them knew. Her head ached.

"Kylie?"

Kylie felt another buzz of annoyance. She could overheat his fidget and burn him. She could make someone come get him. Nobody in the world mattered to her. Not her disappeared sister Isabelle. Not Papa or her dead parents. Not even herself. All that mattered was the cold, pure logic surrounding her current situation and solving the puzzle. Where did Shannon go?

She touched every machine that had access to the outside world. This was the original purpose of her hack, wasn't it? But she forgot why she wanted that access. She didn't need to warn anyone of anything. She needed to find Shannon.

Austin circled her and stared directly into her eyes. An uncomfortable knot twisted in her stomach when she stared back, but Kylie forced herself to do so.

Because Austin *did* matter. She blinked at that. Was she so far in her head that she forgot Austin was her friend? The thought made her palms sweaty with fear.

"I'm sorry," she said, flat as before. "I'm sorry." Better.

"Are you okay?"

She forced a smile. "I get lost sometimes."

"Don't we all." Austin looked around. "If she didn't go up the elevator and she's not in the science wing, then she must have gone into the abandoned section."

"The scary part," Kylie said. Warmth flowed back into her fingers. She flexed the last dregs of connection and pulled open the digitally locked door. "Do you want to go after her?"

"Absolutely not."

Kylie shrugged. She didn't blame him. The mine was darker than any place she had ever been. Darker than the blackest night. Darker than hiding from a scary father in the remains of the lab that was once her home. Darker than even her blackest dreams.

She stepped through the door. "Let's go, then."

Austin followed.

CHAPTER TWENTY-ONE

OLEXIE BURST from hiding and slammed a fist into the man working at the bench. The wail of the alarm pierced the cool garage air and swallowed the man's shout of surprise. Olexie roared.

Ajay's fingers danced over his fidget's controls. "Maja? Help."

The comm was silent.

The crack of weapons fire sounded through their open feed, punctuated by the voices of Maja's team as they maneuvered.

The worker in the garage shrugged off Olexie's onslaught and regained his footing. The Russian snarled like a wolf and swung a wild punch. The worker sidestepped and clubbed Olexie hard on the hip with a long wrench. Olexie slammed the man against a snowmobile, sending them both tumbling over.

"They have three moving east through the lodge," Ajay said to Maja, checking the feeds of surveillance. "I see four outside converging on your location." Two of them stopped in front of the garage door, setting in behind the heavy cover of the sunken driveway. When Maja didn't respond, he said, "Please, Maja. Help us get out of here."

For a dozen rapid heartbeats, Ajay thought she might not answer. She might be bleeding out in the snow or fleeing already. If the rattle of gunfire outside was any indication, things were heating up fast. She could easily retreat, abandoning Ajay and Olexie to their fates.

"Copy," said Maja, finally. Her voice was hard with tension. "Powell, Yates, fall back. Tab, Alvin, take the left flank."

One of the mercenaries outside staggered backward, spraying gobbets of red blood over the stark white snow. Another moved to better cover and returned fire. His position effectively blocked escape out the garage.

"I thought we weren't killing anyone," Ajay growled.

"I thought we weren't setting off any alarms," Maja snapped.

Olexie swore, but Ajay ignored him. The computer he had connected to dropped from the network before the download finished. Liam must have it. He was in the lodge somewhere, but Ajay couldn't see him on any of the surveillance feeds. He scrambled through images, mentally mapping the area.

There!

A thud-crack, and Olexie slammed the worker against the floor. The man gave out a grunt and went limp.

"Did you get what you need?" Olexie asked.

"The alarm triggered a network lockdown," Ajay said. "I need access to the physical machine."

Olexie swallowed big gulps of air. He threw open the door and stepped into the hallway. A wall of warm air hit in a scented wave of lavender and pine. It was an artificial overabundance of what somebody thought cabins ought to smell like. It was stifling.

Olexie limped into the hallway, drawing his large pistol as he went.

"Back! Back!" hissed Maja through the feed, but Ajay didn't think it was directed at him. Through his surveillance access, he saw her teams drawing the mercenaries farther out.

The alarm stopped, leaving the hum of its absence hanging in Ajay's ears. Behind it all, the crack of rifle fire echoed in the distance. Louder weapons rang down the long hall he had just entered. His video feed showed the mercenaries were several rooms away, but they sounded much closer. He cast Olexie a worried look, but the tall Russian shrugged.

Ajay led Olexie to the right, away from the noise. There was one door in his surveillance survey that didn't have video on the other side. A private room, and Ajay figured that would be the one with the best chance of finding the rich man's secrets.

And maybe the old man himself.

The door to that room opened, and Ajay pulled Olexie into a side hall. They waited in the dark, watching Ajay's video as Liam Thompson emerged from the study. His skin was pale and sallow, a bandage covering one arm, and he pulled an IV stand along behind him. The old man wore a loose shirt that left his arms mostly bare. He carried a black pistol and scanned the hallway with dark eyes.

Ajay held Olexie back, placing a hand on the man's gun.

"That's not polite," Olexie whispered.

After a brief pause, Thompson touched his ear and spoke, but Ajay hadn't hacked the audio feed. Thompson turned away and went west through the lodge, away from the gunfire.

Maja's words were a jumbled mess in Ajay's ear. All he could gather was that Alvin and Tabitha were taking heavy fire. Tabitha was injured.

"This is our chance," Ajay said. "His computer must be in there."

Olexie grabbed Ajay's elbow before he could move. "He's unguarded."

He stared down at the gun in the Russian's hand. "We're not here to kill anyone."

"Liam Thompson is not a good man."

"We don't have proof." Ajay had lived his life according to rules, and he had never bought into the idea that people needed to die to make things right. There was always a better solution, and if he didn't do the work to find it, then guilt would eat at him every night until he died. He still pictured Sashi when he closed his eyes. She hadn't been a good person. As her father, at least some of that was his fault.

But her death sat *entirely* on his shoulders. There were

a million things he could have done before she died, and he had failed completely.

Olexie was right. Liam Thompson wasn't a good man. Nobody could be a trillionaire and maintain a high moral ground, not even someone who made their fortune as an environmentalist entrepreneur. The man had sunk corporations and cost millions their jobs. He had backstabbed other hardworking men and women on his way to the top. He had twisted hard at the knife that climate change had put in the backs of the American people, and the ensuing economic strife had been a stepping stone for his rise to the top.

No, Ajay had no illusions that Liam Thompson was a good person.

But he didn't expect what he found when he stepped into the office.

The padded oak chair facing the huge desk had absorbed most of the blood, leaving only a few thick drops to gather on the stone floor. The room smelled of iron, and the warm air from the fireplace burned Ajay's nostrils. There was no body, but there was so much blood. Ajay had never seen that much in one place. He circled the chair and saw two tight bullet holes in the high oak back. The bullets were still lodged in the bloody wood.

"Work," ordered Olexie, breaking Ajay from his spell.

One wall of the room held the massive fireplace, which roared with a huge flame. The opposite wall was a single pane glass window, showing a deceptively peaceful view of the lake shore. The wall opposite the door was covered in huge paper topological maps. The desk was clean, with only a few papers on it arranged neatly in rows. Ajay didn't see a computer there, but a docking station sat to one side on the wide desk. Liam Thompson was a laptop kind of guy. Ajay tried to remember if the man had been carrying a laptop as he left the office, but all he could think of was the bloody chair and the gun in Liam's hand.

The fire popped, and Ajay jumped.

"It was recent," Olexie said, touching the blood. His finger came away with a spot of dark red.

Another wave of gunshots rattled the house. Automatic fire, this time, with each crack echoing against the icy world outside. This sounded closer than before. More dangerous.

Ajay didn't open the drawers of the desk right away. First, he checked for security and locks. On his fidget, he found a near-field signal near one of the drawers. Liam probably had a device he used to unlock that drawer. Ajay attempted to spoof the signal, but it was complex, and every time he was close to cracking it, it cycled to a new code.

"I'm really starting to hate time-cycled locks," he said.

"They don't like you much, either," said Olexie.

Ajay set his machine to cracking the study's local network. Datastore access was close, and with some work, he knew he could wipe their servers. He and Kylie and Austin would be free to leave.

Olexie pulled something from the fire. "He's been burning papers," he said, holding up the ashed remains of a stack of printer paper. "Getting nervous and burning evidence?"

"Don't you think he'd start by burning that chair?" Ajay asked.

"Maybe it's pig's blood."

Ajay stared at the Russian. Nothing on Olexie's face gave a hint that he might be joking. "Do you—"

"Rich people do strange things," said Olexie. "But I'm certain this is a person's blood, and I'm certain that person was murdered."

"Then we might want to hurry."

"Can you open those drawers or not?"

The network hack clicked, and Ajay was one step closer to the datastores. He swiped through a machine identity database, searching for the appropriate device. There was a network access history here. Liam had recently used the satellite access to reach the outer world, but that access wasn't connected in any way to the datastore. That system, in turn, wasn't connected to the surveillance network which he'd already hacked. All these separate pieces didn't talk to one another.

But that's how things were in modern networks. Without a powerful trust system provided by encryption, someone like Liam couldn't afford to put any of his main systems anywhere near the internet.

Another barrage of gunfire rattled the lodge. The fight was moving into the house, and every shot rattled the huge window. Muffled voices rang through the hall outside the study door.

"Status," Olexie said through the comm. When Maja didn't answer, he tried again. "We need more time. Buy us more time, dammit. This guy is as slow as Silas."

"I'm not—"

"Leave it," Maya snapped.

Ajay tried the drawers again. The digital fortress nearly fell, but again the codes changed and he had to start from scratch. "It's too much," he said. "I can't crack it with the resources I have here."

Olexie crossed the room and yanked open one of the drawers with a physical lock. The wood splintered, and the whole drawer flew from the desk.

Empty.

"A waste of time," Olexie spat. "We need to leave." But he continued to search the room.

Another drawer came up empty. Then another. The top drawer contained fancy pens and ink and a few pads of blank paper. Ajay took one of the pens and put it in his inside pocket.

"What?" he said when he caught Olexie's questioning look. "I'm not breaking into the richest man in Minnesota's lodge and coming out empty-handed. It's a nice pen."

"Fine." Olexie smashed another lock and found another empty drawer. In the comm, he said, "Maja, where are you?"

The gunfire had stopped, and there was more movement in the hallway. Ajay froze when footsteps approached the study door. He met Olexie's gaze, and the Russian raised his pistol.

Whoever was outside the door moved away, and Olexie relaxed.

The only drawer left was the one with the signal lock, but Ajay still couldn't crack it. The drawer resisted Olexie's best efforts to pull it open, so he slammed the butt of his pistol against the lock until it shattered. He yanked the drawer open, then a flash of pure white light burst from it.

Ajay took a step back, blinded by a phosphorescent flash. Whatever papers were inside burned to ash in half a second. Bright lights danced in his vision.

The office door burst open, and Ajay looked up to see Liam Thompson standing there with a pistol pointed at Olexie.

"I wondered if you would be able to get into my desk," Liam drawled.

Olexie didn't move.

"Put it down," said Liam. The man's skin looked even more sallow in person. His smile barely touched his lips and didn't even bother moving to his shark eyes. "I'd hate to ask my cleanup crew to work overtime tonight."

Olexie set his big gun down on the gigantic desk. It looked small on that huge open space. Olexie raised his hands in the air, and Ajay followed suit.

"Good," said Liam as he pushed the door closed. "Now, let's have a little chat."

CHAPTER TWENTY-TWO

"I think my battery is dead," whispered Austin.

"Already?"

"It's my dad's old fidget. It barely works anyway."

Kylie pulled him back farther behind the abandoned mine cart. She hadn't thought carts like those were real, but there it was, sitting half rusted out on some metal tracks that ran deep into the rough rock of the old iron mine. Voices echoed down the tunnel, and if she could hear their hushed voices, maybe they could hear hers.

The terrifying dark embraced them for an eternity. Kylie's senses strained against the oppressive black, fighting it as it pressed in ever closer. Panic welled in her chest, consuming her whole body in its mind-shattering noise. Austin must have sensed something because he squeezed her hand and snapped her out of the spiral.

"Breathe," he whispered.

It didn't help. Nothing would ever help.

Then it did. She focused on the sound of Austin

breathing and tried to match his super slow pace. Every exhale was a hot vent of unwanted energy. Every inhale brought cool, dry calm. With Austin's help, she had managed the panic attack without using the machine part of her brain. Time passed.

At first, she thought that she imagined the light in the tunnel, but then one of the voices congealed into something recognizable.

"Do you want to get paid or not?" said Shannon.

A man's voice that Kylie recognized as Samuel, the mercenary who had helped them in the workshop. "We have a contract."

"No," Shannon's voice sounded extra patronizing. "We have a choice."

"This isn't right," said the man. "There's a mercenary code."

Kylie pulled Austin farther back. Farther down. She didn't want him anywhere close to this.

Shannon and Samuel rounded the corner. He held a light in the palm of his hand—his fidget switched to flashlight mode.

"We just got new orders," said Shannon, her voice like ice. "That's your mercenary code."

The man stopped and turned to her. He saw the gun in Shannon's hand the same second Kylie did. "What are you doing?" he asked as if it wasn't obvious.

Shannon's voice shook a little when she spoke. "We follow orders here, Sam."

"No, we don't. Not this order." His voice rose an octave. "We don't do this. Sometimes we get to be on the right side of things, Shan. Sometimes we don't. This is our chance to choose."

"Was," Shannon said, and she shot him in the chest. The light and noise sent Kylie's heart into furious convulsions. Her head spun, and her hands went numb. It was the day when her mother died. She saw her father dead on the floor. Saw her friend Olivia shot in the parking lot. Raw pain and emotion and fear pounded through her whole body. So much fear.

Instinct raged in her head. It stomped down the wildfire of her emotions. Crushed the fear. Her heart rate slowed. She had seen something important. What was it? Her machine brain ran over the conversation again. Shannon pulling the trigger.

Austin placed a hand in hers and pulled her deeper into the dark.

The man hit the floor, and his light went black. After a pause for a long, ragged breath and a whispered apology, Shannon lit her own fidget and dragged the man away. Kylie and Austin listened to her pull the body into a nearby passage. They listened as Shannon grunted with the effort and then they heard the sickening crack as the body struck the stone far, far below.

"They're going to kill us all," whispered Austin.

Kylie couldn't read his emotions. She knew only facts. "No," she said. "No, they're not."

Even as she crouched deeper to hide as Shannon returned to the science wing, the fog lifted and Kylie's fear and doubt returned. She wondered if she was telling Austin something because making him feel better was useful, or if she was telling the truth because it was correct. Sometimes it was so hard to tell the difference.

All she knew was that they needed to contact Papa, but when she reached out again to the machines that had access to the surface, all she found were broken stubs.

Kylie swallowed the lump of emotion in her throat. "He was nice to me," she whispered. Austin didn't say anything. "We need to find a way out."

Austin chewed his lip for several long seconds. "I think I have an idea."

CHAPTER TWENTY-THREE

"I would ask you to sit," said Liam, waving his gun lazily at the bloody chair, "but it seems my cleaning crew was interrupted." He still wore a loose-fitting robe and a thin pair of crescent glasses.

"Falling back," said Maja in Ajay's ear. A quick glance to Olexie showed that he heard it, too. "I'm sorry, Ajay."

"This lodge is where I come to get away from it all," Liam said. "It's very rude of you and your people to interrupt when I'm supposed to be on vacation."

Olexie glanced pointedly at the bloody chair. "Seems like it must have been a working vacation."

Liam's glasses flashed, and his expression went stony. His hand tensed on his pistol. "Olexie Sokolov." Olexie rocked back at the mention of his name.

Liam turned to Ajay. "And Ajay Andersen."

"That's right." Ajay caught a flash of the display in Liam's crescent glasses. They were a much more advanced version of his own cheaters.

"Happy birthday," the wealthy man said with a bemused expression, confirming to Ajay that he was reading an online dossier.

Ajay did his best to keep his own reaction in check. His hands clutched the head of his cane until his knuckles went white. "You're surprisingly well informed for a man without a computer at his desk."

Liam showed his teeth behind thin lips. "I've been consolidating some research lately," he said. "Surely you've heard of my cancer."

Ajay said, "From what I've been told, you *are* the cancer."

That brought a chuckle from the old man. "I suppose it depends on the company you keep. I've always fought against the corporations and those who would exploit the land. That's made me more than a few enemies." At that, he glanced at Olexie. "Some on principle and some more... personal."

"I don't trust this asshole any more than I trust you," said Ajay.

Olexie met Liam's steely gaze. "Maybe you are not as popular as you think."

"I don't know," said Ajay. "The kids seemed pretty impressed."

Liam waved the comment off. "Public speaking is one thing. It's my actions that won my fame."

"A person doesn't get into the business of cleaning environmental disasters if he wants to stay out of the spotlight," Ajay said. "You do it because you want to be a hero."

The pale man lowered himself into his chair, keeping

the pistol pointed at Olexie. "If I'm being honest," he said, "fame was always a motivation. My legacy is important to me."

Ajay clutched his cane. If he could bring Kylie's taser to bear, he might be able to stun the old trillionaire. He couldn't do it with Liam pointing a gun at Olexie, though. The risk was too great. Instead, he said, "Your fans will forget you before the flowers from your funeral die."

"You're right," said Liam. He sank deeper into his chair. The exhaustion showed in deep bags under his eyes. "A true legacy persists." He cocked his head. "Tell me, Ajay. What will people remember when you're gone?"

Ajay glanced at Olexie, who stood stone-faced. "They'll remember me." They wouldn't. Almost everyone had already forgotten Ajay, and those who remembered likely remembered him as a different person with a different name. He had been invisible his whole life, hidden behind a screen and manipulating the world by its digital reins. "They'll remember the harm I've caused."

"People are like that, aren't they." Liam glanced at the wall with the maps. For the first time, Ajay noticed penciled-in markings along the margins. Liam continued, "They need a constant reminder of the good we've done." He set the pistol down on the desk.

Ajay tensed, ready to pounce. He could take one step, jab with the cane, and drop the old man.

The door opened behind him, and Tenen Lang's massive form filled it. "They've retreated," he said. The big man blinked at Ajay and Olexie. "Trouble?"

"Just some thieves," said Liam. "I haven't decided how to deal with them."

"Need any help?"

"You'd best stick around." Liam nodded at Olexie. "I don't like the looks the Russian keeps giving me."

In a smooth, brutal movement, Tenen took a baton from his hip and cracked it against Olexie's collarbone. The Russian grunted and dropped to one knee.

Liam's appreciation was painted in the wicked tilt of his lips. "We are very much alike, Olexie Sokolov. We both seek to make the world a better place."

Ajay involuntarily took a step back. Pain shrouded Olexie's features, but the tall man forced himself to his feet.

Liam nodded to Tenen, and the huge mercenary jabbed his baton into Olexie's kidneys, dropping him again.

"You see," Liam explained, this time addressing Ajay directly, "it is our civic duty to leave this world a better place, but it is our right to be given credit for our influence." Again, he looked at the maps on his wall.

Ajay really studied the map. It was a topological view of somewhere in the boundary waters, but he couldn't see where. The markings in the margin were a series of cryptic numbers and letters. Instructions? Islands dotted the wide lakes, and large swaths of swampy land covered an enormous range of undeveloped wilderness. It was the treasure of Minnesota, this pure, perfect land. Nobody would ever let the likes of Liam Thompson develop his city of the future there.

Yet.

There it was, the sketch of the city center penciled so

light as to be hardly visible, the apartments integrated with natural features, earth and water and mankind joined in perfect harmony.

"This is it," Ajay said, letting some of the awe seep into his voice. "This is your city of the future."

This time, Liam's smile touched the corners of his eyes. "Every resident from now until the end of time will know my story. I started from nothing, built my fortune on the industry of saving the ruined earth, and then constructed a city designed in such a way that humanity would need never destroy the land upon which we live."

"Bullshit," muttered Olexie.

Liam's expression darkened. Tenen cracked the baton over Olexie's other shoulder, and the Russian cried out again. Ajay's breaths came in short gasps at the raw, casual violence. He fought back the rising panic in his chest. There was no way Liam would let them out of this alive.

To Ajay, Liam said, "I still wonder what your part is in all of this."

"You killed a Silas Cardoso."

Liam glanced at Tenen and raised an eyebrow. Tenen gave a quick shake of his head so slight that Ajay might have imagined it. "Maybe this is about your granddaughter?" Liam said. "Is the Russian holding her as a hostage so that you'll work for him?"

"Leave her out of this."

"I think she's already involved," said Liam.

Maja's voice murmured in Ajay's ear, "Buy me sixty more seconds."

"You know about my granddaughter," said Ajay. Liam

had uncovered the first layer of Ajay's identity. Nothing more. "You know I wouldn't put her at risk."

Liam's eyes went cold. "People have betrayed their beliefs for far less."

"Maybe you're right. Maybe Olexie took my granddaughter and her friend. Maybe he knows that they'll be good collateral. But he doesn't know my secrets. Not like you do. If he was dangerous to me, then you're doubly so, even as you build this city of yours. Even long after we're both gone, I still dare not utter one secret of yours because you're perfectly capable of punishing my granddaughter for my sins."

"You make a good point." Liam picked the gun up from the desk. He pointed it at Olexie. "So, what if I don't want you to leave?"

Ajay swallowed. His throat was dry. "I don't understand."

"I know you're a hacker, Ajay Andersen." Maybe Liam knew the second layer of Ajay's identity. "Maybe you're a pretty good one. Come live in my city when it's built. You can have a position of power. I'll put you in charge of the networks. Privacy."

"There's no such thing as privacy," Ajay said reflexively.

"No, of course not," chuckled Liam. "But we need the illusion of it, don't we? Nobody likes to *feel* like they're being watched at all times, but everyone likes to know that everyone else is being kept in check."

"Ten seconds," said Maja.

Ajay did his best to avoid looking at the huge window

but failed terribly. "Tell me something, Mr. Thompson," he said looking out the window.

Liam looked affronted at the intrusion.

"Why does a beloved entrepreneur need bulletproof glass in his country estate?"

Several things happened at once.

With a pop, a web of cracks appeared in the glass near Liam's head.

Olexie kicked backward at Tenen, striking the big man's knee.

Liam flinched from the noise of another bullet striking glass. He swung the gun over to point at Ajay.

Ajay swung his cane hard at Liam's gun hand, hoping for a repeat of his signature disarming move. The bronze lion sang through the air and missed the hand by inches.

Another web of cracks appeared in the window. The bullets weren't getting through.

Liam fired a wild shot at Ajay. Ajay staggered back from the smoke and the noise. He didn't know if he'd been shot. Everything hurt. Every nerve in his body fired at once, in an involuntary echo of the time he was shot a year prior.

But he couldn't let himself pause. He cursed himself for not using his taser when he should have. He brought the cane to bear as if to spear Liam, but the wealthy man had already adjusted his aim and grinned a toothy grin.

Tenen slammed the baton onto the bone of Olexie's shoulder, inches from a hit that would cave in his skull. Olexie brushed off the strike, redirected the bigger man's momentum, and shoved him toward the window.

"Run!" Olexie shouted.

Olexie and Tenen bowled Liam over and struck the window, exploding into the night. The noise and fury rang in Ajay's skull. He couldn't hear anything over the raw thunder echoing in his ears.

The mercenary Chay Quinn threw open the door. She raised two small semiautomatic pistols, aimed at Ajay's head.

Ajay heard the hum of nearby snowmobiles carried on the frigid wind. Fresh snow swirled through the office. He remembered watching Chay casually murder the librarian at the government center. She hadn't paused or shown any remorse. Tenen might be frighteningly huge, but Chay Quinn was a whole new level of terrifying.

They were on the second story. Far enough for an old man to break a leg or a neck or a hip. Far enough that even if he managed not to badly injure himself, he would still have the wind knocked out of him. He'd be left stunned and vulnerable out in the cold.

Ajay met Liam Thompson's gaze. The environmentalist rose from the floor, gasping for breath, with one hand clutching the gun that he didn't seem to understand was still there.

Chay caught him and shoved him away from the window.

Before Ajay could talk himself out of it, he rounded the desk and jumped through the window.

He hit the snowbank hard, but the drifts of new powder padded his landing enough that he didn't break anything. Probably. The impact pounded the air from his lungs, and he rolled over, gasping. Snow piled under his shirt and numbed his arms. He cursed himself for leaving his coat in the garage.

Maja lifted him and slammed him onto a purring snowmobile. The big Russian lay a hair shy of limp on a second one. She pushed a helmet in Ajay's lap and said, "Ride like your life depends on it."

And she twisted the gas on the other snowmobile, launching herself out across the frozen lake.

CHAPTER TWENTY-FOUR

"I READ about old iron mines like this," said Austin. "They connect the levels because it's too much work to move equipment through the elevator all the time. This way they can lower stuff straight down a hole."

"You read too much," Kylie whispered.

"There's no such thing."

They were deep in the mines, past where Shannon had killed Samuel. It was cool in the dry tunnel, and even though Kylie wore her coat, the cold seeped into her bones and made her teeth chatter. Her light wouldn't last forever, and Austin had already his last dregs of power.

Kylie squinted at him in the dim light. "Why would you read if you can watch shows?"

"Who says I don't do both?"

"At the same time?" He was just being ridiculous.

They passed a square hole several yards across that descended into infinite darkness. Kylie held out a hand and pointed. Austin nodded grimly. They needed to get to one level up, not a million levels down.

"It shouldn't be much farther," Austin said. Kylie congratulated herself on being able to notice the fact that he was trying to convince himself of the statement. He wasn't really trying to convince her at all. He was smart enough to know he couldn't do that.

"What if someone's guarding it?"

"Then we'll think of something else," Austin said, based on absolutely nothing. "But I'm not going back to that Shannon lady. She—"

"Gives you the creeps."

"Well—"

"Makes you uncomfortable."

"It's more like—"

"Terrifies you."

"Yeah, that's the one."

Kylie wasn't sure if she had enough power for a trip back, and she certainly didn't want to do it in the dark.

Metal clanged against stone somewhere far behind them, sending a shiver down Kylie's spine. A million years later, Austin took another step forward. It occurred to Kylie that he was the braver of them. Maybe they would find their way out after all.

She still had some pretty serious doubts.

The stairs were crude things shaped in an age when power tools were a fantasy. They spiraled up into the inky black above, and Kylie took the lead. Step after step after step, her numb feet stumbled and her legs burned. It felt like they were climbing a mountain. The cool air smelled of mold and urine.

A voice echoed below, far away and indistinct.

"They're looking for us," whispered Austin. "They figured out we're not in the base."

"They have more important things to worry about." She hoped that what she said was true.

It wasn't. She knew it wasn't.

Kylie's fidget died halfway back to the elevator on the upper level. It flickered twice, each time sending a shock of panic through her chest. Austin, impressively, kept himself calm as it flickered out the first and second times.

But on the third time, it didn't come back, and Kylie could hear the boy's breath growing more ragged and panicked. She took his hand and whispered into his ear, "We've got this, Austin." Probably a lie, but she didn't know for sure, so did it really count?

His breathing slowed.

"I'm sorry I got you into this," Kylie said. "You shouldn't have come over. I shouldn't try to have friends."

Austin drew a deep, long breath, then whispered, "I almost died last year."

Kylie didn't know what to say in response, so she stared into the dark where she knew he still stood.

"Did you know I'm fourteen? I'm only in seventh grade because in second grade they said I wasn't emotionally developed enough. In third grade, they said I wasn't keeping up."

"You're smart," Kylie whispered.

"Not smart enough. Not good enough. Not big enough.

I'd never really made any friends, and every time I started to, they made me switch grades and I lost them all." His voice cracked as he spoke, and Kylie could hear him swallowing back the emotion. "What I'm saying is, I like you and I want you to be my friend, even if it means we have to go through something dangerous."

They sat in the dark for a long time, letting the cold seep into their bones. Far away, voices rose and fell as the soldiers hunted them, and Kylie alternately felt hope and fear at the idea of them succeeding. Still, they didn't give up.

Kylie found Austin's hand in the dark and squeezed it. "I have a machine growing in my head," she said.

He stayed silent, and she didn't really blame him.

"It's experimental, but it keeps growing as I get older, and Papa says it'll cause brain damage pretty soon if we don't get rid of it."

"Really?"

"It lets me talk with computers."

"Is that why you act all funny sometimes? Brain damage?"

Kylie let go of his hand and hugged herself close. She shivered but wasn't sure if it was prompted by cold or fear. "I don't know if I want to get rid of it."

"But it's brain damage," said Austin. "That's kinda serious."

They sat again in silence. The voices grew closer, but she couldn't hear what direction they came from. Everything bounced and echoed around the wide caverns of the old iron mine. Kylie ran her fingers along the metal rich walls and drew a long, calming breath.

"I thought all the bats down in Mystery Cave died a long time ago," Kylie said when the silence became too much.

"They reintroduced bats that could resist the disease that killed the original ones," said Austin. "And they try not to let people bring diseases in anymore."

"It's always people's fault, isn't it?" asked Kylie.

"Pretty much."

Kylie had an idea.

The signals from the machine half of her brain wouldn't travel far down here. If she concentrated hard, they'd bounce off the rock and reverberate back into her skull. All it would do was give her a headache—and let her get an idea of their surroundings.

Kylie reached out carefully at first. There were no devices nearby, and that was so dreadfully lonely. Her head ached at the first touch of the wall, since it pounded the signal back right at her. She tried again, lighter this time. Another direction. She used it like echolocation, and after a few minutes, she could halfway sense the tunnel up ahead. Placing Austin's hand on her shoulder so that he would walk behind her, she moved forward.

It was slow and painful. To get a faster image, she needed to push harder, and as she did, she felt her brain go dull and cold. She tamped down the fear. Cold logic took control and led her to push even harder. She needed to move fast. They had to escape to warn Papa of Shannon's betrayal. If they could get to the elevator, she was sure she could escape.

They avoided a hole in the floor, skirting alongside the gaping fissure. Kylie felt the whoosh of air coming from the infinite empty space. That hole swallowed her signal and didn't bounce it back. She walked with her eyes closed, so she was surprised when Austin let go of her shoulder.

"We're here," he whispered.

Kylie opened her eyes and saw the rust red walls lit by the hint of a glow from up ahead. Her brain felt dull with fog, and she was annoyed that Austin would speak so close to the enemy.

The enemy. Her head spun with ideas on how to solve the problem of these mercenaries. She saw with vivid detail how she might detonate their weapons or lock them somewhere and never let them out. There were ways she could make them disappear if only she didn't have Austin holding her back.

She turned to face the boy and watched as a series of inscrutable expressions flashed across his face. He opened his mouth to talk, but she gripped his arm hard enough to warn him away from it. Another expression. Pain?

Kylie blinked. Pain. She was causing him pain. She let go of his arm and sat on the cold stone floor.

He took her hands in his and tried to look her right in the eyes. It was too uncomfortable, letting him see directly into her like that, so she looked away. Tears tried to force themselves out, but she squeezed her eyes shut and forced them away. She forced everything away. This wasn't a time for tears.

Kylie became aware of a high keening coming from the base of her own throat. She tried to stop it, but it rang louder and louder. They would hear soon. They would come and take Austin away. She needed to get herself under control. Be tough like Papa always was. Smart.

Silence. The knot in her chest loosened, and she drew a long, slow breath.

"I'm fine," she whispered. All she needed to do was find a way out. They could figure out where to go once they reached the surface.

"Found them," called a gruff voice.

Kylie turned to see one of the mercenaries rounding the corner. A smile on his lips showed off his yellow teeth.

He spread his arms and said, "Hey, we found you just in time. Base is moving."

"Moving?" said Austin. "But isn't Mr. Andersen coming back here?"

Shannon stepped around the corner, her hand resting on her holstered gun. That same gun had killed Samuel. Kylie flashed back to a vision of that hand pulling the trigger on that gun, and she knew what she had seen. "Plans have changed, kids," she said. "You're coming with us."

Kylie stared at Shannon's hand. "We're waiting here for Papa."

Shannon gave a slight nod of her head, and the other soldier took some zip ties from his belt.

Kylie bolted, trying to push past Shannon, but the woman was fast. She grabbed Kylie's arm and slammed her against the wall hard enough to elicit a cry of pain.

Austin swung a rock at Shannon's head, but her grip didn't lessen as she dipped out of the way. The other mercenary grabbed Austin and shoved him against the wall. "Best settle down, kid," Shannon said, "You're the one extra here."

"You're a traitor!" Kylie shouted. "A traitor! You work for Liam Thompson."

Shannon pressed Kylie hard against the stone. The Frontier Arms ring flashed on her finger, just as it had when she'd shot Samuel. "My employment is none of your concern."

Austin cursed and spit, but the bigger man bound his hands and shoved him to the floor. Shannon did the same to Kylie.

"Now," said Shannon, "let's talk about how much I don't like babysitting."

CHAPTER TWENTY-FIVE

Ajay had a lot of regrets in his long life. He regretted not giving his wife more priority. His marriage probably would have still ended, but it might have ended better. He regretted almost every interaction with his daughter. The poison of his fatherhood had led to her death, and he couldn't imagine regretting anything more than that.

But this was close.

Ajay regretted leaving his coat in Liam Thompson's snowmobile-filled garage.

The windshield helped, as did the bundled warm layers of flannel Ajay wore. That kept him from instantly dying in the driving cold. Thin gloves covered his frozen fingers—the kind meant to fit underneath bulkier, warmer gloves. The gloves he wore were driving gloves made for a jaunty adventure in a climate-controlled automobile on a cool Sunday afternoon.

They were not meant for ninety miles per hour across a frozen lake on an absolute monster of a snowmobile.

His only salvation was the warm helmet Maja had given him. Maybe his brain would survive long after his body was frozen stiff.

Maja sped ahead of him, blasting through the freshly fallen powder. Olexie clung to her back, flopping dangerously whenever she banked to one side or the other. The rest of the team was gone, dispersed into the wild to reconvene back at the base camp or in one of several secondary points which Ajay had been forced to memorize using a brain which now barely functioned in the excessive cold.

Ajay couldn't hear anything through the padded helmet, but a glance back told him they were already being followed.

They hit the forest, and Maja signaled a stop.

"Where is your coat?" she demanded.

"I was too warm."

"You are the worst field agent ever."

"I was never a field agent."

"Then how were you a hacker?" She jostled Olexie and shoved him toward Ajay's snowmobile. "Take the Russian. I can't move fast enough with him."

"I can't," Ajay said but caught the tall man anyway. "Where are the others?"

"Then leave him in a snowbank," Maja said. Ajay didn't think it was a joke.

"You're leaving us?"

"Go." She pointed down a narrow trail—barely enough to fit the huge snowmobile. "I will lure them away."

Olexie settled onto the back of Ajay's snowmobile with a grunt.

"His collarbone is likely broken," Maja said. "But if you let his complaints slow you, you'll be dead before you freeze."

Ajay flexed his stiff fingers. "That doesn't sound so bad."

Maja shook her head in disgust and settled back onto her ride. With a twist and a hum from her motor, she spun around and blasted back onto the lake toward three approaching plumes of powder.

"You ready?" Ajay asked Olexie.

"It hurts so much," the Russian sobbed.

"Tough it up." He took Olexie's thick gloves, figuring he needed them more than the Russian since Ajay needed to be able to manipulate the snowmobile controls.

Ajay launched the snowmobile deeper into the woods. The going was slow at first, along the narrow trail. He weaved and bumped over ancient oak roots and dodged through a stand of tall jack pines. Moving slower, he sensed a little of the world around them. Needles prickled his fingers as circulation returned. The rumble of snowmobiles echoed through the forest, punctuated by the rattle of automatic fire.

One humming motor approached. Maybe two.

"She only drew one of them off," Olexie said.

"Dammit."

"You drive like an old man," Olexie said as they bumped slowly through the woods.

Then, Ajay hit a straightaway. He unloaded, blasting them forward along a divide between forest and lake. The trail was open here, and well worn. It banked hard left, but the slope kept him rooted solidly on the ground. Glancing over his shoulder, he saw two black snowmobiles emerge from the trees.

He twisted the gas even harder, and his motor whined. The treads slipped as he banked hard across the lake, abandoning the well-worn trail for clean snow.

The pursuers closed some of the distance.

The ache of cold gave way to the heat of adrenaline.

Ajay hit the lakeshore hard, launching off a drift and plunging into dark forest. His snowmobile's yellow headlight danced off trees, barely giving him time to dodge through the dense old forest.

Faster.

The sounds of his pursuers rattled through the forest like bones. They closed. He couldn't possibly shake them. He needed a way to shut them down, but Olexie had left his gun at the lodge.

Maybe he could get lucky.

He spotted the low branch and banked toward it rather than away. "Duck," he shouted to Olexie, not sure if the Russian would hear him.

Punching the accelerator, he hunkered as low as he could. The thick oak branch crushed his windshield and slammed against Ajay's shoulder, but he clung to his ride and somehow kept Olexie from falling. Then, he turned and rode fast and straight through the next clearing.

He heard a shout and a crunch as his pursuers hit the branch, but he had no way of knowing if it stopped either of them.

They hit another lake, and without a windshield, the

full force of the winter wind hit Ajay in the chest. He hunkered as low as he could and pushed the snowmobile fast across the ice. His arms and shoulders grew stiff from cold.

They hit a place where the ice had no snow at all, and the skis of the snowmobile skidded sideways. His treads still gripped, but the front wobbled and lost purchase.

Ajay swore.

Then he lost all control. He slid sideways, punched the accelerator to try to regain a footing, but nothing worked. His snowmobile slid sideways into the bank, sending loose powder everywhere.

When Ajay tried to let go of the handlebars, his fingers refused to move. A shiver thundered through his whole body. He was cold. Too cold. He wouldn't last much longer out here, and he'd fade fast if he tried to fight the wind.

"Hold on," he said to Olexie. His voice was barely a whisper through blue lips.

He watched as a single snowmobile emerged from the woods. It had two passengers. One must have stopped to pick up the other, which explained why they were farther behind. Ajay wondered if it was far enough.

"I'm slowing you down," said Olexie. "Drop me off here and send someone to pick me up when you escape."

"Don't be an idiot," Ajay replied.

Ajay launched the snowmobile up the hill and rejoined the powdery trail. The next section was a hill, and if he remembered it correctly, he just might have enough time.

A shudder ran through his aching shoulders. His muscles seized, and try as he might, he couldn't bring himself to push the snowmobile faster. The buzz of his pursuers approached across the wide lake.

"Go," said Olexie.

Ajay couldn't breathe.

"Ajay, you have to go. You have to move."

"Can't," Ajay managed. His vision grew dim along the edges. He would die there. The pursuers would find him, but he'd already be dead from the cold.

"You are a Minnesotan," Olexie growled. "Be tougher and power through it. Cold is nothing to you."

Cold. The whole world was cold, and Ajay was frozen all the way down to his core. The layers of long underwear and flannel had done nothing against the sharp winter wind. He flexed his fingers as if to improve circulation, but they were so stiff and so numb he wasn't sure if he had succeeded.

"Go, Ajay. For your granddaughter," Olexie urged.

Ajay turned his head to look at the Russian. Even that motion hurt as if shards of ice had buried themselves deep in the muscles of his neck. The old man looked sad—injured and beaten. "Olexie," Ajay said. "You aren't slowing me down."

"Then move."

For Kylie. Ajay cranked the acceleration, crushing the undergrowth as he plowed his own trail through the tall forest. He wove side to side, scraping each time against the orange bark of towering scotch pines. Branches of buckthorn scraped against the underbelly of the snowmobile and tore against the fabric of his fleece.

Gunshots. Bark exploded from the tree near Ajay's head. Then again by his knee.

"Keep going," Olexie spat.

Ajay didn't know how much more he could go. The gunshots ceased as he pulled ahead, dancing in a tight rhythm between trees. The undergrowth cleared, and the pines stood like sentinels at the edge of the civilized world, ready to march at a moment's notice.

Another shot scattered ice ahead of him. The pursuers were too close. Inaccurate as they were, they'd hit eventually. He had to do something.

Then he saw it. By chance, the pines parted for a straightaway leading up to the thick bore of a fallen tree, in front of which was a piled drift of snow.

Olexie saw where he was looking. "Don't—"

His words cut off in a grunt of pain as Ajay pounded the accelerator. The snowmobile launched at its full torque, speeding faster, faster toward the fallen tree. It was an insane move. Ajay had no idea if they'd make it, and he couldn't possibly know what was on the other side of the tree.

But, then again, they had no chance if he didn't try.

Trees flew by, and a surge of adrenaline slowed time. Ajay watched the bark explode a few feet away. Another bullet pinged off their treads. He heard the roar of the snowmobile behind him surge in its own acceleration. He felt the whine of the electric motor beneath his seat as it surged with every ounce of power it could possibly manage.

They hit the snowdrift, and the snowmobile's skis sank into the loose snow.

Then hit the solid drift underneath. The lift was just enough to clip the top of the fallen tree. With one final twist of acceleration, Ajay launched up, jumping a dozen feet before landing hard on the open trail below.

But his tread had disturbed the snowdrift. When their pursuers hit it, their skis sank deeper. They caught, flinging both men and the snowmobile end over end to crash hard on the forest floor.

Ajay didn't pause to see how that worked out for them. He punched the accelerator again and left them in the powder.

"What a shitshow," muttered Olexie. He had one arm in a sling tied closely to his belly. His other hand held a glass of Coke with a twist of lime floating in it.

Ajay and Olexie sat in the Snowbird, a seedy snowmobile bar somewhere in the depths of greater Minnesota. Its customers wore more layers than Ajay had ever seen, and the air hung heavy with the scents of sweat and melted snow. Every surface in the entire establishment was oak, except for the hazy mirror behind the bar. Two shots of vodka sat in front of Ajay.

"Are you sure you don't want one of these?" Ajay asked.

"I can't stand vodka," Olexie grumbled.

"I thought Russians loved vodka."

"I thought Minnesotans loved cold."

Ajay's fingers still ached, and the occasional bone-rattling shiver reminded him that his brush with hypothermia would probably linger for a while. "I'm sorry," he said.

Olexie took a drink of his Coke. "You are a behind-the-screens guy."

"Always was."

"You could not have worked with a coat on."

"I loved that coat." Ajay mostly just hated shopping for new outerwear.

"Maybe you can ask for it back."

Ajay sipped his vodka. It tasted like paint thinner.

"You could have killed Thompson," Olexie said. "This would be done."

"I told you I'm not a killer," said Ajay.

"Now you sit with back to the door." Olexie tapped his temple. "You need to start being paranoid. Everything can always go bad."

Ajay had always thought of himself as one of the most paranoid people around. Online, he always considered every angle before it became a problem. He had scoured government systems, proprietary data collection, and medical records to cover his trail when he left the NSA. He constantly checked his digital signature.

A group of snowmobilers bustled into the warm bar, stomping packed snow off their boots. Ajay fought the urge to turn around to look at them, and instead slipped his cheaters on to watch them on a grainy video. It didn't help. "I'm not good at this," he said.

"Neither was Silas."

Bringing up the dead man didn't help Ajay's mood.

"Cut Ajay some slack," said Maja as she sat down at their table. She slid a data chip across the table to Ajay. "He did well for a first time out."

Olexie scoffed. "He got us caught, and he took forever to hack through their security."

"*I* got us caught?"

Olexie took a sip of his Coke. "Well, I didn't set off the alarm."

He hadn't set off the alarm, either. "Maja must have been spotted." The hairs on the back of Ajay's neck stood up. He slotted it into his fidget and scrolled through the data.

"It wasn't me," Maja said.

"You picked up the data we scraped from his feed?" Ajay asked.

Maja downed the second vodka. "That's why it took so long to get into position outside the window. You had that thing hidden pretty well."

"He still screwed up." Olexie shifted his weight and winced in pain. "We shouldn't have needed a rescue."

Ajay said, "It was top notch network security, and I didn't see you punching your weight."

"I could take that big guy in a fair fight," Olexie growled.

"In your youth, maybe."

"I got us into the house."

"Where we got caught."

"That wasn't my fault," Olexie spat.

"This guy has better security than anything we dealt

with a decade ago. You're lucky I've kept up with tech, or you'd be stuck here with nothing to show." He scanned the new data on his fidget. The outgoing messages they had picked up proved to be trivial. He snapped the display closed with a sharp chop and dropped the chip on the table. "Never mind. We have nothing."

"Sometimes it goes this way." Olexie took another dainty sip of his Coke. "Drink your vodka."

Ajay drew in several shaking breaths, which failed to calm his nerves. His vodka burned on its way down, then burned again as it tried to claw its way back up. "Ugh."

"I told you," Olexie said, "vodka is terrible. You should drink Jack Daniels."

Maja shook her head with an expression of disgust.

Olexie leaned forward with cold shark's eyes. "Why did you pull back right when we got caught? We could have used more distraction."

Maja's jaw tightened. "It wasn't a suicide mission. We followed the plan."

"Plan?" Olexie flicked the data chip toward her. "That wasn't the plan. You left when we needed you." He winced as his weight shifted. "You could have taken the lodge."

"You were caught. They had us outnumbered and outgunned."

"We were negotiating," Olexie spat. "It would have been nice to do it from a position of power." He swallowed the rest of his Coke. "And then you didn't follow through when you had the chance to finish it."

It was Maja's turn to look like a shark. Her freckles

went pale, and the cold in her eyes made Ajay shudder. "There wasn't a clean shot."

"Bullshit."

Ajay slammed a fist down on the table and hissed through his teeth, "Nobody was supposed to get killed."

Olexie rolled his eyes.

"Tell that to Tabitha," Maja said.

"Where did your true believers go?" Ajay asked.

Maja stared at her empty glass. Something in her expression appeared profoundly vulnerable for a fraction of a second before disappearing behind her steely gaze. "When Tabitha got hit, I ordered the retreat. They'll meet us back at the mine."

"Is she going to be okay?" When nobody answered, Ajay continued, "I need to get back to Kylie. I wasn't able to delete Liam's records, so she's still in his system. We're going to need to disappear." Saying the words made it feel too real.

Olexie waved Ajay's concerns away. "The CIA lady can make you disappear, but I don't know that you'd like it."

Maja's hand drifted down to rest on a small pistol strapped to her side. "Olexie," she warned.

Ajay's heart pounded. A cold fear clenched like a fist in his chest. Maja was CIA. Was everything she had done a lie meant to manipulate him?

"Yeah, yeah, yeah," said Olexie. "I'm not supposed to talk about the CIA thing."

"I'm not the only one with secrets," said Maja in a calm voice.

Olexie went very still.

"Guys," Ajay said. "I just want to get back to Kylie and Austin."

Maja said, "You don't want everyone to know what you did for the KGB, do you?"

"That's enough, Maja," Olexie growled.

"Some people wouldn't be happy to hear—"

Olexie slammed a fist on the table hard enough to make their empty glasses rattle. "Enough!"

The corners of Maja's lips turned up in a wry smile. "We'll give you a ride back to the mine, Ajay," she said, now the friendliest person Ajay had ever met. "We'll even help you get established in a new life if you want."

"That really hurt," said Olexie, grasping his wounded collarbone. "Please do not make me do that again."

"And Silas?" Ajay asked.

"We'll take care of the body," Maja said. "And Ajay?"

"Yeah?"

"I'm *ex*-CIA. I'm not working you. I really thought you might be interested in taking up our cause."

"How can I know you're on my side?"

Maja drew a long breath and leaned forward. "I have a family, Ajay. Maybe I don't ever get to see them again, but I love them as much as you love your granddaughter. I fight for their future." She tapped a spot on her wrist and an image of a younger Maya with a man and two young girls appeared on the table.

"How long since you've seen them?" Ajay asked.

"Too long." Maja cut the image. "But that doesn't mean I care any less. I'll help you get those kids back."

He connected to the tavern's network and checked his messages. He didn't find anything from Kylie, though he didn't expect to since the iron mine cut off her access. He also saw nothing from the neighbors who were caring for Garrison, which was well and good. Garrison didn't tend to cause much trouble except for when he really, really did. Ajay missed the dog immensely, even after only a short time away.

He looked up after running some network searches. "There's nothing on the network about a manhunt for us. Sounds like Liam decided to keep things on the down-low."

"Why call the police when he has his own mercenary army?" said Maja as she flagged down a server to order more drinks. "Any word about their location in the BWCA?"

"Not at all. They run mostly off grid. No indication where their base is or where their people are currently located. All I can tell is that Frontier Arms operates around the world and they're actively hiring."

"Maybe you should apply," Olexie said to Maja.

"Will you be my reference?" Maja joked.

"I will tell them that you fail to follow through when you have a perfectly good shot."

"I didn't have the shot."

Ajay looked over the tops of his cheaters.

Olexie gave a half shrug. "I told you before. It's the simplest solution."

Ajay spoke through his teeth. "And I told you I don't do that kind of thing. What makes us so damn holy that we can be judge, jury, and executioner?"

"When dealing with the ultra-rich, it is enough to have motive and opportunity," hissed Olexie. "Especially with the likes of that bastard."

Liam Thompson had said it was personal. Ajay remembered the moment he had said it and rage had flashed over Olexie's face. The countercapitalist wasn't a pure idealist fighting for the rights of the common citizen, but what more was there to his story? The drinks arrived but one look at Olexie's stony jaw and Ajay knew he wouldn't get any more from the old Russian. Not just then.

They sat for a while in silence, sipping their drinks. Maja had been kind enough to order something other than vodka. Ajay thought it might be this rural Minnesota version of an old fashioned, but the whiskey was too harsh and the color was too yellow.

"Tell me," he said, leaning his sore bones back in his chair. "How did people with your backgrounds ever start working together? CIA? KGB?"

Olexie chuckled. "It wasn't long after I became a citizen of the United States. I figured, as a citizen, I ought to be allowed to go to protests. After all, it is one of our inalienable rights."

Ajay saw the big man relax as he recounted his past, but he also watched the feed in his cheaters. There was a rowdy group of snowmobilers drinking a few tables away, a couple whispering intimately in the corner, and a bartender who kept looking at Olexie as if he might not be welcome. Ajay grinned to himself. Who's paranoid now?

"It was a protest for that Bezos thing years ago. People were getting upset that all that wealth was going straight to the moon while people down here starved on their minimum wage jobs."

"Fair enough," said Ajay.

"The protest got violent. Not my fault!"

"I keep hearing that."

"Apparently violence is only sometimes an inalienable right. I neglected that page of the citizen's handbook." He stared off into the distance. "I was one of the few arrested, but that made me look more serious than I really was. In jail, I met some very nice people, and they explained to me all the wonderful things we could do for the world."

"Like more violence?"

"We've never been terrorists," said Maja. "Just people trying to shake the system up."

"With bombs," said Ajay, using his best disapproving voice.

Maja shrugged. "You saw Thompson's army out there. You saw his strike on the government center. Why does a man like that sling around so much hardware?"

Ajay didn't mention that being afraid of terrorists might drive a man to hire mercenaries. "Do you two run CCS?" He had been trying to figure out their leadership structure since he first met Olexie.

"Not at all," said Maja. "We support a greater movement. Together, we run the operation against Thompson, but we don't have any power over anyone else."

"We don't even really have a connection to them," said Olexie.

"Like a terrorist cell," said Ajay.

"Pretty much," Olexie said at the same time Maja replied, "Not at all."

"So, you were arrested and they used that to recruit you?" Ajay tried to steer the conversation back to Olexie's history. "Who recruited you?"

Olexie cast a nervous glance at Maja. "His name was Black. I don't know anything else."

"And you?" Ajay asked Maja.

"Same."

"First name?"

Olexie said, "I thought that was his first name."

"Then what's his last name?"

Olexie gave a sheepish look and took another sip of his Coke.

"You thought his name was Black Black?" asked Ajay.

"American names can be tricky."

Maja rolled her eyes. "He doesn't use his real name. We're doing good work, and we're taking care of a real problem. Thompson is up to something terrible, and that's all that matters."

"And everyone in the org feels the same way?" Ajay asked. "All those true believers you had at the lodge. What did they think they were signing up for?"

Maja said, "They move when we tell them to move. We trust the boss as much as we need to, and we trust our people to get the job done."

Ajay knew better than to give anyone that much trust, but he had to agree that Liam Thompson was up to something bad. The fingers of his left hand danced over the controls of his fidget, then the holographic image over the back of his hand came to life.

"I know what Thompson is doing," he said. "And I think if we get it to your analysts, we'll be able to tell where he'll be next."

CHAPTER TWENTY-SEVEN

THE FIRST THING that set off Ajay's paranoid instinct when they arrived at the mine was the distinct lack of vehicles parked under the old warehouse roof. Only one remained, a massive truck sitting low on its axles near the front of the loading dock. The air smelled of diesel mixed with the cool wet of fresh snow. It was an old smell that Ajay hadn't smelled in years.

It reminded him of Minnesota winters long in the past, when he would watch as the plows trundled through the neighborhoods, clearing snow from choked streets. It was the smell of a snow day, back when enough bad weather meant a day off of school or work. The remnants of that long-ago joy mixed with his current state to make a low-key sensation of dread which lingered like bitter bile on the back of his tongue.

The second thing that set off Ajay's paranoid instinct was the body.

It wasn't obvious at first, but when Ajay shouldered his

way into the office, he noticed a thin spray of red in one corner of the window. Searching the rest of the building, he found Walt with his mop of steel gray hair matted against the side of his bloody and ruined head.

Ajay fought the urge to vomit. Dead. That kind old man, his body askew and discarded in the corner. Ajay checked the elevator controls. They had been set to override, meaning the elevator could be controlled inside the mine.

Someone was still down there.

Ajay worked the controls, bringing the elevator to the surface, and then switching it back to the internal override.

"Dead," gasped Ajay as he stepped back outside. "Walt's dead."

Olexie shot a glance at the mine elevator as it clanged into place at the top of the shaft. "What do you mean?"

Maja stepped out of the sedan they had taken from up north. Hours had passed in transit, and each hour had only served to grate at Ajay's nerves.

Ajay stalked across the windy hilltop to the mine entrance. "The elevator operator's dead," he said. "And we're going down there to get Kylie and Austin."

Maja easily caught up to him. "Ajay, we can't go down there."

Ajay spun on her. "We can and we will. If they're still down there, we're bringing them back. I don't care who's in the way. If not," Ajay jabbed a finger at her, "then we're going to find them."

Maja opened her mouth to respond, but Olexie slapped her on the back and said, "Let's go, then."

"If there was an attack, the team would fall back to a secondary location," Maja said as they rode the elevator down.

"What about the kids?"

"They will have brought them along," said Maja.

Ajay's heart pounded in his chest. It didn't feel right. He'd left Kylie in an unsafe location. Again. All he wanted was to keep her safe, but even that simple goal slipped through his grasp.

"This is why I should always bring my kid with on missions," he muttered.

"Good advice," Olexie said, laughing.

The technology that ran the elevator might have been the original hardware of the iron mine, which was over a hundred years old, and it sounded like it. When they had ridden down earlier, the old man in the control building had operated the elevator, as it had been done since the mine was in operation. Ajay watched the lights on the retrofitted panel as the elevator slowly descended.

"Take this." Maja pressed a small pistol into Ajay's hand.

He looked down at the gun. It sat like a turd in his palm and gave him about the same rush of power. "I don't shoot," he said.

"You'll shoot if you have to."

"I probably won't." He wouldn't. Ajay wanted to explain to her *again* that he'd always sat behind a screen. He'd been responsible for terrible things, but there had been a long par five between his actions and a living human being. "That's just not who I was."

"You'll shoot someone if you need to save your grand-daughter," growled Olexie as he took up position inside the elevator. He winced with every movement, and his mood was starting to deteriorate rapidly. He hefted a large pistol he had taken from Maja's supplies.

But Olexie had a point. Ajay kept the gun pointed to the ground and leaned his cane against the wall so that he could operate the elevator.

"Stop one level up," Maja said, ice in her flat eyes.

"Why?" asked Ajay.

"If there's anyone down there, they'll be waiting at the elevator. They probably heard you bring it to the surface."

The metal levers of the elevator control were so cold they burned his already frostbitten fingers. The elevator didn't use a straight vertical shaft. It descended at a slight angle, giving Ajay's stomach a slightly odd twist as it rumbled down its track.

The only light was a dim incandescent bulb wavering in the top of the elevator, and through the metal grate, he could see the nearly half mile of rock as they passed to the world below. It was an almost inconceivable amount of stone when he thought about it too hard. Its existence was crushing. Yet, the elevator rattled and descended even further.

"I don't like this," muttered Olexie. "Where has everyone gone?"

"What about the owners," Ajay said.

Olexie raised an eyebrow.

To Maja, Ajay said, "Olexie said your people were squatting here. Someone else owns the actual mine. Who?"

Maja stared at the stone as it slowly slid past. "I don't know."

Ajay pressed her, "You're CIA. You can come up with a better lie than that. Who uses the mine to store equipment?"

She pressed her lips into a tight line.

"Maja," Olexie growled.

"Liam Thompson," Maja said.

"What?" shouted Olexie.

"It was so that we could keep an eye on his movements."

"Just fucking great," Ajay said. He stuffed the pistol in his pocket so that he could manipulate his fidget's holographic projector. An image of the map on Liam Thompson's wall appeared on the moving stone, complete with the cryptic instructions. He found his image of the soil map and set it as an overlay.

"My people went through every box that he had stored here," Maja said. "There was nothing incriminating. Nothing dangerous."

"How much do you trust your people?"

"Implicitly."

"Fuck," Ajay said after plugging their GPS location into his map.

Olexie cast him a sideways glance. "What?"

"We know that Liam is trying to build his city of the future, and his map had a branch of instructions I couldn't interpret before." Ajay highlighted the Soudan Mine on the map. Interpreting the series of numbers, he found the corresponding county roads and rural streets. They lead through northern Minnesota to a spot at the edge of the BWCA.

"I don't get it," said Olexie. Maja folded her arms and scowled.

Ajay pointed at the image with the tip of his cane. The non-rubberized tip clacked against the metal grate. "The instructions start here. This is the staging area for the project."

"That brings them to the edge of a lake."

"A frozen lake."

A smile spread slowly across Maja's face and for a brief second, the wrinkles in the corners of her eyes melted. "Brilliant," she said, but Ajay didn't know if she was referring to his discovery or Liam's plan.

"The map on the wall didn't match the official maps online," the Russian said. Ajay was impressed that the old man had made the attempt.

Ajay continued, "They don't fit because this section isn't on any of the public online maps. It's the old copper-nickel site, and it was scrubbed from all the copies."

Olexie nodded. "That's why he needed the paper copies."

"To make sure his plan would really work," Ajay said.

"And he wanted the rest destroyed so he could control the whole message."

"But why kill those librarians?" Ajay asked. "Why not just sneak in at night and do it quietly?"

Olexie said, "Lives are nothing to a man as rich as Thompson."

It didn't sound right to Ajay, but he didn't see the

benefit of pressing the point. "This is an extremely difficult region to approach with heavy equipment, due to the lakes. It's mostly water all the way north from here. Soil surveys were for various locations around the site, including every-thing around this lake here, and this calcareous fen."

"The what?" Olexie asked.

"Calcareous fen. It's an extremely rare type of wetland, and it's even more rare this far north and east."

"Oh, okay," Olexie deadpanned. "That explains everything."

Ajay jabbed a finger at the map, excited to show Maja and Olexie how the pieces were finally fitting together. "If my interpretation of the instructions is right, they're going to work around it. Here, here, here, and—"

Maja slammed the elevator controls. The elevator jerked to a stop, and Ajay's projection shone out into the black mine tunnel. "Explain later," Maja said. "This is our stop."

Ajay closed his projection, activated his flashlight, and stepped out of the elevator.

CHAPTER TWENTY-EIGHT

"Where are we?" asked Ajay as he stepped out of the elevator. The rough-hewn walls glistened slightly with damp, and his whispers were swallowed by the expanse of darkness up ahead.

Maja held a boxy pistol in two hands pointed down at the floor. "This is the storage level. It's about fifty feet up from the labs."

Ajay said, "But it's empty."

Olexie leaned against a wall, sweat beading on his forehead, despite the cool cave air. "Why?"

Ajay edged forward and to the right as Maja took the left. He set his fidget to its highest light projection and panned it across the wide, empty corridor. "There's nothing here."

Maja shushed him.

Fresh scrape marks marred the rocky floor, evidence of large equipment being moved recently. Crates, Ajay thought, and some of the tread marks hinted at a Bobcat or maybe a full-sized forklift. "Did CCS store equipment here?"

"Some," Maja said. "The whole level had matériel in it, but most of it belonged to Liam."

Ajay drew several long breaths of the cool air. "We need to find Kylie."

"I'll scout ahead," said Maja. "There's another way down."

"Or there's the elevator," Ajay said through gritted teeth. He could only picture Kylie down there, afraid and alone. What if she were injured?

Olexie nodded to Maja, who disappeared down the wide central corridor. The tall Russian stepped between Ajay and the elevator. "She'll come through, Ajay."

"I don't trust her that much."

They waited in tense silence for several minutes. The million pounds of stone compressed Ajay's thoughts into a diamond-hard point aimed directly at finding Kylie and escaping. He pictured Walt's ruined face in the dark shadows in the corners of the stone passages. Kylie was in danger. He needed to find her as soon as possible. His palms grew slick with sweat and his heart raced.

"My girl's down there, Olexie," he finally said. He clutched his cane until his knuckles turned white. "I need to get down there now."

Olexie raised an eyebrow. "Be patient."

"Patient?" Ajay muscled past the big Russian. "I've been patient. I've helped you on your little assassination mission against all my better judgment, and I think I've been plenty patient." He stalked back to the elevator. "Are you coming with me, or not?"

Olexie batted his hand from the controls. His face was inches from Ajay, and he spoke through clenched teeth. "This is where we trust Maja. She knows what she's doing."

"The CIA spook?" Ajay asked. "You, a former KGB thug, are telling me to trust a former CIA operative."

"I was not thug."

"The point still stands!"

Olexie's lips turned up in a snarl. "Walt is dead. Equipment is missing, our people are gone, and we haven't gotten any messages about any it. If they had to leave without warning, they would have left a signal for us. It's probably not safe to go straight to the lab."

"Last I checked, Kylie and Austin were down there. I don't care about your messages or your soldiers or your equipment. Do you understand? If I know Kylie, she's still hiding down there, figuring out ways to avoid whoever the hell killed Harry." He shoved Olexie back a step. "I. Don't. Care. You countercapitalists can go on your way and fight all the injustice in the world. You can be terrorists if you like. All I want to do is find a nice, peaceful place to raise my granddaughter and live out my retirement."

"Sunshine and roses," grumbled Olexie.

"That's right."

"You don't get it, then," Olexie said, his shoulders slumping. "I thought after seeing what we do, you would get it."

Ajay threw up his hands. "I don't. I won't. Just leave us alone."

"There is nowhere safe so long as they are out there," Olexie snarled. "There's no way to live out your life in peaceful retirement when someone like Liam Thompson can swallow up your money, burn down the forests, and build his city of the future without ever thinking about the real consequences for regular people."

"Is that really so bad, though?" snapped Ajay. "A city of the future isn't going to hurt people. If anyone's going to build a city that doesn't damage the environment, it'll be that asshole Thompson. He loves trees more than anything."

"Not more than anything," said Olexie.

Ajay stared at the big man for several seconds. "No, you're right. Not more than his legacy. I think we saw that well enough today." He snatched the elevator control and switched the lever. The machinery clunked into place, but the door didn't close. "But his legacy is tied to the environment. He's motivated to do the right thing."

"So is everyone else, and we see how that goes."

"Yeah." Ajay hit the button to move the elevator.

Olexie gave a roar and slammed the controls from Ajay's grasp. "That's enough!" The elevator's movement stopped.

Ajay clumsily swung his cane at Olexie's head.

Olexie raised an arm to block, but it was the bad arm and caused more pain than the cane would have. The Russian howled and staggered backward.

Ajay pressed his advantage. "You were always an asshole."

"I am injured," Olexie pleaded.

"Back when you attacked the States with your vicious propaganda campaigns." Ajay jabbed at Olexie's injured shoulder. "You killed people, Olexie. Not soldiers on the battlefield or government leaders. You killed regular people in their homes. Where was your 'right thing' then?"

The big Russian turned so his good arm could fend Ajay off. He stepped out of the elevator. "I did what I thought was right!"

"You were wrong."

"You were no better," Olexie spat. "Whole fields burned because of your hacks. Children starved when you toppled our agriculture. Did you ever think about that? You care so much about this granddaughter of yours? What about my granddaughters? What about my children who suffered for decades because of the ego of the mighty United States?"

Ajay pounded the elevator lever with one fist. "That wasn't me."

Olexie roared again and kicked the elevator door. He prevented the mesh gate from swinging shut, but the elevator's mechanisms ground noisily. "You were the worst of them, Ajay Andersen. You did your country's bidding so long and so well that you didn't even know you were fighting on the wrong side."

"The wrong side? You've joined my side. What does that make you?"

The elevator started to slowly descend, even though the door was still open. "The sides weren't America versus the world. You were on the side of the corrupt against the innocent. You were the side of the oppressors."

Fury bubbled up in Ajay's belly. He stepped up face to face with Olexie Sokolov, rage burning like molten lava in his chest. "You hypocrite!"

Olexie grabbed Ajay's flannel with one meaty fist and pulled him from the elevator, throwing him to the hard stone. Then the elevator descended, leaving a black gaping void through the open gate.

"Goddamnit," Ajay swore, pulling himself to his feet.

Maja watched from the corridor with a smirk on her face. "He outsmarted you, Ajay."

Ajay rounded on her, cane clutched in one hand. "You're going to get me down there. I want Kylie back right now."

Maja pointed at Ajay. The wrinkles at the corners of her cold eyes deepened. "That'll be a good distraction," she said. "I found the back way down. Follow me."

She led Ajay and Olexie down the corridor to the right.

Which was why they weren't near the elevator shaft when it exploded, shattering stone and shaking the very core of the iron rich earth. All the lights died, and the air filled with choking dust.

And everything went black.

CHAPTER TWENTY-NINE

"The consolidation is complete," said the voice. Kylie recognized the deep woman's growl as Shannon from the mine. She wasn't near the log cabin where Kylie and Austin had been caged, but her voice rang through the signals dancing around the small encampment. "The camp is secure."

Austin poked at the fire heating the potbellied stove in the center of their little cabin. The iron poker was smoking hot already, but the dancing fire kept his attention. "We could sneak out the window."

"And the girl?" said another woman's voice on the comm channel. It was a strong voice, and Kylie thought she recognized it, but from where? "Is she safe?"

"The kids are fine," snapped Shannon. "Once the charges are set, we'll blow the reservoir, and then we should have enough staff to bring them to you."

"Kids?" The woman sounded like she disapproved. "There was only supposed to be a girl."

"Well, the girl brought a friend. Some black kid."

There was a pause, and Kylie wondered if she should interpret the long silence as disapproval. Then again, with the throbbing ache in her skull, she interpreted almost all emotional signals as disapproval.

"Maybe if we attack the guard with a hot poker, we can escape into the woods," Austin said, waving his poker like a sword. "And then walk back to town."

"We're a hundred miles from a town," said Kylie. It was late and she was tired. Her brain wasn't capable of offering any sympathy to the boy, no matter how desperate or scared he was. Only cruel logic. "Even if we escaped, we'd be killed by the cold. That's why they took our coats."

"I'd be fine," Austin said. "I'm immune to the cold."

"She doesn't have any friends," the strangely familiar woman on the comm finally said, "and this isn't the kind of thing someone brings friends to."

"Maybe she was lonely."

"Kylie is the most important part of this mission. Bring her to me immediately."

"Thompson needs us around," Shannon said. "We're behind schedule after the thing at the wolf lodge."

"What if we stole one of those flying drone cars?" said Austin. "I bet I could fly one of those."

"Have you ever flown anything?" asked Kylie.

"I drove the riding lawnmower once."

"I don't care about Thompson," said the woman on the comm.

Shannon growled, "We have a contract."

"Void it."

There was another silence on the line.

"Do you think we can convince our guard to help us?" Austin asked. "That Shannon lady seemed pretty stone cold, but some of the other mercs didn't seem all that thrilled about having us around."

"Were they unhappy about keeping us, or unhappy about keeping us alive?"

"I don't know."

"That's a pretty important difference."

"I suppose."

"Then maybe we shouldn't count on their help."

Austin jabbed at the fire, sending sparks flying.

Shannon said, "You don't have that kind of pull, boss. Nobody voids a contract like this."

"Just get her to me, Shannon," said the woman.

The connection clicked off, and Kylie blinked several times very fast. Her skull ached from the prolonged use of her tech, and she wasn't sure if she was causing permanent damage to her brain. She could listen to comms and see through video feeds without much effort, she found. If there was heavy encryption, it hurt to break it. If she wanted to manipulate the mercenaries' feeds, that cost her even more. She could deal with a headache. The fear of doing real damage weighed more heavily.

Fear of Papa's disappointment was the absolute worst and made her angry.

She couldn't interpret Austin's flurry of emotions in his expression and actions. Was he afraid or thrilled or sad? Not happy. She could see that much. Her first real attempt at making a friend and she already knew he was going to hate her forever.

Kylie blinked again, and parts of her brain clicked back online. She opened her mouth to speak but closed it again when a sudden realization washed over her.

"I know that voice," she whispered.

"Huh?"

"I was listening to a comm," she said dismissively. "Shannon was talking to her mercenary boss, but it doesn't make any sense, because I know who the boss is."

"A friend of yours?" Austin asked warily.

"No," said Kylie, "a sister."

CHAPTER THIRTY

AJAY'S EARS rang like a hearing aid malfunction, and his head ached like his brain was three sizes too large. He pressed his palms to the cold stone and pressed his aching body from the floor.

Then he flopped back down. The room spun out of control. Dust choked the air.

Maja emerged from the haze, a long pistol held in a relaxed grip. She cast a glance his way with a cold expression in her eyes. He thought he saw something there. Distaste? Disapproval? Then she moved past through the wide corridor.

Her three grenade-sized drones circled her, lighting the space ahead without ever really illuminating her. Ajay watched her from the floor, unable to force himself up.

What if Kylie had been down there?

Had the explosion killed everyone down below? Had there been anyone down there? The thoughts spun through his head like a fast drive through a heavy blizzard. An empty ache pierced his chest when he thought of Kylie dying in a place he told her was safe. Maybe Olexie was right. Maybe there wasn't anywhere safe in the world for Kylie so long as there were people willing to exploit others for their own gain.

But what could he do? He chewed on all the wrong choices he'd made over the years. His career, his personal life, his parenting. He'd fucked it all up and never once thought he was doing the wrong thing.

Olexie took Ajay's elbow with two hands and heaved him to his feet. He pulled him away with a grim expression. It didn't matter if they disagreed. They would work together.

For now.

They moved down the long corridor, and Ajay saw more evidence of large equipment being moved. The rock of the floor and walls showed signs of more crates. More machines.

"What was stored up here?" Ajay's voice sounded hollow in his own ears. He felt like he was shouting, but it sounded muffled.

"Quiet," said Olexie.

"This is important."

"Quiet," Olexie tightened his grip on Ajay until it hurt.

Ajay decided to be quiet.

They proceeded down the corridor, drones advancing ahead. They zipped around corners and shone light on nooks and crevices that wouldn't have been visible if the only point source of light had been Maja. It was a slick system, Ajay thought, and he almost wanted something like that of his own.

No, that's not right. Even in his fear and grief, he wanted toys to play with. Maybe in his backyard. He wasn't some countercapitalist avenger out to bring justice to a broken world. He couldn't afford to be that. All he cared about was finding Kylie and keeping her safe.

Olexie's grim face was covered in dust. He held a pistol in one hand and squinted against the reflected light from the hovering drones. What had Ajay done to hurt Olexie back when the Russian was still the enemy? The tall man kept dropping hints about it as if it might be something Ajay remembered. He didn't. Ajay knew he had hurt people over the years. A person can't get into the kind of aggressive hacking he'd used without some collateral damage. He had always done what needed to be done for the benefit of his country. He was a patriot.

Then again, so was Olexie, and Olexie had changed.

Ajay took the gun from his pocket and held it in his right hand. His cane felt awkward in his left, but he would manage. He set his hearing aid so that it would alert him of movement, then filtered out the buzz of Maja's three drones. The air hung heavy with ash and dust, and the lights from Maja's drones cut through it like knives.

They moved forward as a group, scanning the long corridor. Maja's drones checked side passages, darting in and returning at her command. Soon they came to a place where the floor dropped away, straight into the stone.

Maja peered down the hole and sniffed the air. "This

leads to the lower level, but we don't have a way to climb down. There are stairs farther back."

"Send a drone," Ajay said.

She shook her head. "Can't. I'll lose signal before it reaches the next level. We have to walk back to the stairs."

"How long will that take?" asked Olexie.

"Too long," said Ajay. Any time was too long. "Transfer one of your drones to me."

After a brief hesitation, she complied. Ajay took the drone, which was the size of his palm, and connected it to his fidget and glasses. With a little configuration, he was able to give himself a view of the drone's video and audio feed. He cast that feed to Olexie and Maja, so they would see as well.

The drone's scripting language was a more modern version of a language he once used to subvert industrial robots. Within a few minutes, he discovered a cache of automated routines—basic building blocks for an algorithmic search program. He slotted the pieces in place, telling it to descend until it couldn't and then map the halls below. Once he was fairly certain it would work, he powered up the drone and cast it into the pit.

His video feed flickered, then failed. The signal was lost.

"Now what?" Maja asked.

"We wait," said Ajay.

"Those are expensive, you know."

Ajay had no idea. "I'm aware."

Olexie sat against the wall. "We can still go down the back entrance to the base."

Maja shook her head. "The air quality is going to be terrible down there. We don't have respirators."

She was right. The air was getting worse. If there was a fire below, they'd suffer from the smoke and soon run out of oxygen.

Ajay ran his fingers through his hair, dislodging a cascade of grit. Minutes passed, and worry ate at the hollow behind his chest. What if he had put Kylie in danger? What if she was dead or dying down below and there was nothing he could do to save her? What if the drone didn't make it back?

"I mean," said Maja, "*really* expensive. It's some of the most advanced drone hardware available on the military supply market." The two remaining drones orbited her head.

Minutes passed, and the gray haze grew thicker.

"They rigged the elevator to explode when it hit the floor below," said Ajay. "Why would they do that?"

"Proof against anyone following up," Maja said. "Covering their tracks."

Ajay turned to Olexie. "You fought pretty hard to keep me from going down there."

"We shouldn't split up."

"Are we going to talk about how we get out of here without an elevator?" Ajay asked.

"There's a ladder," Olexie croaked. "In the elevator shaft."

"We're half a mile down."

The Russian shrugged, winced, and said, "It could be worse."

"Yeah, I could have a broken collarbone. How are you going to do this?"

Olexie met Ajay's gaze with a hooded expression of grim determination. "When something needs to be done, it will be done."

Ajay coughed. Dust caked the inside of his lungs and made his mouth taste like blood. Hard stone clacked against his boots as he circled the pit. What if he had misinterpreted the drone's command structures? What if something down in the lower level had broken the drone.

What if Kylie was hurt down there?

He heard the scuff of a boot against stone and looked sharply up at Maja. She was still. Olexie was still. Had he heard someone else? His heart pounded in his ears, hammering a sharp staccato rhythm that resonated against the rust red stone. His breaths came in long, slow rasps—gulps of smoky air that threatened to send him into fits of coughing.

He couldn't afford to cough. He couldn't afford to make a noise at all. He pressed a finger to his lips to signal silence from Olexie and Maja and listened.

There it was again. Distant. Farther along the corridor away from the elevator, someone moved. The hissing cadence of a harsh whisper danced along the edges of his hearing. He could have imagined it.

No. It came again. The tap of a boot against the stone.

Ajay drew Olexie to one side of the corridor where an abandoned mine cart provided some small shred of cover in the open space. Maja recalled her two remaining drones and extinguished their lights. The three stayed in silence.

Ajay then realized his hands were empty. His cane and pistol were on the rock where he had set them so that he could program the drone. He crouched down and eased forward, toward the pit. Another step. Then another. It had to be close. He searched with his fingers for the gun. Anything.

"Quiet," hissed a voice at the very edge of Ajay's enhanced hearing. "Someone's up there. Jan flank left. Sean, go left. Stay alert."

The scuff of more quiet footsteps. The brush of fingers against cloth. Ajay forced his breaths to come slow and steady so that they might be quiet, but he couldn't hear over the thunderous pounding of his heart.

There! His fingers brushed against the hard stone. He probed from memory and found his pistol, taking it in his hand.

There were at least three of them, and they moved so quietly he struggled to pinpoint them in the wide corridor.

Except for one. His hearing aid located the man's rasping breath. Ajay could kill that man. Turn the tide of the battle before it started. He swallowed back his fear and tamped down the impulsive urge. It came from a place of fear, and he knew not to trust it. This wasn't a time for rash decisions.

What if they weren't the enemy? What if these people were survivors of the attack?

But what if they were the people who had set the explosives? They were likely the drivers of that final vehicle. They might know something of Kylie's location—if she had been taken or if she was down below in the explosion.

All Ajay wanted was answers, and a bullet in the dark wasn't going to get him that.

A light in the corner of Ajay's cheaters flickered.

"What was that?" someone hissed up ahead.

Ajay's light flickered again, then his scout drone's footage started playing across his eyes. A dim glow from below bounced off the haze but didn't reveal the intruders.

He saw the corridors from below projected into his left eye while his right scanned for the way back to Olexie and his cover.

Then, the drone burst from the pit, and its spotlight pierced the smoke. It revealed a man in black fatigues carrying a rifle. His face was covered by a black balaclava. He was a step away from the pit. A few more seconds, and he might have fallen in.

The man raised his rifle, pointing it at Ajay. There was a moment when Ajay could have fired. Could have still had the advantage of a first strike.

But the video played in his left eye, and he couldn't keep himself from watching for Kylie. The corridors below were thick with smoke, but the drone's advanced imaging showed shapes even through closed doors. It panned through the science wing, skirting past still-burning piles of slag and debris. It scanned corpses near the exit to the unfinished section of the mine, then darted through the halls toward the elevator.

"Don't move," said Olexie, lazily pointing his pistol at the man in fatigues. Olexie sat with his back against the stone wall. "We have some questions."

The man didn't lower his rifle. Ajay felt the weight of

its grim finality. That was a high-powered killing machine. He wouldn't even have time for regrets if that man decided to fire.

Maja's other two drones launched from their perch on her bandoleer. They darted around the room and illuminated two more of the intruders. "Back down, Nick," she said.

In his video feed, Ajay watched the recording of the drone bob as a roaring flame disturbed the air currents. It swept through the small kitchenette and scanned each of the sleeping quarters. Two more corpses lay in their beds. Adults. Not the children.

"What happened here?" Olexie asked Nick.

"Never mind that," Ajay interrupted before the man could respond. "Where are Kylie and Austin?"

Two more men appeared at the edge of the hazy dark. Five in total, outnumbering their wounded and exhausted three. Ajay didn't like those odds, even if he had managed to get the drop on them, which he had not.

"I don't know what happened to the kids," the man said.

"You can lower your weapon," Maja said. She had her gun pointed at one of the others.

Nick didn't lower his gun. "We were attacked."

"Fuck," said Maja.

"They locked us into our quarters and rigged the place to blow." He indicated the others with a nod of his head. "We only got out because Sayid had the override to our door."

In Ajay's video, the drone floated through swirls of

thick black smoke. Its scanners mapped the large room of the science lab and flagged the corpses of seven more bodies. Gunshot wounds glowed with red indicator lights. Not trauma from the explosion. Many had been shot in the back. Several had been kneeling when it happened. None had been locked in.

"Where did they go?" asked Ajay. His arm was shaking from fatigue, but he kept the pistol leveled at the man across the pit. "Where did they take the kids?"

"I told you," said Nick. "I don't know."

In the video, the drone flagged a fire burning near a cache of fuel. The electrical system's liquid fuel reserve. Ajay's heart skipped. He had to remind himself that the drone had already returned. The fuel hadn't ignited while it was down there, or it wouldn't be feeding him the video.

Nick took a step back but kept his weapon raised. "Did you do this, Maja?"

Olexie said, "Don't move." The tension between them was palpable.

Maja disappeared into the smoke. Ajay still saw her in the corner of his eye, but the drones cast no light that direction. She stayed in shadow.

Ajay's video didn't have an audio component. He hadn't instructed it to collect one, which was fine because he couldn't afford such a distraction at the moment. It did, however, indicate noise with visual cues. A pounding came from one of the doors, followed by a voice which appeared as text on the bottom of the feed.

Let us out, the text said. *Please. The smoke is getting in. Coughing. The smoke.*

"Was anyone else left down there?" Ajay asked, trying to keep his voice from shaking. His heart slammed in his chest and the back of his throat tasted like acid. "Is this all of you?"

Nick looked at Ajay from the blank expression of his ski mask. "There wasn't anyone else."

The drone continued down the last hallways of the science wing of the mine. It passed the exit and slipped into the tunnels of rough-hewn stone covered in discarded mining debris. Ajay's mind raced. They couldn't have left without hearing those people behind the door. Those people needed to be saved. They were trapped. They were dying.

In the drone's recorded feed, Ajay saw who was down there. The drone spied them through the narrow vent in the door. Four people. Alvin, Tabitha, Powell, and Yates. Maya's four true believers. The core of the CCS cell.

Nick was killing them.

Which meant Nick was responsible for the attack, and therefore responsible for whatever happened to Kylie.

Ajay raised his gun, finger on the trigger. "Who do you work for, Nick?"

Nick glanced Maja's direction. "I think you and I both know you're not in a position to be asking that kind of question, old man."

"What did you do with Kylie?"

Before Nick could answer, an explosion of ash and heat burst from the pit between them, and the whole mine was swallowed in roiling black smoke.

CHAPTER THIRTY-ONE

THE CUT on Liam's cheek would not stop bleeding. He pressed gauze to the wound as his drone car brushed the tops of the pines in the early pre-dawn light. Those damn old men had violated his house. His sanctuary. The offense of it all burned like a wild parsnip rash, but Liam wasn't driven by revenge. He wouldn't let this get to him.

Every time he pulled the gauze away, it tugged at the wound, and the bleeding started anew.

It had been hours since the attack, but his nerves still ached from the adrenaline of raw terror. The explosion of his window brought fresh urgency to his plans. Death by cancer approached, but death by assault was already here. There were those in the world who, through raging irrationality, despised his success. They sought to destroy his legacy.

Tenen greeted him as he stepped from the drone. The rotors spun down and folded, their warbling hum echoing off the snow-covered trees surrounding the old logging camp. A second drone stood nearby on the more exposed charging pad, its rotors frozen with packed ice. He would need to have someone clear the ice from that machine as soon as possible. It wouldn't take long, but Frontier had only sent the bare minimum to do this job. There would be discussions about that. Liam never settled for the bare minimum. He needed to make sure his functioning drone car stayed sheltered from the snow. A brilliant man always planned ahead.

With a swipe through his fidget's holographic display, he sent the drone to circle the encampment and make its way to the solar charging pad. Once there, it would keep itself warm for his arrival. Once he finished inspecting the work along the ridge, he would want to leave immediately.

"Status?" Liam asked as Tenen drove him along the edge of the reservoir. They passed through a scraggly stand of pines around a granite boulder the size of a small house. His people worked in the nearby woods, placing the charges according to his calculations based on the paper maps from the library.

"Our people are wrapping up the last of the business at the mine, and the remaining explosives are on their way."

A few minutes later, Tenen parked the truck among a dozen other vehicles. Liam stalked through the old logging camp toward the dozens of identical white tents that marked the mercenaries' presence. This Frontier Arms organization ran a tight ship, he had to give them that. "I've been made aware that some of your people are working on something other than the task at hand," he said. "That's not acceptable."

Tenen didn't say anything for a long time. Liam noted as the big man glanced at one of the log cabins as they passed. The mercenary—Chay Quinn—lazed in front of it with an assault rifle in her lap.

"We picked up a couple kids," said Tenen finally, "but it's not for a side business. They're insurance against certain factions who oppose you."

"I won't stand for kidnapping."

"It's for your own good."

"My reputation is all that matters, and this does *not* help."

"Neither does murder."

"That was necessary."

"You don't need to have anything to do with this."

"I have *everything* to do with this." Liam threw his bloody gauze to the ground. To hell with bleeding. "This is *my* operation, Lang. If you get caught trafficking children, it's on *my* reputation."

"Sir—"

"Get rid of them," Liam spat. "Now."

For a moment, Liam thought the big mercenary might protest. As if Liam hadn't bothered to acquire a contract that allowed for his unlimited power over the group. As if the negotiations hadn't specifically included the execution of certain illegal activities. *That* was risk enough to Liam's reputation, but this—Liam could not abide by the kidnapping and imprisonment of children in the camp that would one day become his city of the future.

"Get the remaining charges set," Liam said as he stalked away to his cabin. "We move forward with the plan tonight."

CHAPTER THIRTY-TWO

Black smoke billowed from the square hole.

"The fuel depot," Ajay coughed as he scrambled away from the plume of smoke. "It must have blown."

A wave of heat belched from the pit, and black smoke rolled in a wave across the ceiling. Nick was gone, disappeared behind the column of ash and heat.

Olexie fired three thunderous shots into the smoke. "We need to get out of here."

Smoke swallowed Maja's drones, casting the cavern into a roiling storm cloud of shadow.

"This way," shouted Ajay. He set his drone into follow mode and ducked back down the corridor.

He only got a few steps before gunfire erupted behind him. He dove back behind his cover behind a mine cart, followed by Olexie. Sparks flew off the mine cart as flakes of rust pelted Ajay's face.

"Don't move," Maja whispered through the comm.

"They have visual enhancement to let them see through the smoke."

Keeping low, Ajay snatched a glimpse of the corridor. The hole in the floor formed a choke point. Smoke billowed from it, rising up and around, and then shunting away down the corridor. To either side were ten feet of open space without cover.

He could breathe, as long as he stayed low, but it still burned at his lungs.

"Let's talk about this, Maja," called Nick from behind the wall of smoke. "Just let us past and we'll pretend like this never happened."

"You shouldn't have let it come to this," called Maja.

"They could let us leave first," muttered Ajay.

"Nick, you asshole. I thought you were on our side," said Maja.

"It's just business," Nick called. His voice was muffled as if he spoke through a mask.

Business. He was Maja's hired help, along with half the people working down there. This was an inside job.

"Who do you work for?" Ajay asked.

"If you'd asked me that last week, I would have told you Red Horizons," Nick said, "But I guess Frontier Arms is buying up everyone in town, aren't they?"

"Let us leave," Ajay said.

"Nick has no intention of that," coughed Olexie. The big man didn't look good. His skin was pale, and the sweat on his brow mixed with smoke and ash.

The air was hot. Ajay covered his mouth as best he

could with his shirt, but every breath was like inhaling razor blades.

Across the corridor, Maja rose from her cover behind a fallen stone and fired two shots. Someone on the other side screamed, followed by a flurry of movement.

"Dammit, Maja," called Nick. "What are you doing?"

"Try to move up again and you'll get worse."

"You killed Sayid!" Nick's voice had a high edge of panic.

"I know." Maja touched the controls of her fidget. Into the comm, she whispered, "Cover me while I move the drones into position."

Olexie gestured to Ajay, instructing him how to move. Ajay crawled several feet behind the cover of the mine cart, raised his gun, and fired several quick shots into the billowing smoke.

The return fire was immediate. The rattle of automatic fire roared through the mine, forcing Ajay to adjust the feed on his hearing aid. He wanted to hear where the shots came from, but the ferocity of the attack was too much. When it died down, he shuffled sideways and fired more wild shots.

This time, the response was different. Two mercenaries fired from either side of the column of smoke. While Olexie dealt with them—his shots went wide and Ajay almost thought the big man might faint—Nick leaped through the churning column of smoke. He wore heavy goggles and a respirator, and his assault rifle was trained on Ajay as he landed.

"Got him," whispered Maja through the comm.

It wasn't a noise. Not really. It was a thump, like a hammer to the chest and the release when one's sinuses clear after a bad infection. The pulse hit the space behind Ajay's eyes like the rapid depressurization of a particularly turbulent airplane. A wave of dizziness struck, and Ajay rocked back on his heels, falling solidly on his rump.

Nick got it worse. As Ajay watched, the man swayed, grasped for a handle on something—anything—and fell backward into the pit. He didn't even scream before landing with a solid, sickening thump that echoed up through the smoky halls.

Ajay straightened, trying to follow, but another wave of dizziness held him down.

Maja disappeared into the haze to the left of the column. Gunshots echoed in an eerie call and response. Pop-pop. Pop-pop. A ragged scream cut through the smoky mine and was cut short.

Then it was done. Maja emerged from the smoke.

Ajay coughed until his lungs ached. "There were others down below."

"They're dead," said Maja. She took Ajay's arm in her iron grip, dragged him toward the elevator, and handed him his cane.

"But they were trapped. And Kylie—"

"Wasn't there," grumbled Olexie. "They took the kids away."

"How do you know that?"

Maja spun Ajay around and looked him in the eyes. "What's so special about the girl, Ajay?"

A shiver ran down Ajay's spine. Maja was his best bet

for getting Kylie back, but he still hesitated to tell her anything. Something still didn't click, and he couldn't bring himself to let Maja in on all his secrets, even if Silas had already told her something. "She's my granddaughter."

Maja shook her head. "There's something more. Silas hinted at it. Why does Liam want her so badly?"

Ajay pulled away from Maja's grip. "They were planning this all along, weren't they? Even before we left."

"Maybe."

"Nick was supposed to be working for you."

Maja glanced at Olexie, then back at Ajay. "I think we need to go to ground."

"Absolutely not," Ajay snarled. "We're going after them."

"We're outgunned. Half our people turned on us and the other half is dead." Maja gestured at the gaping maw of the corridor behind them. "Nick and his goons weren't alone. They had help, and they were likely just the last cleanup crew."

Never mind that they were all dead and couldn't talk. "What do they want?"

"You tell me!" Maja shouted. Her voice grated against the stone walls. "Why do they want to control you so bad that they're willing to kidnap your granddaughter?"

"You think this is about me?" Ajay shouted. "I'm an old hacker. A *retired* hacker. I'm all but useless in an operation like this. What could they possibly want from me?"

After a long and heavy pause, Olexie said, "Retired men can still be dangerous."

Whoever kidnapped Kylie must have known who she

was. They must have wanted to grab her because they knew what she was capable of. The corporation that had made her had others, too, but Kylie's sister Isabelle was the first.

Who had known she would be in the CCS headquarters? More importantly, who knew about her location in the base but hadn't known about her life in Bemidji? If kidnapping had been the plan, an ambush outside of school would have been much simpler. No, this had to be something else. These people planned their violent takeover before Kylie and Ajay arrived on the scene.

When they reached the elevator shaft, Ajay saw the ladder on the sloped side of the shaft. The very idea of climbing it exhausted him, but one look at Olexie told him he wasn't the worst off.

"Will you make it?" Ajay asked, coughing until his head felt like it might burst. He spit a muddy stream of saliva. The smoke was thinner near the elevator shaft, but it still smelled like a particularly unsuccessful bbq night at the Andersen residence.

Olexie closed his eyes and breathed. "I think so," he said. "I think so."

"Good," said Ajay. "Because I know where we need to go next."

"WHAT DID you do to Nick back there?" Ajay asked as he climbed into the passenger seat of the truck. His arms felt like noodles at his sides, and he was almost ready to collapse and die. "With your drones."

Olexie flopped into the back, grunting in pain.

Maja started the truck. It roared to life, and then the diesel engine settled into a steady rumble. She backed slowly out of the garage and crunched across the icy gravel. Their headlights danced across the snowy pines. She hazarded a glance at the drone in Ajay's lap. "Subsonic pulse with a mix of microwaves just for fun. Screws with a person's balance. It's temporary."

"Mostly," said Olexie from the back seat.

"Mostly," agreed Maja. "Sometimes it's not so tempo-rary, but that's usually if you get hit with all three." She mimed surrounding a target and firing at it from all sides.

A twist of nausea danced on Ajay's stomach. He was more than just tired from climbing out of the mine. He was physically and emotionally exhausted. "It wasn't temporary for Nick."

"He had other issues," Olexie said.

"Don't worry," said Maja. "A hit with one of these just makes you stumble around for a while, and you weren't even in the direct line of fire."

"That's not what I'm worried about. You killed those people down there. Shot them."

The truck lurched as they passed from the gravel road to a poorly maintained county road. Maja punched the gas and the drone of snow tires on asphalt increased in pitch. "Would you prefer I tell you I disabled the rest of them without killing them?"

Ajay considered it. "I don't want you to lie to me."

Olexie barked a laugh and clapped Ajay on the shoulder. "She is CIA, old friend. She's always lying to you."

Ajay turned the drone over in his hands, inspecting the tiny weapon mounted to its carapace. "It's really non-lethal?"

"Better," said Olexie. "Nobody hit with these could ever work anything other than a desk job." He tapped his head. "Permanent disability. Dizziness. Nausea. All that good stuff."

"That sounds horrible."

Olexie winced as they hit a rough patch of highway. "If you think about it, it might increase their lifespan." He chuckled to himself about the idea. "Unless they get a brain bleed and die. Let's call it *less* lethal. Like a taser."

"Better for everyone if you just shoot them," said Maja. "But it does have its tactical uses."

"Desk jobs wouldn't be so bad," Olexie muttered.

Ajay tended to agree. Probing in the drone's programming interface, he found the routine for the pulse attack. It had a list of warnings three miles long, which he didn't bother reading. "I'm keeping this one," Ajay said.

"They're very expensive," said Maja. She eased the truck around a bend. The roads had been cleared since the storm, but another blizzard approached from the west. "And you don't know how to run them in a combat operation."

The argument didn't find any traction with Ajay. "I couldn't do it," he mumbled, finally. "When I discovered that Nick and his people had betrayed your group, I still couldn't shoot him." He looked down at his knobby hands.

Maja said, "You just need practice."

"I've hurt people before. Killed. But it was never right there in someone's face. I never pulled the trigger and watched someone die."

Maja said nothing for a long time. She placed a warm hand on his shoulder, and it was all he could do to keep from breaking down.

"I'm sorry," said Ajay, choking back a sob. "It's just not something I can do."

Maja drew a deep breath. When she spoke again, it wasn't the hard professional voice Ajay was used to hearing. It was soft and kind, like a friend of fifty years consoling him for his loss. "There might be a time when you have to decide. You can either be the person who pulls the trigger, or you can be the person who catches the bullet." She glanced back at Olexie. "It sounds like a warning, but it's not. Either choice is valid, depending on your values. You just need to decide what those values are. In the mine, you were responsible for Nick's death. You lured him out. I pulled the trigger on the drone, but you made it happen. It was the right decision. They never would have let us out of the mine."

Ajay deciphered the map instructions as Maja drove into the small hours of the night. Exhaustion and adrenaline warred in Ajay's skull, and eventually, exhaustion won out. He only woke when the truck slowed as Maja drove into a small, snow-filled parking lot at the end of a long tunnel of pines. The lot brushed past, and she hit the icy lake. Their truck's tires skidded on the bare ice, but she turned into the skid, regained control, and continued across the wide expanse of ice past a dozen tiny ice shacks that stood like lonely sentinels in the moonlight.

"They're out early this year," said Ajay. There had been an early cold snap, prompting cries of climate change and an incoming ice age. Hyperbole as far as Ajay could tell. The world had finally reacted to real climate change. This variation in the winters was nothing compared to the catastrophe of the early thirties. He consulted his instructions. "The location is due northeast from here, but we're going to have to skirt those islands."

"You're sure about this?"

"I've studied the maps from Liam's study," said Ajay. His head felt like fog and his tongue was a slab of cardboard. "I compared it to the information you had at the mine. It's a match, and the indication on Liam's map showed an old logging camp that wasn't on anything online.

It's been wiped from all the mapping tools, aerial photography, and historical documents."

"The only existing copies would have been on paper," Olexie muttered from the back. "You really think your granddaughter and her friend are there?"

"Liam grabbed her. I don't know why yet, but his people were already embedded in your operation."

"What a clusterfuck."

"Go to sleep, Olexie," said Ajay.

"I can't. I need to post on social media."

"Now?" Ajay asked.

Olexie shrugged, staring into the simplified interface of a fidget Ajay had not seen before. "We might need my protesters."

Maja rolled her eyes, and Ajay took the hint to drop the topic. It was past midnight, and they were in the middle of nowhere. There would be no groundswell of protesters to back them up, no matter what Olexie claimed.

To Maja, Ajay said, "He's right about why they wanted to destroy the government records. The fallback would be to duplicate the online copies, which have already been modified by Liam's team. The modified versions show a much more questionable history for this area. It's not even clear that it's really part of the BWCA in those documents."

"Aren't the boundary waters pretty well defined?"

"Not really," said Ajay. "Not after decades of legal erosion by mining companies trying to force their way into the edges of the wilderness. The map shows the winter road through this part of the BWCA. It's the same road that the old copper-nickel mining companies wanted to use to establish a mine in the area north of the camp. If we take this path, we'll find the camp. That has to be where Kylie and Austin are." Ajay didn't want to think about what he would do if they weren't there.

The car skidded again, but Maja controlled the vehicle with expert skill. On their right, the first island passed, the branches of its aspens grasping at the sky like skeletal claws. A deer stood at the edge of the forest, watching them with curious eyes.

"You think you'll get them back without killing anyone," Maja drolled.

"I'm not going to shoot anyone." His grip tightened on his cane. "But I'm not saying people won't die."

"Like Chernobyl," Olexie said from the back seat.

Chernobyl. The memory left a sour taste in Ajay's mouth. What did Olexie have to do with Chernobyl?

Maja mused. "Did you cause the spill?"

"Of a sort," said Ajay, "but not the one you're thinking." He pressed his palms to his eyes, trying not to pay attention to the sounds their vehicle made as it rumbled across a section of ice as clear as glass. "Cleaning up Chernobyl was something of a vanity project for the Russians. The site had a tourist revival back in the twenties, so people were thinking about it again. Someone came up with a way of detecting and purifying radioactive waste, so Vladimir Putin wanted to make a triumph out of the biggest embarrassment Russia has ever suffered."

"Second biggest," grumbled Olexie from the back seat. "There was the 1980 Olympics."

"Right." Ajay cleared his throat. "The hockey game. I had nothing to do with that. Anyway, the Chernobyl cleanup wasn't entirely popular. There were protests. People were starving and suffering from disease. Russia was on the brink, just like the rest of the world, but Russia was spending a fortune to a new startup to clean a city that was only a tourist attraction because it had been left alone for so long.

"At that time, the United States was negotiating with Iran over a nuclear deal. Russia was, to put it lightly, complicating things. We needed a distraction so that we could lock down a deal. It turned out there were a number of easy solutions around Chernobyl. The Russian people brought everything to the table. It likely would have tipped even if I hadn't touched anything."

"But you did," said Olexie. His quiet voice held a measure of threat.

"I did." Ajay swallowed, his throat even dryer than it had been before. "Yeah, that was me."

They passed a peninsula where the pine forest stretched out into the frozen lake. Great drifts reached like tendrils out onto the ice, stretching to grasp anything they could atop the frozen lake. Maja's driving took them in long loops around the heaviest drifts, navigating them safely out past the worst of it into the untouched wilderness.

"It doesn't take much to turn protests on the verge of riot into something resembling revolution," said Ajay. "It'll never turn into a real revolution without strong leadership, but the chaos is there. There's this kind of entropy inherent in a country that has suffered abuse for too long. One that has been ruled from the top rather than ruled by the people. I didn't put any of that there. I only gave it a nudge.

"The process they used to clean up Chernobyl didn't eliminate the radioactive waste. Interestingly, they used a kind of nanomachine to collect the worst of the material and move it to a central location. There, it was contained and processed. But, you see, none if it was *safe*. Every step in the process had flaws, from the programming of the nanomachines to the temperature regulation of the collected waste product. All I had to do was cause a big enough problem to set off some alarms—"

"And the country spent a year in violence." Olexie sat up in the back seat. He no longer appeared sallow and weak. Rage burned in his bloodshot eyes.

"I underestimated the powder keg," said Ajay. It had been a blip of regret at the time. He'd felt a mix of pride and awe every time he saw reports on how Russia devolved into chaos. Every time a government official was dragged into the street and shot, he wondered if he had been the cause.

"Did you underestimate the accident?" Olexie asked.

"Excuse me?"

"The accident. The one you caused which spilled radioactive material on a thousand protesters. The one that was covered up by Russian officials and made to look like a minor inconvenience in an otherwise successful project."

"I think people knew it wasn't successful."

"Did they? It's still touted as one of Russia's greatest achievements." Olexie leaned forward. "It's one of the reasons I defected."

Ajay swallowed the lump in his throat. There was something Olexie wasn't telling him, and he didn't like it. "If people believed that the accident was nothing, then why all the riots? Why the year of chaos?"

"Tradition."

"I think people knew, even though official channels covered it up. People talk. Not just on social media, but in backyards and offices. They talk in punk nightclubs and in the privacy of their own homes. How did you learn about this if not through back channels?"

"I learned from my sister," Olexie growled, "before her bones crumbled and her face fell off."

Ajay twisted around to look the enraged Russian in the eyes, hoping to spot some flaw in the big man's anger. Some hint that he was lying or wrong.

But there was nothing. Olexie whispered, "She suffered. Her hair fell out and her teeth bled. Over the next weeks, her body failed from the radiation. By the time I spoke to her, she was almost unrecognizable." He swallowed. "It was a bad death."

They rode in silence for a long time, and Maja kept casting Ajay glances that he couldn't help but read as accusatory. Why couldn't he pull the trigger if he was such a killer? Such a monster?

Maja took their vehicle through a low drift, following the rugged tracks of a much larger vehicle. Another pair of tracks converged with theirs, then another. Up ahead, the converged tracks rolled around the long end of another pine-filled peninsula. A cluster of stones at the point marked the bend where the tracks disappeared into the white distance.

"I'm sorry about your sister." Ajay had done his job, and the hack had been a success. More than a success. It had helped him rise through the ranks of his division and focus on the kind of work he enjoyed most. Now, all his success turned to ash. "Now I know why Liam said your purpose here was personal."

"Because of you?" Maja asked, not taking her eyes from the cracked ice.

"No," said Ajay. "Because the cleanup of Chernobyl was Liam Thompson's greatest achievement, and I didn't cause that accident. All I did was control its timing. I had some influence on its severity, but it was going to happen whether I influenced it or not. It was always going to be bad. It was always going to be the focus of a powerful government coverup—one that too many people knew was false."

Olexie drew a long, slow breath. Some of the color drained from his face. "There is nothing quite so dangerous as a shared lie discovered."

"Nothing quite as valuable as information, either," Maja said.

Most of Ajay's years behind the screen blurred together, but the attack on Russia was one he remembered perfectly. It was the moment his career at the NSA had turned worldwide. Until then, he had been picking apart criminal networks and investigating irregularities in internet service providers. When the organization shifted to an outward focus, he had thrived.

That Russian job had been his legacy through his whole career, even though it had been a carefully guarded secret. Underneath it all was what he had just revealed to Maja and Olexie.

"Timing," said Ajay, the realization clearing the last dregs of fog from his brain.

Maja hazarded a glance at Ajay.

"That's why Liam is here right now. The storm will blot out the skies. There won't be any drone or satellite coverage of the area. He can start whatever he wants up there as long as the storm covers him."

"The storm won't last long enough," said Olexie.

Ajay twisted around to look at the Russian again. "What if he faked a disaster? What if there really was a mine up there? A secret one. They might have left a ticking time bomb of an environmental disaster."

Olexie scratched his chin. "There were legal fights about copper-nickel mining up there. The environmentalists won every time."

"But what if they didn't?" Ajay brought up the soil map, which still made little sense to him except for the basic topography of the land. "The ground is frozen, so the wastewater won't infiltrate if there's a big spill. Cleanup would be easy for Liam and his team as long as they get it done before the thaw. They have these detailed soil maps so they know exactly what they're doing when it comes to getting that work done. The ice road over the lakes even lets them move equipment in cheaply."

Maja said, "Why have a spill at all?"

"He needs an emergency. Nobody's going to let him

build his city under normal circumstances, but if there's a dire and verifiable emergency, they'll sign off on anything."

"Then he's going to need to move equipment and people," said Olexie.

"Exactly. And all that movement will be a cover for establishing his construction. By the time spring comes, he'll have a foothold on this segment of the BWCA. The thaw will make sure he has all summer to keep building, since the ice road will close. He's crippled the paper record, which means the legal challenges will take years. Decades."

"Generations," said Olexie. When Ajay shot him a questioning look, he added, "Let's be honest about the American legal system."

"Fair enough," said Ajay. "Kids born in his city will be in college before the legal wrangling gets close to finished. It'll be impossible to shut it down by then. He will have conquered a significant portion of the boundary waters and left a legacy that will remember his deeds forever."

Maja looked at him for a long time, but when Ajay tried to meet her gaze, she turned away.

Ajay sat in silence as Maja rounded the last peninsula. Ahead, a thin wisp of smoke rose into the gray sky. Light flakes hovered in the morning sky, suspended and still. They were there, finally, and Ajay didn't know what he wanted to do. When they had set out, all he wanted was to get Kylie back and return to a safe retirement somewhere.

But remembering the Chernobyl job and hearing what Olexie said about it stirred something deep in his chest. Did Liam Thompson really deserve this legacy? Did he get the privilege of carving up Minnesota's greatest treasure to build his name into something that would last forever? The thought of it bothered Ajay, but he didn't see what he could do. He couldn't topple everything. Not with Kylie and Austin still in danger.

Ajay spoke into his comm unit, which ran through a filter and then uploaded to the truck's radio. When he spoke, he heard his own voice, but the transmission was an accurate imitation of Nick's gruff voice. "On approach with the last of the supplies from camp," he said. "Permission to park this bad boy?"

Empty air hung over them as they rumbled forward over the frosted ice. The vehicle's black tires crushed over the thick snow compacted by a dozen big vehicles passing the same path in the past day. As they approached the old logging camp, Ajay could make out separate buildings nestled among the trees. The ice road they followed led up the shore and straight through the camp.

"Permission granted," came a voice over the comm.

"We're in," said Ajay.

Olexie placed a big hand on Ajay's shoulder. "Remember my sister," he grumbled. "Think about how you killed her to build your career. Consider how she died horribly because you wanted a slightly better chance at negotiating with another country." He swallowed more painkillers from a small white bottle. "Think about her when you are deciding whether or not you can kill someone, Ajay. The enemies here are nothing but a drop in the ocean of blood on your hands."

CHAPTER THIRTY-FOUR

Kylie was cold, and she didn't like it. Snow found its way into her boots ten minutes into their walk, and now both her feet were numb. She held Austin's hand tight as they made their way through the snowy forest. The faint signals of faraway computers faded into the distance, and even when she tried her hardest, she could no longer sense what was happening back in the logging camp. All she could feel was the gun that the jerk kept poking into her back and the chattering comm unit he had plugged into his left ear.

She recognized the man who had dragged them from their cabin and ushered them out into the frozen woods. He was the man who had almost killed them back in the government center. He still wore the same ring, and one of his arms was in a sling.

"You should have told Jason Smit that you liked him," she whispered to Austin.

"No way."

"Why not?"

"I heard he was a jerk," said Austin after some consideration. "Anyway, that's way scarier than this."

"Quiet," snapped the mercenary. He jabbed Austin with his rifle. "Keep walking."

"Are you going to shoot us?" Kylie asked, earning a horrified look from Austin. "What, it's a valid question." She genuinely wanted to know. "You wouldn't shoot us before."

"I said be quiet," said the man.

"That's not a yes," Kylie told Austin. "So, when we get home, you should talk to Jason."

Austin stared at her.

"He's not going to shoot us," said Kylie. "Are you?"

After they had walked for a few more minutes, the man said, "I follow orders." He had a bruise darkening the left side of his face, and Kylie wondered if it might be related to his hesitation earlier. "I'm taking you to a new cabin."

"That sounds like a lie," Kylie said.

Austin said, "I don't think Jason Smit even knows who I am."

"Yeah, because you're afraid to talk to him."

"He's intimidating!"

The man let out a frustrated growl. "Kids," he said. "You will shut up right now, or I swear I will shoot one of you."

"There's no other cabin, is there?" Kylie said.

"No," the man said, "there's not."

Kylie listened to the quiet woods for several seconds, tuning her ear until she could hear the chatter filtering through the man's comm. "You're not supposed to shoot us," she said. "You'll get in trouble."

"My boss was pretty clear."

"But his boss said something else," Kylie said. "Who do you want to follow?"

Austin whispered frantically to himself, repeating something that Kylie couldn't quite hear. She thought it probably had something to do with Aunt Candice. When their guard didn't respond to her comment, Kylie finally allowed herself a tiny sliver of fear.

And with that sliver came a roiling wave of terror. She couldn't handle this situation. She and Austin were kids, in the middle of a vast wilderness with a bunch of heavily armed mercenaries, and she didn't even have a coat. Terror shuddered through her bones, riding the waves of guilt. Guilt at getting Austin into this. Guilt at making their situation worse by ignoring her own rightful fear. She should never have tried to talk her way through this. She should never have tried to make a friend.

Because of that, her new friend was going to die.

Isabelle hadn't said to save both children. She had said to save Kylie. If that was really Isabelle on the other end, somehow commanding these mercenaries, then she didn't care at all about Kylie's new friend. She would never care about Kylie's friends. They were nothing to Isabelle.

They pushed their way through the dense undergrowth into an open clearing. The heavy pine canopy shielded the space from the falling snow, leaving a lightly dusted field of amber needles over the knobby, shallow roots of the trees. Kylie stopped as she stepped into the clearing. Her hands were shaky, and her heart pounded so hard it hurt. She had to run. Had to flee as fast as she could before the guard killed them both and left their bodies to freeze here in the woods.

The mercenary stepped into the clearing behind them, cursing at the dense patch of buckthorn. Kylie could feel Austin's stare burrowing into the side of her face. He must have figured out that this is where they die. What did he expect *her* to do?

"What would Aunt Candice do?" Austin whispered to himself.

Kylie blinked. Her head throbbed, and her eyes unfocused. What would Candice do? "She wouldn't be afraid," Kylie whispered.

Austin swallowed. His eyes were so wide his whites showed all the way around. It was almost cartoonish. "She'd die," said Austin. "She'd die in the woods and be buried, and the FBI guys would never find her. There wouldn't be witness protection. She would just be gone."

Kylie tried to wrangle her fear again. She tried to use the machine part of her brain to tamp it all down and smother the all-consuming fire. Her fear burned like ice through her spine. It devoured every attempt at logic and reason. She couldn't *think* with it raging through her veins. How could she?

She stood next to Austin in the empty clearing. Sharp flakes of crystalline snow hung suspended in the still air as if time in their snow globe stood perfectly still. She took her friend's hand, sure that it would be the last moment she ever held a friend's hand, because how could she ever have a friend after this? If Austin died here, she would swear off people forever. She'd sink into the numbing fog her sister had lived in for so long.

Only, she couldn't do it. She was too weak to fight the damning fear. Behind her, the mercenary breathed raspy breaths of ice-cold air.

"Are you sure?" he asked, speaking into his comm.

Kylie hadn't heard the other half of that conversation. With the fear pulsing in her brain, she had no access to the signal. It slipped through her fingers even as she tried to regain a shred of control. Was the mercenary's boss sure? Of what? Kylie didn't *want* to know.

Austin squeezed her hand tight, but Kylie realized it was a response to the crushing force she was applying to his. She tried to command her hand to release him, but it didn't work. Nothing worked. A snowflake burned a horrible death by landing on her nose. Its friends drifted aimlessly around, uncaring of their companion's demise.

After a hundred years, Kylie breathed again. She tilted her head and snuck a peak behind.

The mercenary wasn't there.

CHAPTER THIRTY-FIVE

"Surveillance drone swarms are like schools of fish," said Ajay as he synced the last of Maja's drones with the local swarm. They stood behind a row of trucks at the edge of the windy logging camp. Cold bit into Ajay's fingers, and his knuckles ached with every gesture. "Each one acts as an individual, but it behaves in a way that moves as a contiguous group. Each one says, 'Give me space,' at the same time as it's saying, 'Stay close.'"

"Like people," Olexie said.

Ajay continued, "It lets them cover the area completely without having to take direction from a central controlling system. That makes it harder to compromise the whole swarm, but easier to integrate with it."

Maja looked over Ajay's shoulder as he worked, a tight frown on her pale lips. She wore a ski mask, as did Olexie and Ajay. It wouldn't be a great disguise if anyone cared to look closely, but along with the extra coats they found in the back of the truck, this might buy them the extra time they needed to find Kylie and Austin.

"You'll be invisible," Ajay said. "If your drone is part of their swarm, then you're walking around in a little bubble that we can visually filter."

"Fine," said Maja. Her voice was like ice.

Ajay released the drone into the air, where it hovered over Maja's shoulder. As she moved, it kept its position relative to her. Ajay and Olexie had their own miniature followers.

"What is the plan?" Olexie said.

"I need more information. Codes, locations, timing. All of it."

Maja's expression didn't change.

"Kylie won't be safe until Liam is stopped," said Ajay. "Neither will Austin, for that matter."

Maja said, "You're not telling me something."

He wasn't.

"You need to trust us." Maja took his hand. "Ajay, we can't work as a team unless you tell me everything." She drew her weapon, checked the clip and the chamber, and holstered it again. "Liam will just try again. We need to confront him directly."

"He's waiting for the cover of the storm. Once he has that, he's going to go all in, but if they miss that window, it could be weeks before he gets another good storm to cancel their activity from low satellite surveillance. By then it might be too late for his people to get the foothold that they want. Either way, this will buy us plenty of time for Olexie to spread footage out to the world. These mercs might be experts at quashing data leaks, but they've never gone against The Ghost of Lenin."

Olexie chuckled. "They won't see what's coming."

"But for that to work, we need information." Ajay thumped Olexie in the chest with the bronze lion head of his cane. "I'm not your nemesis, Russian. I never was. I was a patriot, and I believed in what we did, but I never hated you." He drew a long, cold breath. They were in a concealed corner of a section of the camp dedicated to parking huge black vehicles, but their isolation wouldn't last long. "I still believe. To an extent."

Olexie started to respond, but Ajay held up a hand to silence him. Something in the chatter in his earpiece caught the attention of his automated routines. Ajay brought up the flagged dialog.

"Come back," said a voice. Ajay thought it sounded like Tenen, but the inflection was off. "Leave the kids there."

"Are you sure?" said a voice that Ajay didn't recognize.

"I'm not fucking around," said Tenen. "Get back here now. It's time."

Ajay swiped through commands on his fidget. His bare fingers were cold, but he couldn't move quickly enough with gloves on. He found the ping locations of the comms that were speaking. One of them was the man with the kids. He was over a mile away from camp. The other signal —Tenen Lang—originated somewhere else. Far away. Too far.

A drone, high above the camp. Ajay couldn't pinpoint its location. Not without a deeper delve into the datastream. All that mattered was that the signal came from far away. Tenen wasn't in the logging camp.

"We need to move," said Ajay. "The kids are north of the camp. Maja, you need to find the codes for the explosives. I can't hack those with my current resources. I'll circle around north of town. Olexie, do you think you can sabotage their driving fleet? If we need to escape, I don't want anyone following."

Olexie fixed Ajay with a scowl and disappeared into the increasing storm.

Maja clenched her jaw. "Olexie's wrong, you know."

"About what?"

"We don't change when we retire. We're the same people our families learned to despise when we did what we did." She checked her pistol and straightened her coat. "We don't get forgiveness just for wanting it."

"Sometimes penance is too much," Ajay said.

Maja gave him a weak smile. "I was going to say it doesn't hurt to try, but I guess if it doesn't hurt then you're not trying."

"I have something," Ajay said, bringing out the data chip Kylie had given him. "Silas brought it to my house."

Maja looked at the chip with sad eyes. "That got the old guy killed, didn't it?"

"I think so, but I haven't seen anything worth killing on it. It's an employment roster." The snowflakes swirled around him. "And some research that could help Kylie." He sighed. "I don't know if it will, though. I wish I knew what to fight for."

"Maybe your penance is not knowing."

"I'm not sure if I can handle that."

"Penance is always too much. That's why nobody ever does it." With that, she turned to make her way across camp.

Ajay blinked as he watched her go. Her words had a morose finality to them that he didn't like. On a whim, he clicked the data chip in place and started a scan of the information there. The process would take some time, since it had to decode each row of the database as it searched. In his visual field, he brought up a view of Maja as seen by her drone.

Then he made his way north. Snow danced around his feet, and he did his best to avoid using his cane. His hip ached, but he walked upright along the edge of the camp. The few other mercenaries he saw didn't give him a second glance. He limped from behind one log cabin to the other, forcing his way through tangled shrubs and heavy drifts.

The snow stilled, and for a few seconds, Ajay could see where the road ran north of camp. The wastewater reservoir sat surrounded by a wide earthen dam, the road running along the length of its rocky ridge. Liam's mercenaries were setting explosives around the rim, working furiously in the oncoming storm so that they might destroy the one thing holding the polluted waters at bay.

If Tenen wasn't close, then he might be at that site to the north where they were setting up the explosives. They might be much further along on the task than Ajay had hoped, ready to blow the reservoir at the start of the storm. Ajay looked to the north, barely able to see the glacial erratics that marked the start of the ridge. The enormous granite boulder stood sentinel against the oncoming storm.

Or maybe Tenen's emergency was something else. Maybe they were behind schedule. After all, they had needed the explosives that were stored in the mine. Those wouldn't have arrived until a few hours before Ajay and his crew.

On his tiny cheaters, Ajay saw Olexie creeping across the logging camp. He walked upright and strong, as if he belonged there. The tall Russian fit right in with the quasi-militant group, something Ajay would never be able to say for himself. His fight for his country hadn't involved boot camp or physical training. It hadn't included poise or weapons management. He felt naked among these mercenaries. He couldn't imagine Olexie or Maja deferring to him. Why would they?

Maja strolled through the center of camp with her mask off and snow landing on her gray-blonde hair. A soldier greeted her—a woman that Ajay recognized from the government center.

Chay Quinn. The woman who had shot the innocent clerk for no reason.

"What the hell?" Ajay recentered his video feed. "Maja, what are you doing?"

Maja leaned forward and whispered to Quinn. "It's time I had a chat with Liam." Together, they approached the larges cabin in the camp.

Ajay blinked. What did she mean? Was Quinn betraying her boss? Liam was there.

And so was Tenen. The big man stood in front of the

cabin as they approached. He had a rifle hung loosely across his chest.

It made no sense. Maja working with Quinn? Tenen was local and not sending a signal in remotely? Liam Thompson was stepping out into the swirling cold, greeting the three killers as if they were all family.

"Olexie," Ajay hissed through his comm, directing the signal so it would only go to the Russian. "Who told you to visit the government center yesterday?"

"It was Maja," Olexie replied.

"And who hired all of CCS's mercenaries?" But Ajay knew the answer. Maja had been in charge of it all.

In the video stream provided by her personal drone, Maja pressed a finger to her ear. "Don't forget to ask who set up your comm units, guys."

"Why, Maja?" Olexie rasped.

"This is the only way. I'll get Liam to free the kids and I'll get to retire with my family." Maja said. "Sunshine and roses, you know?"

"And then you die," muttered Ajay.

"We'll have to see about that part." Maja turned, winked at her drone, and, with a swipe of her hand, cut off his feed.

A flash of movement danced across the edge of Olexie's video feed. Olexie glanced up at his drone and bolted for cover. Gunshots rang across the camp, but the Russian was already gone. He returned fire, ducked, and moved away. If his collarbone bothered him at all, he no longer showed it.

"Plan B," Olexie said through the comm.

"Plan B?" Ajay gasped. "We don't have a Plan B."

"You'd better think of one." He rose from cover and fired three shots. A mercenary dropped, spraying bright red across the pure white snow. "Quickly might be nice."

Then, the snow started falling in earnest. A wall of white swallowed the world.

"I think we're in trouble, Russian," Ajay said.

"I don't think we've ever *not* been in trouble, American." With that, Olexie launched himself at the enemy.

CHAPTER THIRTY-SIX

Kylie dropped to her knees. All the world was white, and the wind and snow erased their tracks. She ran her numb hand over the rough earth, touching the bumps where the snow was slightly more packed. It might be a footprint.

It might not.

Icy wet soaked into the knees of her pants, and the cold wind blew straight through her sweater.

Austin sat in the snow next to her in his bright orange shirt.

"Aren't you cold?" Kylie asked.

"I'm immune, remember?" But he looked scared. Scared and tired.

"I'm sorry," she whispered, but she didn't think he heard. It still counted, though. She took some satisfaction in that. It still counted.

"It's not your fault," he said. Apparently, he had really good hearing. "Bad stuff just happens."

Kylie gave up on trying to track the way back to the camp. She didn't even know if she wanted to find her way back there. Not that there was anywhere else to go. She looked at Austin. The boy wiped the tears and snot from his face and stuck out his chin. He was a brave boy. They were going to die there in the cold of the heavy snow.

She said, "It's all my fault because of what I can do."

He shook his head. "I used to think that after my grandma died." He looked up into the falling snow. "It was when I was little, and I missed the bus, so she had to come pick me up. That's when she got in a car crash."

Kylie felt his grief like a knife in her heart. She resisted the urge to use the machine in her brain to shut it down. "But that really isn't your fault. This is different."

"It was bad weather," Austin continued. "And it *was* my fault for missing the bus. I didn't want to get on that stupid bus again, and instead of just toughing it up, I hid behind a tree. They told me later that the bus driver knew I was hiding, but he drove away anyway."

"I can hear computers," Kylie said. "And I can control them with my thoughts. That's why they want me. That's why they think I'm dangerous. This has nothing to do with you. I feel so bad that I got you pulled into danger. This never should have happened."

Austin stared at her for several long seconds. "You can't help who you are."

Kylie hugged herself close. Snow swirled all around, blotting out even the closest trees. If she could be someone else, would she? Isn't that what Isabelle did? Papa said he had an operation that would fix her.

Austin put an arm around her shoulder. The snow wasn't too cold. They could survive out there a while. Maybe once the storm was done, they would be able to find their way back.

But then what?

"It gets worse," she whispered. When he didn't say anything, she continued, "Whenever I use my power, my head goes numb. I stop feeling anything."

"That sounds nice."

"It's like building a wall around myself that makes everything bad go away. Fear, pain, hate. Gone. I only get pure logic.

"That's the stupidest thing I've ever heard."

She pulled away from him. "Excuse me?"

"Not feeling anything? That's not logical at all. It would be more logical to feel everything. You're probably shutting off your feeling because you're afraid it might make you fail, but you're wrong." He looked away into the pure white forest. "That's what I did for a while, too."

"This is different."

"Not really." Austin pulled away and looked at her.

She didn't meet his gaze because she couldn't bear how uncomfortable it would be. "Did it work?"

"Feelings don't go away. You're just bottling them up."

"Maybe I'll just bottle them up forever."

He opened his mouth to protest but closed it again when she grinned at him.

"Whatever's in my head makes it happen automatically. And worse than a regular person. I don't know. I'm pretty broken, Austin. I don't think you'd really want to be my friend if we get out of this."

"Why not?" He looked around. "Our friendship has been fantastic so far."

She smiled again, but the tears that ran down her cheeks were sad ones. "This is the best friendship I've ever had," she sobbed. It was true.

He hugged her close again, and she cried on his shoulder.

"So it's agreed?" he said, finally, offering a fist to bump. "Friends forever?"

Kylie didn't even hesitate. She bumped his fist hard and pulled him back into a hug. "Till the end."

A gust of wind blew through the forest, and for a second, the air around them cleared. Kylie listened as hard as she had ever listened, tasting the noise hanging in the winter air and feeling for anything familiar in the signal waves. Her senses touched upon something familiar. Something she'd known for a long time that had brought her equal parts comfort and frustration.

It was Papa's hearing aid. The comm signal drifted over her in the clearing, faint and faraway, but clear in its direction.

"Dammit Olexie, you're going to get yourself killed," she heard Papa say.

"This way," Kylie said to Austin. "I know where we need to go."

CHAPTER THIRTY-SEVEN

"Dammit Olexie, you're going to get yourself killed." Ajay hobbled quickly along the outskirts of the camp, finally circling around to where he could see the tall Russian.

And Olexie stepped into the center of camp with his gun raised and a smug smile on his bruised face. "New plan. I'll buy you some time."

The Russian was a force to be reckoned with. No doubt about that. He stomped through the blizzard, a ghost in the raging storm. His gunshots thundered—both echoing against the merciless sky and muffled by the all-encompassing snow. He punched bullets into one vehicle after another, smashing windshields and puncturing engine compartments.

Olexie roared into the white void. "Come get me, assholes! Bring me Liam Thompson's head!"

He shot the first mercenary to step out of the pure

white. Bullets tore through the man's chest and neck, spraying red onto the snow.

But the falling snow covered all, and the blizzard quickly swallowed all the death Olexie dealt.

Ajay tore himself from the grisly scene. He made his way quickly around the outskirts of the camp. There was no longer a need to be quiet. Olexie's fury covered everything, drawing the attention of the few mercs still left in camp.

"Papa," crackled a faint voice in his ear.

He froze where he stood, halfway between the cover of two log cabins. "Kylie?"

"Papa, we're coming toward you."

Ajay blinked tears from his eyes. "You're both okay?"

There was a pause. "Pretty much."

"Stay away. Things are bad here."

After a pause, Kylie responded, "They took our coats."

Olexie's gun clicked empty, so he dropped it into the snow and charged forward. He slammed into a big merc who, emboldened, was just rising from his cover behind one of the big black vehicles. Olexie lifted the man and threw him down hard onto the frozen ground.

Ajay ran for the next cabin. "I'm on the north side of the camp, sweetie." He didn't know which vehicles Olexie had violently disabled, but it couldn't have been all of them yet. "We can run." To hell with shutting down Thompson's operation.

An explosion shook the camp. Orange flames danced against the falling snow. A wave of heat rolled through camp.

"Things are getting a little exciting here, Kylie. How long can you stay away?"

"Too late," said Kylie. She stood at the edge of the forest and now talked with her regular voice. Ajay swallowed back the temptation to chide her for not having a coat. Next to her, Austin stood with a stick held like a club. "We want to help."

Ajay raised his hands and motioned them closer. "Oh no. You can't help. This is getting dangerous. Wait there and I'll—"

Another explosion. A shockwave popped Ajay's ears, and he staggered backward, falling when the rubberless tip of his cane slipped on some ice. "Dammit," he said. Pain blossomed in his knee where it struck the ice.

Kylie and Austin helped him up. His hip and elbow and ego all hurt, but it was the last one that pained him worst.

"Papa, we can't let them blow up the reservoir," Kylie said.

Ajay brushed the snow from his coat. "You need to escape." He looked to Austin for backup, but the kid was no help. He had a determination on his face that Ajay didn't think was possible. "You both need to go somewhere safe."

"But I need to hack their explosives," Kylie said.

"No."

"Papa," she hissed. "There's no time for anything else."

No time. Ajay gripped his cane in both hands. No time. He'd had time his whole life. As much as he'd wanted of it. What had he done with it? Nothing. He had supported a corrupt system. He had hurt people who didn't deserve to be hurt. Every decision he made through his long career at the NSA had been designed to move himself upward in the ranks and consolidate his country's power. At first, he had told himself that being higher up the food chain would allow him to do more good.

Higher up the ranks never made things better. It never gave him the power he wanted to make the world a better place. Even at the height of his career when he had finally driven the stake through the cryptography-based digital ecosystem, he had done so out of desperation. It had never been about making the world a better place. It had been about escape and change and fear.

Now he was retired.

And it sure as hell wasn't all sunshine and roses.

"All right," he said.

The camp was quiet. Ajay hazarded a look around the corner of the nearest cabin and saw Olexie standing before Maja. She looked up into his face with the kind of smug satisfaction that made Ajay want to spit. They were surrounded by mercenaries, all with automatic weapons raised.

And Liam Thompson was there. He was buried in an expensive-looking coat, but his head was bare to the cold wind. Snow collected on his thin eyebrows.

"You can't hack the explosives, though," Ajay said. "You'll hurt yourself."

"It won't," said Kylie. Already, her voice sounded flat to Ajay. She had been using her power to speak through his hearing aid. It was already affecting her. "It won't hurt me, I promise."

Ajay wanted to tell her she was wrong, but he didn't know enough about what was in her head. All he knew was that Isabelle had used her ability, and it had damaged her. What if the two girls weren't the same? What if there was a difference with Kylie that allowed her to push herself without damage?

But Ajay preferred to be cautious when the consequence was brain damage. He couldn't allow her to risk it.

Austin said, "She has to make her own decision."

Ajay blinked at the boy. "This is serious business."

"It's *her* brain."

He looked to Kylie, then back at the boy. How much had she told him? His argument wasn't a good one. Not by a long shot. Ajay met Kylie's gaze, forcing her to look him in the eyes one more time before using her powers. It clearly made her uncomfortable, but she could do it.

With a slight buzz, Liam's voice filtered through Ajay's hearing aid. A hint of cruelty twisted his words. "You really thought you could stop the future, didn't you, Mr. Sokolov?"

There was a pause for a moment, then Olexie said, "It wouldn't have been any fun unless I tried."

Ajay heard Maja speak through Olexie's feed. "You need to pick up Andersen. He's the dangerous one." She sounded harsher than before. Cold.

Liam scoffed. "Are you kidding?"

"He could hack the explosives that are still here in the camp," Maja said.

"You told me he was harmless."

"Trust me, you want him."

"There's no way he can hack the charges," said Liam. "It would take him hours, and we'll have everything in place by then. I installed the world's most advanced security system on the blasting plugs. He could have direct access to the Cube, and he'd still struggle to crack the encryption fast enough to blow us up."

"He's the one you want," said Maja.

After a pause, Liam said, "Tenen, please go round up the old man."

"Yes sir," said Tenen. He took Olexie by the arm and yanked him away. Olexie howled in pain. "I'll just use this guy to help me find him."

Liam nodded.

"Great," whispered Ajay. "That's all I need."

He brought up his fidget display and checked the local networks. Sure enough, there were several. He guessed at which one might contain the explosive charges. There were dozens of them. Separate. Complex. Heavily encrypted.

Shit.

He wasn't going to be able to hack those. His signal could reach the ones at the nearby reservoir, but he couldn't disable them. Not remotely. The security was too tight. Without even trying to crack the code, he could tell that the gigabit rotating keys were too much for him. He needed another answer.

Or a better hacker.

"Kylie," he sighed. "Do you really think you can crack the explosive charging caps? Turn them all off?"

Her eyes glazed over for a second. "It'll take time."

"I think we don't have much of that."

"We have to hide," whispered Kylie. Her lips were blue. She pulled Austin closer to the nearest cabin and touched the lock. It was a metal doorknob with a physical lock. She shot a questioning look at Ajay.

Ajay took his lockpicks in frozen hands, not sure how long it might take to gain entry. The alerts in his systems now warned him of approach. The mercenaries were looking for them, slowly working their way through camp and soon they would round the cabin and discover the intruders.

He sent his drone higher into the snowy sky. Its fancy video rig penetrated the snow as easily as it had the smoke, and with a couple of swipes at his fidget, he sent it to cause distractions around the adjacent cabin.

The first tumbler clicked into place. He felt it deep in the joints of his left hand. The next immediately followed.

Then, nothing. He adjusted his pressure and tried again.

"They're coming," whispered Kylie.

Ajay glanced at Austin, who looked about as scared as Ajay felt. The boy toyed with his inert fidget and stayed close to Kylie as if she might protect him.

"Son," said Ajay, "if things get bad, I need you to run for the woods. Just get away. Find a place where you can stay warm enough that you can outlast the storm. Just stay away from the mercs."

Austin nodded, wide-eyed.

Another tumbler clicked into place, but it wasn't the last one. The lock still held. Careful not to release the tumblers that had already fallen, Ajay started his drone's routine. It coughed like an old man on a frigid winter day.

"Over here," said a voice around the corner. They had been closer than he'd guessed, but he heard their padded footsteps as they retreated to resolve the noises from Ajay's drone.

A subsonic pulse shook the falling snowflakes. His drone retreated across the camp, but Ajay couldn't watch its progress. He concentrated on the lock. His fingers no longer felt anything at all, and snowflakes that landed on them took a good long time to melt. He pressured the torsion wrench a little less, hoping to slip the final tumbler in place.

All of the tumblers snapped closed.

"Dammit," Ajay said under his breath.

No choice but to start again, but when he put too much pressure on the wrench, the tumblers wouldn't fall into place. He tried harder. His fingers were numb, and his aching joints shook from frustration.

He was failing. This would be the end because he couldn't do this one simple task. He was never meant to be a field agent. He wasn't trained for this, and his career had never indicated that this might be what he would need to do.

Then again, retirement wasn't a continuation of a person's career. It was a chance to learn new things and establish new goals.

It was sunshine and roses.

Then you die.

Ajay drew a deep breath. He was never trained to be in

the field, but that didn't mean he couldn't start. He paused a moment to let his fingers absorb the numbness. He moved the torsion wrench the merest millimeter, giving it the lightest touch necessary to put pressure on the tumblers. One fell into place, then another. A second later, the third, then the fourth.

The door opened. Kylie and Austin slipped inside, and Ajay followed, pulling the door closed.

When his eyes finally adjusted, Ajay gaped at the shelves lining the cabin walls. Rows upon rows of explosives sat open to the air as if there were nothing more normal than to have C-4 on display for any visitor to pick up. As Ajay's fingers warmed and pinpricks of pain ran down to his digits, he wondered at the audacity of the mercenary group who had left all this dangerous material with nothing guarding it but a single physical lock.

"Work here," said Ajay to Kylie. "Austin, I want you to watch out for her."

"Yes, sir." Maybe he was a decent kid after all. "I'll do my best."

Ajay took a small lump of the C-4 and shaped it with his hand. Maybe it wasn't C-4, but Ajay had no way to know one way or the other. It could be a massive store of Silly Putty as far as he could tell. He picked up a brick with an attached charge. "Can you sense this one?"

Kylie nodded, glassy-eyed.

"Good. They'll all be just like this. The most important thing is to disable the closest explosives, starting with the ones right here in this cabin and proceeding to the ones over on the ridge."

"What are you going to do?" asked Kylie.

Ajay pocketed the brick of explosives. He hefted the smaller lump of C-4 in one hand and his cane in the other. Bad ideas rolled around in his head.

"I think it's arts and crafts time," he said.

CHAPTER THIRTY-EIGHT

Liam Thompson didn't know if he could trust the mercenary Chay Quinn. She wasn't like Tenen. The wiry woman could be efficiently cruel, but Liam didn't like how she operated at her own pace. She made decisions all on her own, and while they were often the right decisions, they tended to also be the most violent option. One look at the scar that ran across the bridge of her nose and Liam knew she was dangerous. Unsavory.

Take that business back in Bemidji. Liam had told the team to make sure there were no witnesses, but that didn't mean anyone needed to die. She had willingly revealed herself to the clerk, forcing her to kill the witness. Yes, Tenen had done the same with the woman he had interrogated, but that was different.

Tenen now dealt with the Russian, leaving Liam alone with Chay Quinn and Maja Berg.

And he *knew* he couldn't trust Maja Berg.

The retired CIA spook came across well enough. She spoke with sincerity and laid all her motivations on the line. She had the casually charming smile one would expect of a duplicitous snake. She had betrayed her allies and her entire organization. He had no doubt she would try to betray him.

Quinn shoved Maja in the back. "Move faster."

"It's not good to hurry in this weather," said Maja as they walked along the ridge. "You'll slip and fall."

Liam wished his people would work faster. The final steps in his plan had to happen under the cover of the storm. If they could get everything in place and set off the explosives, he could then start his final phase. The anticipation of it brought energy to his limbs that he hadn't felt since long before he had started treatment.

Now, it was almost complete. The charges were nearly in place.

"Do we have the last charges prepped?" he asked through his comm.

"Loading them onto a different truck," said the mercenary. Liam hadn't expected this man's nasal voice to respond. Where were his people?

"Where is Shannon?" Liam asked.

Shannon's voice came through the comm crisp and clear. "Where are those kids, Thompson?"

Liam didn't need to answer her. "Get those last charges placed," he said. "That's an order."

"My boss tells me those kids are the priority, sir."

"I'm your boss and I'm telling you to set the charges." This insubordination was not acceptable. If things were going to go down differently, Liam would have needed to fire her. As it was…

"Where are the damn kids?" Shannon snapped.

"I sent them away, and you should be thankful. You no longer need to play babysitter."

There was a long pause on the line before this man's nasal voice piped in again, "I'm almost on my way with the last charges. Leaving in five minutes."

"Make it two," Liam snapped.

They walked along the final stretch of the road that ringed the reservoir. With the heavy snow, he couldn't see his people, but the goggles he wore gave him a hazy idea of their locations. One group worked near the towering granite boulders where snow melted into the orange waters. The reservoir failed to ice over early due to the sulfides in the tainted lake. It made him sick, seeing pollution like this. Long ago, that sense of disgust drove him to build his empire, and even now, after a whole life of cleaning up other people's messes, he still felt that same horror. People who used the earth like this deserved to die.

That was why he needed this legacy, he told himself. So people remembered how to do the right thing after he was gone. That was why he had to build this city, and if this needed to be done, then the way to make it happen might carry some risks.

If everything went according to plan, he wouldn't need to destroy anything.

"So, do we have a deal?" asked Maja. "Let the kids go and give me a share of your city."

"You want control over my city when I'm gone?"

"A single voting share."

Liam stopped and peered at her through the snow. "And what reason do I have to trust what you show me?" The bitch threatened to upend his plans. Another reason not to trust her.

"Easy," Maja said. "If I have a voting share, I'll be able to bring my family into the city. Why would I risk the chance at a peaceful retirement?"

She had a point. He had a council of seven already. Leaders who would see the project forward when Liam was gone. They were all selected as the perfect people to pursue his legacy. They weren't exactly loyal, but he had leverage over them. The owner of Frontier Arms would never betray his own company, for instance. He glanced at Quinn. Her face didn't reveal her thoughts.

"That will leave us with an unfortunate number of council members," Liam said. "Even numbers can be troublesome, you know."

He started moving along the ridge again. His newfound energy was fading fast, and he still had some distance to walk before they arrived at the landing pad. He was starting to regret not taking a truck.

"Then kick one of the others off the council," Maja said casually as if it meant nothing.

Liam barked a laugh. "Any one of them could betray me as easily as you. Why would I take that risk?"

"Because I can give you something they can't."

Quinn narrowed her eyes. Liam thought he saw displeasure on her features, but she quickly returned to her neutral expression. She was professional if anything.

When Liam didn't ask what else Maja could offer, she continued unprompted, "I can prove he gave you cancer. In his own words."

Liam stopped. It took a moment for her words to sink in, and he covered for himself by peering through his goggles at the workers on the ridge below. "So, it was really him? Olexie Sokolov caused the accident?"

"No," said Maja. "You were wrong."

Liam bristled at the statement. "Explain."

"It was Ajay Andersen." She swiped through the controls of her machine and played a recording.

Ajay's voice projected from her device. "The process they used to clean up Chernobyl didn't eliminate the radioactive waste. Interestingly, they used a kind of nanomachine to collect the worst of the material and move it to a central location. There, it was contained and processed. But, you see, none if it was *safe*. Every step in the process had flaws, from the programming of the nanomachines to the temperature regulation of the collected waste product. All I had to do was cause a big enough problem to set off some alarms—"

"And the country spent a year in violence." Olexie Sokolov's voice sounded ragged and raw.

"I underestimated the powder keg," said Ajay in the recording.

Maja cut the feed. "He admitted everything. You wanted me to tell you everything Olexie said about Chernobyl, but this is what you wanted, wasn't it? And it turns out Olexie wasn't even the right guy."

Liam's hands shook. He tasted blood. It was a trap. The

CIA agent was trying to get him to confess. "The Chernobyl job was completed without incident. A smashing success. I wanted to know if Olexie Sokolov was still spreading lies."

"That's a wonderful line for the press," said Maja, "but you and I both know the truth. The failure dosed dozens of protesters. Their families had to be silenced, and their loved ones paid off. But people know how to keep things quiet in Russia. It was standard procedure to keep the accident under wraps."

It had been so long ago. "It doesn't matter how I got this cancer."

"No, I suppose not," Maja said, "but now you know who is responsible."

"No Olexie Sokolov?"

"It was the American all along," said Maja. "Is that any surprise?"

Liam stared at the sky. "You expect me to care about revenge? I'm not doing what I'm doing because of some petty vendetta. I do this because I love our Earth. I built everything that I've built because I've always wanted to do the right thing. You think I care about who gave me cancer?"

"You had me follow Olexie all this time. I infiltrated their whole organization just for this."

"You infiltrated them because I didn't want them interfering."

After a slow breath, Maja said, "I think you care. I think you want revenge."

They walked in frozen silence for a time. Liam

watched a mercenary setting charges near the big granite boulder, carefully placing everything up according to his calculations. The soil was perfect for this work. It would liquify at the first hard impact. If he could hit enough of it at once, the whole reservoir would flow out into the land below.

It was the perfect emergency. With the land frozen, the sulfides wouldn't penetrate the water table. The precious calcareous fen would be perfectly safe for the next four months. Then, as spring melted the soil, the landscape would die. Minnesota would beg him to work fast, and to do that he would need to set up a small community. He would need to move equipment into the area and construct systems to process the contamination. The infrastructure he built would become the framework for his utopia.

Liam would live long enough to watch as the first residents of his city refused to leave. He could orchestrate the first protests as they declared this new place their home. They would build according to his designs, but he would never see the city's completion. He would die knowing the inevitability of his success.

He was surprised to discover the rage that burned in him when he thought about it. A glance at Quinn told him nothing. Her flat expression could have been carved from stone.

"Fine," Liam said. "I'll give you your spot on the council. You have proven yourself."

A hint of a smile played across Maja's freckled face. She displayed smug and caring all at once.

"You won't be sorry."

"No," Liam said, "I'll be dead."

"Is that what you thought in Chernobyl?" Maja asked. "Or were you too naive back then to consider that someone might want to stop your good works at all costs?"

Too naive. He had been far too naive back then. Bitter rage burned in the back of Liam's throat, but he swallowed it back. He wasn't going to jeopardize his city for the sake of petty revenge. He was far too good for that.

"You're right," he said. "I thank you for the information, Maja Berg, but Mr. Andersen will get what's coming to him soon enough." He started again toward his landing pad. "Come, we can finalize the paperwork to put you on the council."

A single gunshot split the night and echoed across the stony ridge.

Maja collapsed to the earth, blood blossoming from her pale temple to darken the stark white snow.

Quinn kicked the corpse over the ridge, and Maja's body tumbled onto the slushy shore below. She turned her flat gaze on Liam. "The council has decided it's not taking any more members."

Liam's heart pounded in his chest. He hadn't ordered the kill. Control slipped through his fingers and would disappear if he didn't grasp for whatever he could. "It's for the best," he said, nearly choking on the lie. "We have work to do."

CHAPTER THIRTY-NINE

Kylie fell into the zone almost immediately. The dull calm washed over her, and the cramped cabin dropped into the background of the million inputs from a million sources all around. Surveillance drones fed her a hundred visuals, comms buzzed with voices, and all the digital talking of hundreds of charges chattered in her senses.

She saw Maja's body fall off the ledge into the orange slush reservoir through the eye of a drone. A twinge of regret tugged at her heart—the memory of Olivia, who she had also watched die.

Kylie choked and fell from her trance.

Austin held both her hands and looked straight into her soul. Kindness. Concern. His emotions were there for her to read, but it wouldn't last. Once she stomped down her feelings, she would lose her connection with her new friend.

She blinked away the tears. "Sorry, I'll try again."

Kylie forced herself to feel what she had felt that day

Olivia died, if only for a second. Grief clenched like a fist in her chest. It only relaxed when she looked at Austin again. This was for him. She would do everything to help her only friend.

Kylie took Maja's drone as Liam Thompson and the murderer Chay Quinn fled into the snow.

"Why are you looking at me like that?" Austin asked. His voice brought Kylie back to reality for a fraction of a second.

"I'm trying to remember you."

"Oh, okay. That's great."

The second of Maja's drones followed Olexie. The big mercenary—Tenen Lang—kicked the fallen Russian in the ribs. Blood muddied the fallen snow.

"Open the channel, asshole," said Tenen.

"Go to hell," Olexie said, his thick Russian accent muddied by the slur of a concussion.

"You should have stayed in Russia, traitor." Tenen kicked him again.

Kylie took Maja's drone from Olexie, cracked open their security barriers, and handed both to Papa. He would know what to do with them.

They didn't need to go far to find him. Papa walked through the thick snow in the center of the camp. He would come across Tenen soon. Why wasn't he hiding?

And she hadn't even started on her task.

"Seriously," said Austin. "Are you all right?"

She met his gaze. Something fluttered in her chest. Affection. Friendship. She could measure how much her brain was retracting from the world by the feeling she still had for her friend. She still cared about him. If she could maintain that, maybe using her power wouldn't hurt her brain as much. Maybe her mind could stay intact.

"I'm fine," she said. Her words tasted strange in her mouth. "I'm trying to hack the charges and disable them so we don't blow up."

"Oh, um." Austin twisted his fingers together. "Great."

"People are coming," Kylie whispered. "They're outside."

Then, she was gone. She found the charges drifting on a network datastream. They were legion—a thousand babbling voices uttering a thousand half-formed poems in the nonsense language of a deeply encrypted sequence. She picked one from the mass. It wasn't armed but would speak on the network to anyone with the trigger. What a strange design. Kylie pondered its curious nature for several nanoseconds before daring her first attempt at a hack.

Keys were nothing but numbers. Long strings of data, which didn't need to be exactly matched to their locks but needed to be close in oddly specific ways. She didn't need to guess the encryption key that was set by the legitimate admin. She only needed to guess a key that would fit the compressed hash used by the internal logic to check the key.

It was still too much. She couldn't guess the answer. That was impossible.

But she could guess *all* of the answers.

Her head throbbed. She looked at Austin and his face doubled in front of her. He scrunched up his eyebrows. What emotion was that? Who was he? She shuddered.

Something strange slipped like a steel tentacle across the inside of her skull. It hurt. Everything hurt.

She almost had the number, but then the next second ticked on the clock and the key changed.

A breath escaped her lips like a gust of the frozen wind. "I can't," she said.

Austin took her hands. Concern. That's what was on his face. "You can do it, Kylie. I don't know how this works, but I know you're the smartest person I know. We're going to get out of this, and you're going to fix everything."

The crushing weight of everything kept her from responding.

"All you gotta do is manipulate time and space with your psychic powers," he whispered. Maybe he was joking. Was he smiling?

Wait—was that a Star Blade Princess reference from the second season when Princess Tiara used her blade to cut through the fabric of time? Kylie blinked.

He kept talking, but his words descended into dull background noise. Kylie reached for the charge again, listening to it as it clicked from one encryption key to the next. How long could it keep up this rapid pattern? It must be synced with the trigger somewhere. No doubt Liam Thompson held that still.

She tried again, but this time the number switched before she was even close. Whatever quantum strangeness happened in her brain still took time to work. She couldn't resolve the key quickly enough before the charge rolled over to a new key. By the time she finished, she was wrong. Every time.

Her head hurt so bad.

There was a noise outside the cabin. Kylie looked through the surveillance network. The mercenaries were one cabin away.

Shannon was with them. She held an automatic rifle as she opened the cabin door. Three other mercenaries followed her, closing off the other exits from the cabin as she searched.

They would come there next.

One of the big black trucks roared to life in the parking lot. It rumbled low to the ground, and Kylie knew it was packed with a dozen more charges. She could hear them asking for their impossible keys. Panic washed over her like a wave in a hurricane.

"You got this," said Austin, holding her hands. "I'm going to distract them to buy you more time."

Kylie blinked. "What? No—"

He was already at the door. "It'll be all right," he said, and he disappeared into the storm.

Kylie's mouth went tacky. She heard Papa's voice shouting through the storm.

"Let him go, Lang!" Papa shouted into the wind.

Tenen Lang turned toward the voice and squinted into the blowing snow. His knuckles cracked. "There you are," he said. "I've been looking for you."

Kylie turned her attention to the charges. She needed to work fast.

The modified tip on Ajay's no longer clacked irritatingly against the hard earth. Each step was steady and sure, and the material didn't slip at all, even where the ice shone through the fresh blowing snow. He made his way forward, tracking toward the last ping he'd received from Olexie's comm. First thing was first. He needed the Russian's help.

If Olexie was still alive.

The roar of a vehicle cut the winter winds. The black truck burst through the snow drifts across the camp and Ajay dove into a drift to avoid it. He rolled and thumped his hip hard on the icy ground, biting back a cry of pain.

Nothing made him feel quite so old as hurting his aching hip. "All right," he said. "Let's do this." He forced himself back up.

With a swipe at his holographic display, he summoned all three drones. After the other two had come to him, he had thrown together a few quick routines, and they would have to do. There wasn't time for anything else.

He stepped forward until he saw the giant figure in the cowboy hat standing over Olexie. He pushed the drones forward and used their lidar to render an overlay of the scene in his cheaters.

"Let him go, Lang!" he shouted into the wind.

Lang looked around as if he couldn't track the source of the sound. He shouted back, "There you are! I've been looking for you." He dropped Olexie in a heap.

As a gust blew across the open yard, Ajay stepped backward until the blowing snow closed around him. He watched Tenen through his cheaters, as he was rendered by the three drones, but he couldn't see the big man without the augmentation. His fingers hovered over the drone controls, but he couldn't trigger the pulse attack. Not with Olexie so close.

Tenen drew a long pistol, pointed it at a drone, and fired. The crack-boom thundered over the rushing of the wind, but the bullet missed its mark. Ajay pulled his drones back and hurried clockwise around Tenen's location, keeping himself hidden in the blowing snow. His only chance was to be a ghost in the frozen night.

"I'll give you a chance to leave," Ajay shouted into the wind. His drones caught his voice and projected it so that the mercenary couldn't follow him by sound. "Walk away, Lang."

The big man edged forward, peering into the driving snow. "You're not the only one with a tech advantage, old man." He looked straight at Ajay. "Come out and let's have a little chat." He trudged forward through the snow.

But Ajay was on the move. He used his cane to steady

his steps, making his way through past the tracks of the big vehicle that had just driven past. He could still hear it roaring up the ridge in the distance.

"I've got nothing against you, son," Ajay called out. Nothing specific. Not yet.

Tenen strode forward through the snow, closing the distance. Closer, Ajay looked in horror at the tech bristling from the big man's dark sunglasses. So much for being a ghost. Tenen could see through the driving snow.

Ajay ran. His hobbling gait was nothing to Tenen's long loping walk. The big man hit him like a truck, slamming him hard and driving him into the snow. Tenen pistol-whipped Ajay hard in the back, the grip of the gun digging into his shoulder blade. Ajay cried out despite himself as he was ground into the snow's cold embrace.

This was not going according to plan.

Tenen kicked Ajay's cane and sent it flying into the snow.

"Maja told the boss all about you, you know," said Tenen. He pressed his knee to Ajay's back, driving his head into the frigid snow. "He just radioed in and told me to make sure you died. Big bonus in it for me. Too bad your Russian buddy wouldn't open a channel to help me find you. Could have made this a lot faster."

Ajay waved his left hand, showing the holographic display over his hand. He tried to speak, but the snow muffled his words.

Tenen chuckled to himself. "It's not an easy job, you know, working for an asshole like Thompson. It's times like these it's worth it, though. We get a little action, fire a few guns. Blow up some trees. Never thought I'd get to do that kind of thing on Thompson's contract, but I can't say I'm feeling bad about it."

Tenen eased up, and Ajay gasped a half breath. "You shoot me, and my drones will strike," he said.

The mercenary leaned in harder. "Shoot? Why would I do that?"

Ajay's vision blacked at the edges. He'd instructed the drones to attack in unison if Tenen shot him. A backup in case things went south. With the last neurons available to his oxygen-starved brain, Ajay regretted that programming decision. Tenen could easily overpower him without resorting to something so crude as a gun.

Ajay tried to bring up the next backup plan. The worst backup plan. Tenen saw the flash of the fidget display, let out a harsh laugh, and tore the device from Ajay's hand.

"No need for that." He leaned harder, and Ajay lost the last gasp of breath he didn't know he had left. "Look at it this way, this is better than waiting for that kid of yours to smother you in bed with a pillow."

Red, raw heat rushed to Ajay's face. He burned at the mention of Kylie.

"I'm not sure what I'll do with her. The boss wants her dead, but Frontier wants her brought in for some reason. I guess it'll just be something they can work out in contracts." He seemed to consider this. "If she survives today, which I guess isn't looking very likely."

Ajay choked with rage and pushed as hard as he could against the big mercenary. Every ounce of pressure was met with a pound of returned force. He could do nothing, and the effort he poured into escape only served to lessen his reserves.

"What's that?" Tenen mocked. "What did you say?"

Another vehicle roared to life a short distance away. Its engine loped and knocked as if something was seriously wrong with its internal combustion. The wind blew, and Ajay felt the last dregs of energy sapping from his limbs. He was done. Helpless.

Dead.

"Retirement's not all it's cracked up to be, is it?" asked Tenen. He slammed a fist into Ajay's head.

Ajay mouthed the words, tasting them as they bled out into the heavy white snow. His hearing aid popped and went silent.

Tenen watched with half-lidded eyes.

This was the end, and as much as Tenen Lang weighed him down, he felt crushed even more by the weight of his regrets.

He never thought about legacy. That wasn't what had ever mattered. Not really. Ajay always knew he would never be remembered when he died. What mattered was the impact of his life. He had lived his life thinking he was a positive influence on the world. His work for the government had furthered order and law. It had pulled the world back from the brink of anarchy.

But had it? Had he just been supporting people like Liam Thompson, who, though they purported to believe the best things, used the world and its people like disposable garbage?

Now that he was done, there was so much more he wanted to do.

The world spun as the black overtook him. Something in the hollow of his chest popped, and pain blossomed out through his limbs.

The engine roared again, its knocking, hobbled thrum sounding in the empty white void of the snowstorm. It was close.

Closer.

The air stilled. The snow stopped.

Then, Tenen's weight lifted from Ajay and a gasp of frigid air crashed into his lungs. His vision cleared, and he tried to force himself up. What was that noise? Knocking? Was it the engine?

But the engine wasn't the combustible engines he'd known thirty years ago. It was a massive electric motor, designed for torque and efficiency. It was a combat vehicle. It didn't knock like a broken combustion engine.

He pushed himself up onto his knees, still staring at the bloody white snow compressed in an impression of his face. Knocking?

No.

It was gunfire.

Olexie shoved him back to the ground. "Look out, old man," he hissed. "Things are getting interesting."

Tenen stood in the center of the camp, both hands on the grip of his long pistol. He squeezed off one shot after another, punching holes in the silver vehicles parked in a semicircle between them and the makeshift car park. A shot thunked into Tenen's armored coat. Then another.

His return fire caught a beast of a man in the shoulder, and blood sprayed through white tactical gear. Another shot exploded another man's neck. Tenen fired with ruthless efficiency, falling into an aim and fire pattern that didn't pause just because he was getting hit. These people —whoever they were—were fully focused on him.

Which was why they were open to the flanking maneuver.

Through the crystal-clear air, Ajay watched as a dozen mercenaries launched a volley from the cover of the cabins. Bullets punched into the new vehicles and slaughtered the militants there.

"Who?" Ajay croaked.

"I told you I had protesters who could come to help."

"Is that what you call this?"

"Armed protesters," Olexie said, spitting blood. "This is America!"

Ajay blinked. He couldn't draw full breaths due to the pain in his chest. A popped rib or something, maybe. Whatever it was, he didn't like it.

This was his opportunity.

There were at least ten protesters left, and half that lay bleeding or dead on the ground. They wouldn't last long against the assault. Ajay got his bearings, peering around at the snowy ground. It had to be around there somewhere. He grasped through the heavy snow.

Tenen repositioned, taking cover behind a heavy drift. Crimson blood seeped from a wound somewhere in his left arm, but he reloaded in a smooth movement and circled his attackers.

He was distracted. That's all that mattered. Ajay grasped through the snow.

"What are you doing?" Olexie asked. The big Russian's face was a mosaic of bruises and blood.

"My fidget," said Ajay. "It's around here somewhere."

"Here," Olexie said. He tossed Ajay's fidget to him. "Tech addicts," he spat in disgust.

Ajay caught the device and slipped it onto his left hand. His fingers were stiff, and the aches were sharp knives driving straight through to the bone, but he manipulated the login sequence from muscle memory.

The drones still hovered at a safe distance, but now Tenen was distracted.

Ajay moved them in, one at a time. They swooped close to Tenen and hovered only a short chip shot away.

One fell into position a few feet from Tenen. Then the second.

Tenen fired at the protesters, punching shots into the center mass of a woman in layers of flannel. She fell, dead before she struck the blood-speckled snow.

The third drone locked into position.

Ajay hit the subsonic pulse. It struck Tenen like a hammer driving in a nail. The big man dropped hard and fast, his nose bleeding and his eyes shot through with blood. His knees struck the ice, then his head smacked the snow. The pulse washed past Ajay and Olexie, and he was glad they were both still on their knees. Dizziness spun the world, and when it was done, the snow fell hard again, and the world disappeared behind its white curtain.

CHAPTER FORTY-ONE

Kylie watched the world as it crumbled apart.

Liam Thompson stood at the landing pad with Chay Quinn and a weaselly-looking man with close-cropped hair. Chay ignored Mr. Thompson's shouts, stalking past without paying any attention to his words. Kylie wished she could have that kind of confidence. Froth flew from Mr. Thompson's mouth, so Kylie knew he was really angry, but Quinn pretended like he didn't even exist. The other man watched in silence.

The other mercenary ran to the truck, got in, and drove back down the edge of the reservoir, the way he had just come. He had given Mr. Thompson and Quinn a ride across the ridge, speeding up their travel time significantly. Yet another reason Kylie needed to hurry.

This was the truck that ran heavy with explosives, and Kylie could sense their charges refusing to speak with her.

There were two drone cars parked in the landing zone next to the newly arrived black transport vehicle. One was caked in ice, and the other slowly turned its rotors. Chay shouted something at Mr. Thompson and entered the running one and launched into the pure white sky. Soon, she was too far away for Kylie to sense. She had escaped.

Mr. Thompson hollered at the sky, but Kylie didn't think his rage would do any good.

A mix of relief and fear and disgust mixed in Kylie's chest. Instinct told her to shunt those feelings aside, but she didn't do it. If she did, she would lose Austin.

Austin ran through the forest, pursued now by only Shannon. The others had returned to the logging camp to fight a bunch of new people. Cruel Shannon mocked Austin as she tracked him through the heavy snow. Kylie could see them through drones flying high above, but she didn't have an easy way to help her friend. A crippling wave of helplessness washed over her. Her sister would be able to summon Thunderhead drones, dropping explosives wherever she liked. Kylie couldn't do that. They were too much. Too far.

Austin burst out of the forest and skidded across open ice. Turning, sliding, scrambling, he darted to the side and back into the forest. Lumps of ice clung to his pants and the loose cloth of his bright orange shirt.

"Do you know anything about hypothermia, kid?" Shannon called. "Because that's how you're going to die if you keep running off into the woods with no coat like this." She held her gun at her side and walked with long strides through the forest.

Austin hit a ravine and leaped into it without breaking pace. His boots slipped when he landed in the deep snow below, but he righted himself and kept moving along the length of the channel.

"First you'll feel cold," said Shannon. "Then your fingers will start to get stiff and you'll shiver." She stepped to the edge of the forest, out from under the thick canopy.

Kylie took the opportunity, switching her full focus to the surveillance drone hovering above. She instructed it to fly full speed at Shannon. It accelerated, faster and faster.

Then, it hit.

And Kylie was blind. The drone was destroyed. She instructed another drone to the area and returned her focus to the camp. The second drone would take time to relocate Shannon and Austin.

The explosive charges were too difficult. Too tricky. Their rolling encryption keys changed too fast, and she couldn't break them in time without perfect timing and a lot of luck. She had taken one down, but there were so many remaining. Another almost fell, but there were dummies here as well, and she couldn't see the difference until she cracked them. She wasn't enough. She couldn't do it. Not with less than a second for each key. Not with the strange rapid synchronous key change.

The timing had to be perfect to make that encryption work, but it prevented anything she could manage. Again, she felt so helpless. Tears ran down her cold face.

A vague awareness of a fight happening in the camp drifted into her consciousness. Gunshots rang out through the storm. A reprieve in the snowfall showed her three new vehicles in town, with a dozen men and women fighting around them. The new people shouted about their boundary waters. They shot from behind the cover of their vehicles, but they weren't going to survive. Not with the mercenaries coming up behind them.

Kylie wasn't sure if she cared. She couldn't care about *everyone*, could she? Where was the logic in that? What was the function?

No. That wasn't right.

The drone she had sent to find Austin showed him panting from his run, scrambling up a short cliff out of the ravine. Shannon still followed, limping and bleeding now. The drone Kylie had crashed into her hadn't stopped her, but it at least injured her.

In the camp, the new people were getting slaughtered. Papa lay with Olexie, huddled behind a drift.

She felt the pulse in her own chest when Papa triggered his drone's weapons on the big mercenary. It rattled the windows and made her whole cabin shudder.

This couldn't distract her. She needed to disarm the bombs. Raw, bloody emotion welled up in the back of her throat. Kylie's fear for Papa, for herself, for Austin all boiled up into one gasping sob.

She bent her power to the next charge, giving everything she could possibly give. The numbers spun through her head, and the pain that had been an ache transformed into something much sharper. Damaging.

Kylie didn't care.

The charge fell, but as soon as it did, she saw that it was a decoy. All that for nothing. It was nothing but a repeater, listening for a heartbeat somewhere in the world and prepared to send an explosive signal if the heartbeat were interrupted.

It wasn't a decoy. It was a backup trigger, and she didn't know how many of them were out there. She tried to tell Papa, but his hearing aid was no longer listening.

She collapsed back into the corner and wept.

There just wasn't time.

CHAPTER FORTY-TWO

AJAY JUMPED into the first of the three vehicles and threw his cane onto the seat. There was nobody there to argue with him. The protesters still fought the mercenaries, but those who weren't dead were pretty darn distracted. Without Tenen to provide flank, the struggle had devolved into a standoff, with neither group gaining the advantage they needed to finish the other.

"They are fine," Olexie assured him as he climbed in the passenger side. "Just drive."

Ajay punched the accelerator. The big machine leaped forward, blasting past the still-swooning Tenen Lang. The pulse hadn't killed the big man, but he wouldn't be aiming a gun anytime soon. Maybe never.

A surprising pang of guilt burned in Ajay's chest. Olexie was right. Facing someone directly and pulling the trigger was much harder than doing it remotely, even though Tenen had just tried to kill both of them and Ajay's move probably hadn't been lethal.

They rumbled along a road out of camp. Ajay pushed too fast, too risky. Snow fell in a pure whiteout, but the vehicle's lidar gave him an image overlay on the windshield. He made his way along the ledge well enough. His heart hammered in his chest.

"Thompson will escape if we don't stop him," Olexie said. "And once he is gone, he'll trigger the explosives."

"But they aren't all in place yet."

"Half the explosives are still back at the camp, but the ones on the ridge are plenty to weaken it. He'll have his disaster."

"And his legacy."

Olexie nodded. The old Russian looked diminished in his seat. The wounds on his face and hands already blotted his thin skin. One eye was swollen shut, and whenever the vehicle hit a bump, he winced.

"Will you make it?" Ajay asked.

Crimson alerts flashed across the windshield. Ajay yanked the wheel to the right, veering off into the ditch as another vehicle blasted past. He hit a rock, and a crack sounded from somewhere deep down in the vehicle. Olexie screamed as he slammed against his door. Ajay braced himself, pounded the brakes, and brought them to a stop a long putt from the sharp drop-off.

"Are you okay?" he gasped.

Olexie didn't respond. Ajay checked the man's pulse. Weak, but still there. He scanned the area for the other vehicle. Nothing. Where was it going so fast? They were almost to the landing pad, according to his maps. Was Liam in that vehicle? Ajay doubted it, but if the rich man fled in such a hurry, he'd certainly set off the explosives soon.

Ajay had a choice. Continue to the landing pad or follow the vehicle. Either way, he could be dooming them all.

The choice was his, but when had he ever made the right decision? He could doom them all if he chose poorly. It would be an appropriate endcap to his long life, wouldn't it?

He punched the gas. The truck groaned as it returned to the path and pressed forward toward the landing pad.

CHAPTER FORTY-THREE

Time.

Kylie needed time. The realization hit like a segmentation fault. What had Austin said? If she could cut through time and space, she could do whatever she wanted. What did he know? She couldn't get the timing right to hack these stupid things. They were too hard.

Austin.

She caught a glimpse of his orange shirt under the snow. He huddled down, hiding at the top of the ridge, but it wasn't good enough. Shannon climbed the steep slope, hand over hand. It was harder for a bigger person. The thin trees jutting from the bank didn't support her weight. Slick ice covered the slope.

But Austin wasn't hidden well enough. Shannon would spot him as soon as she reached the top. His orange shirt was too bright, and Kylie could see it through the light dusting of snow he'd piled on top of himself.

"You'll feel warm toward the end," shouted Shannon.

"Are you feeling that yet?" She pulled herself closer. Austin was almost out of time. "Is your mind starting to slip? Let me save you, kid. I can help."

In a matter of seconds, Shannon would find Austin, but he bought Kylie time. That was all he was trying to do. Buy her time.

It wouldn't be enough. She needed to let him know that he didn't need to sacrifice himself like this.

Shannon hauled herself up the final feet to the ridge of the ravine. She panted with the effort, great clouds of cold breath billowing around her face.

"Where did you go, you little shit?" she growled as she drew her pistol. "I'm going to watch you freeze to death."

Kylie adjusted her drone, looking for an angle where she could try to ram Shannon again. She couldn't find it. She couldn't help Austin, and she was losing precious seconds.

Shannon spotted the orange under the snow. A sly grin spread across her cruel face. "Nice try, asshole." She kicked the snowbank.

Her foot sank in too deep, overbalancing her.

From a nearby drift of snow, a shirtless boy launched himself screaming at the mercenary. He shouldered her as hard as his skinny tween body could possibly shoulder someone. Shannon yelped in surprise and anger.

Then she toppled over into the ravine, tumbled down the steep slope, and slammed against the frozen earth. When she landed, Kylie saw there was something terribly wrong with the woman's leg. Her scream of frustration and rage echoed against uncaring trees of the old forest.

Austin shivered as he retrieved his orange shirt from the snowbank. He had bought her some time, but what had it cost him?

Time.

Kylie couldn't help Austin.

But maybe she could manipulate time.

AJAY DROVE onto the snowy landing pad, stopping the truck across from the one remaining drone car where Liam Thompson cranked the final rotor in place. As he did, a fresh swirl of snow blotted out the rest of existence. Olexie slumped over in his seat, but the tall Russian's breathing had steadied.

"I didn't peg you as the kind of man who did his own repairs," Ajay shouted over the wind as he stepped from his truck. He leaned heavily on his cane, and the newly fashioned tip gripped the packed snow easily. The three drones sat inert in the truck's cab. Their batteries were too dead to be much help, but he only needed to buy Kylie more time to disable the charges.

Liam glanced up from his work on the drone car. With a stiff, clumsy movement, a Sig Sauer pistol appeared in his thinly gloved hand. The wrench he had been holding disappeared into the snow. The rotors started to spin.

Ajay didn't slow until they were only a few steps apart.

"It hurts, doesn't it?" He let his shoulders sag, as if in defeat. "All this regret we carry at the end of our lives."

"Funny you should mention that," shouted Liam. His voice was a muddied mess in Ajay's ear, but that was because his hearing aid wasn't working. "Your friend Maja had some interesting things to say about my cancer."

"Did she say you deserved it?"

"She claims you caused it."

Ajay paced, not approaching the wealthy man, but moving slowly through the calf deep snow. "Chernobyl," he said, finally, when the pieces fell in place. "You were there. That's why she decided to turn on us."

"She turned on you long before that."

Ajay remembered when he had first met Maja. She hadn't mentioned his birthday, which she would have if she'd just learned of him. "She knew who I was the whole time, and she was playing both sides."

"I thought it was Sokolov. She was there because I wanted proof."

"And she brought in more of your people because she could."

"You can't trust someone like that, you know," Liam said. "The only thing she ever wanted was to be seen as a good person by her family. Now they'll never even know that she died fighting for them."

Ajay remembered the data search he had started when they arrived. He checked its results and wasn't surprised at what he saw.

"Silas figured it out when he hacked Frontier Arms." Ajay remembered the drunken footsteps leading up to his front door. She had used her drones on him, but with an old man like Silas, the attack had proved lethal. "And that's why she didn't kill you at the lodge."

Liam spread his hands, palms up. "It's hard to build a reputation for saving the world when all you're doing is murdering people in their vacation homes. A life in the CIA taught her enough about that."

"Instead, she wanted something big like your Chernobyl cleanup."

"Chernobyl was my greatest achievement," said Liam. He blinked hard against the falling snow, ignoring the goggles that dangled around his neck. "But the day I visited happened to perfectly line up with the day everything went bad, as if by fate." He gestured at Ajay with the gun. "That timing was your fault, I hear."

Ajay stopped circling. He was directly upwind from the wealthy man, and the gale at his back drove razor sharp ice directly toward Liam. "I'll add that to my list of regrets," Ajay said.

"Will you?" With his right hand, Liam drew a cylinder from his pocket. The trigger. "My last charge is being placed as we speak. You must have passed him on his way there. Would you like to see what it is to have regret before I kill you? When I pull this trigger, it's not just going to blow the charges around the reservoir."

Ajay blinked, shattering the ice crystals that were forming on his lashes. "Those explosives in the cabin—" A flush of heat burned in Ajay's chest. Kylie and Austin were in that cabin. Olexie, the protesters, and all the mercenaries would be caught in the blast. "You're going to kill everyone."

"There isn't any other way."

"You're planning on killing your own mercenaries and blaming it on their incompetence." The cold penetrated Ajay's chest. "You don't want witnesses to ruin your legacy."

"A clean exit." Liam glanced at the drone car. Its rotors hummed now, almost fully warmed through. "There are loose ends that I'll have to take care of, of course."

Ajay inched his hand to his coat pocket. "There's something you might want to know before you pull that trigger." From his pocket, he drew a charge with half a lump of C-4 still stuck to it. "If you pull that trigger, I won't have much time to regret anything, and neither will you."

Liam's eyes went wide. "I'm dying. What do I care if it happens sooner?"

"Like you said. There are loose ends." He tossed the explosive at Liam's feet.

Liam's lips twisted in a sneer. "I'm not falling for that. You've disabled it."

"Olexie is right," said Ajay, stepping closer. "People like you, you take and you take and you take, and in the end, you have everything. But a person can't live that life without wondering what else is missing."

The trigger shook in Liam's hand. How much longer before he pressed the button, regardless of the threat of the C-4?

"The cleanup won't happen if I'm dead," Liam said. "The organization. The drive. It all comes from me."

Ajay punched his cane into the deep snow, leaning on it as if it was the only thing keeping him up. Maybe it was. His knuckles ached from the cold, and the pain in his hip burned down to his marrow. "You missed it all, Liam. Everything. And now you're risking your reputation by causing an environmental disaster of your own?"

"It's not going to be a disaster," said Liam. "Not really. We've falsified the digital documents to make it look like a bigger risk than it is. It *looks* like the soil here will suck the pollution straight to the water table, but it won't. It's fifty feet of heavy clay here." He waved the trigger at the ridge. "That berm is clay soil that will liquify if vibrated correctly. Even if we fail to clean this up before first thaw, the damage will still be minor."

"That's why you needed to destroy the physical records."

"Inelegant, perhaps," said Liam.

"And you had the librarians murdered because you didn't want them remembering anything from those documents. Your legacy was more important than their lives."

"I wanted that done at night!" shouted Liam over the howl of the wind. "It's not my fault my mercenaries decided they were too busy. It's not my fault they botched the whole job and had to kill the witnesses." He waved his pistol at the skies.

Ajay saw his chance. He popped his cane up, held it with two hands, and swung. He missed Liam's right hand with the trigger but slammed against the forearm of the man's gun hand.

Liam shouted in surprise and stumbled back. Ajay

pounced, grasping the gun and shoving as hard as he could. The gun fired once. Twice. The thundering shots echoed against the distant trees. A gust of wind scoured the two old men.

A sharp twist, then the gun was gone, swallowed by snow. Ajay swung the heavy bronze lion on his cane, but in the close quarters he couldn't get leverage.

Liam, weak as he looked, fought like a feral cat. He kicked and clawed at Ajay, pounding his already aching skull and driving a knee into ribs that already screamed in protest. Ajay's air left him, and he fell backward to the snow.

Snow swallowed the world, falling so thick that Ajay almost couldn't see Liam standing above him. The drone car hummed nearby, its loping motors hissing through the falling ice.

Liam kicked Ajay in the ribs. His boot crunched into already-bruised flesh and Ajay had to fight the urge to vomit. He couldn't draw a breath. Couldn't react. Another kick snapped his head back and sent the world spinning.

Ajay rolled away. Tried, anyway. A stomp landed a hair's breadth from his fingers. It would have broken them all. He still couldn't breathe.

"This is all your fault," hissed Liam as he landed a bruising kick on Ajay's thigh. "You and that Russian. I'm glad you're both here. Maja did me a service by bringing you." He attempted another kick, but Ajay managed to get his cane in the way. "I would have given her everything, you know. I pay my debts."

Ajay swung his cane at Liam's knee, but he was weak.

It did nothing to slow the next kick, which landed hard on Ajay's ribs. Liam snatched the cane away and took a step back.

He stood over Ajay with the trigger in one hand and the cane in the other. "If there's one regret I'll have," he gasped, "it'll be that I wasn't able to make both of you suffer more for what you've done." He stepped to his drone car and opened the door, throwing the cane inside. "When the world was struggling to do the right thing, you were on the side of oppressive governments and strong corporate interests. You were a catalyst for a poison that is killing this world."

Ajay gasped and tried to rise from the snow. Blood shone against the white backdrop, and he wondered how much he had lost. His muscles were weak and his head swam. By the time he was standing, Liam Thompson was already in the air.

The wind and snow stopped. The environment once again helped the man who had exploited the passion of true conservationists. All his life, Liam had profited from that passion. He had created a veneer of environmentalism, cleaning up the highest profile messes while all of the real problems went untouched. Now, all Liam regretted was that he couldn't live forever as the patron saint of environmentalism.

Then again, Ajay wasn't much better. The rich man's accusations weren't far from the truth.

The drone car rose into the sky, a white blur against the roiling gray. Ajay squinted up at the vehicle as it lifted away and banked out over the orange reservoir.

Ajay had stalled all he could. He'd given Kylie as much time as he possibly could, but he hated what he knew he had to do next.

Liam swung back around, lowering his drone car along the side of the landing pad.

"You want to watch," Ajay muttered. "You want to watch me die." He opened his fidget's holographic screen.

He saw Liam through the clear class of the drone car's cockpit. The bruised and battered entrepreneur watched with a dead, heartless expression. Ajay met the man's gaze, refusing to look away for what came next.

"You take and you take and you take," Ajay shouted, "but one day you'll find that you've taken too much."

With a flick of his aching fingers, he summoned the controls for his high voltage taser cane and pushed a trigger.

The simple circuit wasn't anything fancy. Kylie hadn't had a lot of time to rig the stunner, but she hadn't needed it. The signal from Ajay's fidget reached the cane at the very edge of its range. It ran through its simple logic and opened the single switch. Fifty thousand volts coursed through the tight circuit, completed by the moldable lump of material Ajay had used to fix the missing rubber tip that Kylie had broken.

Ajay hadn't been sure how much of a bang a racquet-ball-sized lump of C-4 would make, but it was enough.

More than enough, really. The drone car exploded over the lake, and the wave of force and heat washed over Ajay, rocking him back on his heels. Debris rained down over pure white snow, most of it sinking in and disappearing as if nothing had happened.

Ajay had killed a man. A raw pang of guilt gnawed at his chest, even though he knew Liam had not been a good person. The world would be better without Liam Thompson's attempts to build a legacy no matter the cost.

"My biggest regret," Ajay muttered to himself, "is losing that cane."

He turned to limp back to the truck. Then the whole ridge exploded.

CHAPTER FORTY-FIVE

AJAY LAY on his back and stared up into the empty sky, trying to get a mental grasp on whatever had punched him so hard.

She was dead. That was the first thought that waded hip deep through the mud of his brain. "Sashi," he murmured. No, that wasn't right. Sashi *was* dead. He had watched her die. "Kylie?" he said into his comm.

The only answer was a wave of static wind, but he wasn't sure if it was in his comm or a permanent new feature of his skull. He forced himself up to a sitting position. Except for the persistent sharp pain in his ribs and a deep fogginess in his head, he didn't seem to have any new injuries. Everything hurt.

He looked at the explosive charge, which still sat next to his bare hand half buried in snow. A little of the fog cleared from his skull. This charge hadn't exploded with the rest of them, but what about the charges in the logging camp?

"Kylie?" he said again, tapping his hearing aid. The device clicked when he pressed a finger to it. "Kylie are you there?"

He closed his eyes, fighting off the parental fear. This was the terror he felt every time she left for school. It was the horror that gripped him like a fist every time a milestone told him that she was getting older and more independent. It was the fear that had crippled him as a parent, and it was the fear that he constantly fought as a grandparent raising a child with special needs. All he had wanted for his daughter was that she stay safe, and he had watched her die. All he wanted was for his granddaughter was for her to thrive and—

"Papa?"

"Oh, thank god," Ajay gasped. His heart unclenched. "You're alive."

"I changed the time," she said. Her voice didn't have the flat monotone that she usually got after using her abilities. "Using the drones."

Ajay choked back a million questions, and settled for, "What?"

"The surveillance drones. I used a layer of them around camp to cancel out the GPS time sync signal and then I used another layer to mock up a new signal. I changed time by a second, so when the heartbeat trigger fired, the charges were on the wrong cycle of their encryption sequence."

Ajay blinked slowly. He was sure her words were something he could grasp, but his head wasn't fully functional. A heartbeat trigger. That's why it exploded when Liam died. The idiot hadn't told anyone. "You found the clever solution."

"But, Papa, the reservoir is broken. I couldn't stop those."

Crap. Ajay's fidget flared to life on its own. Kylie's instruction, probably. It showed the ridge, now with a significant chunk of its soil sloughed away. A growing gush of orange water flowed from the broken earth to spread across the forest floor downhill.

The pollution would kill the land, and Liam Thompson wouldn't even get his city. Maybe he was right that it wouldn't immediately sink into the groundwater, but it would flow across the soil. It would seep into the local lakes and kill the fish. The slurry leaking out of the reservoir would ruin a large portion of the BWCA.

Maybe Liam had a plan to stop it, but those plans died with him. Ajay was responsible for this now, and there wasn't any time for regret.

He picked up the unexploded charge. "What happened with this charge?"

"That was the one I hacked the old-fashioned way," Kylie said. A hint of pride glowed in her voice.

"Can you make it explode on my signal?"

Kylie hesitated. "Yes, but Papa—"

"Don't worry about me. I'll be far enough away." He placed a pin on the image of the ledge above the reservoir leak. "I'm going to place it here. If what Liam said is right about the soil, the whole section will liquefy."

"Hurry."

Ajay saw why she said it. In the time they had been

talking, the flow had almost doubled. Sludge flowed faster from the hole than before, spreading like blood across the fallen snow.

He jumped into the truck and slammed the motor into gear. Thick tires peeled against the snowy landing pad. The damaged machine clunked noisily, but it still ran.

"Wake up, Olexie," he said.

The Russian blinked warily at Ajay. "I'm awake."

Ajay tossed the charge into Olexie's lap. "Roll your window down."

Olexie peered cautiously at the charge but did as asked.

The ridge road was rough, and every bump sent fresh waves of pain through Ajay's ribs. He tore through fresh snow where the road fell away completely, hoping he wouldn't hit a deep ditch or a gaping hole hidden by the drifts. Thick tires threw liquidized mud as he powered through the flowing soil. They blasted through a snowbank, sending fresh cold flying through the air and in through Olexie's window.

"What is the rush?" Olexie slurred.

As they rounded the ledge, Ajay veered right and left the road. Their truck bobbed and jerked through the snow. Ajay muscled his way through, punching the torque as hard as he could to avoid getting wedged into the broken, steaming rocks. They splashed through the orange slurry as the side of the truck was pounded by the increasing flow.

Rock and clay sluiced away from the embankment, widening the hole. Ajay powered up the slope, sliding, but always moving up.

Then, Ajay saw it through the torrent of blowing snow.

The granite boulder, the sentinel, after all the explosives and all the damage, stood propped on a narrow ledge of semi solid earth. It seemed out of place, a heavyweight among the crumbling destruction all around. Gray and strong against the pure white sky, it stood watch against the ensuing ruin.

And all it needed was a nudge.

"You've got to be kidding," said Olexie.

"One chance."

"There's no way." Olexie hefted the charge in his hand. "I have a broken collarbone."

Ajay smashed the truck through another snowdrift, but the drift wasn't entirely snow. The bumper scraped off rock and dirt, jarring the big Russian in his seat.

"It's not broken, though, is it?" Ajay said.

"It's badly bruised."

"Uh huh."

"It hurts a lot." Olexie rubbed the injured area. "It was dislocated. The big guy popped it back into place."

"I thought you were being tough back there, pushing forward with broken bones." Ajay steered into a skid to regain control and then veered upslope some more. He had to get as close as possible or it wouldn't work. "But it was the opposite. You were playing up a lesser injury. Making excuses for your failure."

"A little," Olexie said.

"You were hoping for an excuse to stay out of danger. You're actually a coward, aren't you?"

"I don't like to say it." Olexie gave Ajay a sheepish look. "I was behind a screen as much as you were."

"You manipulative son of a bitch." He thought about it for a second. "You climbed that ladder with a dislocated collarbone?"

Olexie hefted the charge, testing its weight. "Maybe I'm pretty tough after all."

"Just throw the goddamn charge."

Ajay veered as close to the base of the boulder as he could, and Olexie threw the explosive. It smacked into the smoldering muck.

Ajay cranked the wheel and drove downslope. The truck rumbled and shook as they sped away. He touched his ear to get the connection with Kylie. "Now," he said.

The explosion sent mud and rock pelting against the back of their truck. Ajay spun out of control, the back end of the vehicle finally slipping loose from its tenuous grip on the slick earth. It skidded to a halt ten feet shy of the ledge's perimeter road, where slushy tracks still shone wet against the clean snow.

With the truck stopped, he got a view of the granite boulder. The explosion at its base had blasted its side, but it was still completely still—still an inert sentinel against the raging storm. A pit formed in Ajay's stomach. They hadn't done enough. The waste slurry would spill out into the land and soak into the soil. It would destroy thousands of acres of the BWCA, creating a zone of death and destruction rather than the pure, primal wilderness it had once been.

And Ajay had murdered the one man who might have been able to clean it up. Liam Thompson was dead, and the organization he ran wouldn't react quickly enough without him.

Then, the boulder started to shift. Slowly, like the toppling of a giant, it nodded forward across the top of the embankment. Seconds passed. Orange slurry flowed below as the granite took its sweet old time.

Once its center of gravity tipped, the boulder fell hard and fast. The shockwave of its impact rocked the truck and send another wave washing over them.

The flow stopped. Ajay let out a breath.

He turned the truck around and drove back to the logging camp, where he found Olexie's protesters rounding up the remaining mercenaries. Tenen Lang lay on a stretcher, weeping quietly.

And he found Kylie. She ran into his arms as he dropped down from the truck, hugging him until it hurt.

"Where's Austin?" he asked when she let up enough to grant him a breath.

She stepped back. Tears welled in her eyes, but she blinked them back. It struck Ajay that she was showing her feelings, even after all that hacking. He'd never seen her separate hacking from the monotone voice and almost robotic affectation. Yet, here she was, feeling everything, even the bad stuff, after one of the most elaborate cracks he'd ever seen anyone perform. She was truly an amazing kid.

"I was afraid to look," she whispered. "After..."

"I understand," Ajay said. He pulled her in for another hug. She cried on his shoulder, and he buried her in his warmth. They would need to leave soon, but for now, they could take a moment to gather themselves and feel whatever it was they needed to feel.

When Kylie finally pulled away, she swallowed once and looked at Ajay. "Okay. I can do this. I'm going to find him."

She closed her eyes, and a serene expression crossed her face. The expression melted into one of confusion. "Where?"

"What's she doing?" said Austin from the edge of the woods. He wore his orange shirt, and his face was red and raw from the cold. His cornrows were covered in frost.

Kylie's eyes snapped open. She ran to Austin and crushed him with a hug.

"I'm not quite immune to cold," he said, shivering.

"Well," Ajay said, a tremendous weight lifted from his chest. "They made it." A single sob choked him. "Thank god, they made it."

Olexie slapped him on the back. "Field agents don't usually bring their kids to work, but I'm glad you did."

Ajay wanted to respond that he wasn't a field agent and never would be one, but that didn't ring as true as it used to. He was retired. Life didn't have to be all sunshine and roses. It could be whatever he wanted.

Maybe sitting still was no longer his thing.

CHAPTER FORTY-SIX

"I buried my shirt in snow," Austin said. "Then when she found it, I ran up behind her and pushed her back into the ravine."

"Very clever, son," Ajay said. "And brave. They found Shannon in that ravine. She had a broken leg, but she'll otherwise be fine." He wasn't sure what the protesters would do with the mercenaries they'd rounded up, but he imagined it wasn't flat-out murder.

They rode in a self-driving rental car, a white sedan with leather seats and too many cup holders. The children sat facing backward because Kylie insisted that it was safer. They both huddled in their coats, which Ajay had located in one of the cabins. Olexie had rented their current ride to take Ajay, Kylie, and Austin home, while he stayed up north to deal with what he called a spectacular coverup. After taking the time to ensure that Kylie was purged from Liam's computers, Ajay had agreed that it was best for everyone if they leave.

The car pulled up to the front of Austin's house, a small yellow rambler buried in newly fallen snow. He looked at it for several long breaths before saying, "Thanks for bringing me along, Mr. Andersen."

"It wasn't intentional," Ajay grumbled. "Are you sure your parents won't be upset you're getting home so late?"

He shook his head. After charging his fidget in the car he had contacted his parents to tell her when he'd be home. Ajay wondered what kind of home life let a kid spend so much time away. Didn't they worry? Not that he really was in much of a position to judge parenting skills.

"It'll be fine," Austin said. Then, more hesitatingly, he added, "Kylie, are you busy tomorrow?"

She swallowed hard. "I don't know."

"I was wondering if you wanted to come over to watch Star Blade Princess. I just finished the second season."

Her face lit up. "Oh, I love the third season. That's the one where—"

Austin covered his ears with gloved hands. "Don't spoil it!" And with that, he ran up his snowy sidewalk and disappeared into the house.

"You made a friend," Ajay said as the car pulled forward to their house. He connected to its data storage and purged all evidence of their journey.

"Yeah," Kylie said as if the thought had never occurred to her. "I did, didn't I?"

"It's going to hit him," Ajay said. "Everything that happened. He seems fine now, but he's going to need to process this."

"I know," she whispered, and Ajay believed that she probably did. She would need time to process it, too.

Together, they trudged up their snowy sidewalk—it really had snowed a lot in the past couple of days—and, finally, returned home.

Everything was exactly as they had left it, except for two things.

The first was a note on the table, sealed in a plain white envelope. Ajay opened it with shaking hands once Kylie was in her bedroom, wary of all the dangerous things that could be placed in such an innocuous package. Anthrax or radioactive substances or a wide variety of contact poisons. He tamped down his paranoia. If someone wanted to kill him, they would have had an easy enough time.

Inside the envelope, was a single sheet of paper, covered with curling penmanship. It read:

DEAR PAPA,

I hope you find this.

I'm sorry you had to get involved. It would have been better if you hadn't. You once told me to become whoever I wanted, and I've chosen a life for myself that is going to lead to great things. I think we both know what I'm capable of.

You have my research. I don't see any reason to take it back from you. Kylie needs to decide what to do with it. The rest is payroll information on Frontier Arms. I'm sure you understand how dangerous that is.

Stay away from Frontier Arms. We're going to make the

world a better place, Papa. It's going to be amazing, and I'm going to lead them there.

Thompson's city of the future would have been a good place for my vision to thrive, but there will be other opportunities. Liam Thompson wasn't the only wealthy benefactor willing to fund the revolution.

With love,

Isabelle

AJAY STOOD with the paper in his shaking hands for a full minute before folding it and putting it away. He would need to deal with Isabelle at some point because something Liam had said still bothered him. Liam hadn't sent Tenen to search Ajay's house. The big mercenary had always worked with two bosses.

Isabelle had sent the man. She had had Kylie relocated when the mercenaries turned against CCS in the mine. It was Isabelle whose information Silas had stolen when he found out about Maja and located Ajay's home. In her effort to keep her sister safe, she had endangered her even more.

The girl was pretending to be much older than she was, and with her abilities, she could convince almost anyone of it.

But she was over her head, and she would clearly need help soon. Ajay wondered how he could ever hope to provide that help. How dangerous would Isabelle become? Ajay didn't know the answers, but he knew he would need to figure it out.

The second thing that had changed in their home was in the backyard. Ajay saw telltale footprints through the heavy snow, softened at the edges by the intervening drifting. When he made his way out through the bitter wind to the shed, he found no corpses at all.

Somehow, the missing body didn't make him feel better.

———

KYLIE WAS LATE. After a Sunday of watching shows with Austin, she'd slept in Monday morning. Ajay watched her stuff papers into her backpack, slip on her fidget, and scramble for her coat.

The doorbell rang.

Ajay forced his sore bones up from the comfortable chair—he had to work to forget that a few days ago it had had a body in it, but he still needed a comfortable place to sit, so there it is. He opened the door.

Austin stood on the bottom step with a grin on his face. "Can Kylie walk to school?"

Ajay nodded. When he turned, Kylie was there and ready to go. He held up a hand to stop her.

"What?" she asked, her voice bristling with annoyance.

"Are you going to hack into the school's system?"

Her expression clouded over.

"You don't need perfect grades," Ajay said. "But I want them to be *your* grades."

Kylie drew a long breath, then said, "But—"

"There are some cases where the clever solution doesn't work. Sometimes only the truth will do."

She scrunched up her face. "Fine."

"Good." Ajay held out the white envelope to her. There was a bulge in the middle. "You should have this," he said. "It's a letter from your sister."

Her jaw dropped, but she recovered quickly. "Thanks," she whispered. She opened the envelope and peered at the bulge. It was the data chip that Silas had brought. "Is this—"

"Yours. You decide what to do with the info on it." Ajay swallowed, even though his throat was suddenly parched. "And it's a lot more than just details about your biomodifications. It contains a full roster for Frontier Arms, complete with paid informants. Big stuff. Dangerous."

She raised her eyebrows.

"I trust you, Kylie," he said. "I trust you with all of it."

Austin had a very serious expression on his face when Kylie stepped outside. "Should we work on our papers tonight?"

"What are you going to say about Thompson's speech?" Kylie gathered up her backpack.

Austin licked his lips, then said, "I'll probably say that he was one of millions of people who cared about our environment and tried to fix it over the years. The only difference was that he figured out how to take people's money for it."

Kylie scrunched up her face thinking about this, then nodded. "Yeah, that sounds about right." Together, they disappeared out into the cold outdoors.

Ajay went back to his comfy chair and brought up his holographic display. On it was a list Olexie had sent him of the world's most powerful people. The richest, the most politically influential, and the most dangerous corporations. In one list.

It wouldn't be sunshine and roses digging up info on the members of that list, but Ajay vowed that he wouldn't trust Olexie's judgment on any of them. He would do his own research and come to his own conclusions about who on the list abused their power. Who on the list deserved the kind of correction that only the world's best hacker could provide. It wouldn't be easy, but it might be important.

Maybe he could make the world a better place.

The television played its news cycle over and over. The nation mourned the loss of Liam Thompson, who had finally succumbed to the great equalizer named cancer. He had been a hero environmentalist, and his legacy would be the many locations on Earth that he had saved from impending doom. Around the world, people would be safe in their homes because he cared enough to help them. It was all lies, of course, but Ajay didn't care about any of it. What a person did to make the world better mattered more than what people thought about it.

Garrison rested his head on Ajay's leg, his warm jowls still slobbery after an extra-large breakfast. Ajay rubbed behind his dog's ears. "I know, big guy," he said. "You did a good job holding down the fort."

Ajay selected the first name on the list and started to dig.

I was a little conflicted when I decided to make the main antagonist of this story an environmentalist. On the one hand, the environment is important to me, especially in places like the BWCA where a pristine wilderness is constantly threatened by factors of profit and greed. Mining efforts are constantly attempting to whittle away at the edges of the land and get at the precious resources within. Climate change threatens everything.

On the other hand, I really do believe that climate solutions that drive profit are the ones that will really move the needle. Liam is a villainous representation of that, but, really, a climate initiative that creates jobs and drives profit is the one that anyone can get behind. Those solutions exist, and I have hope that they can succeed.

But, everywhere that there is profit, there is opportunity for exploitation and abuse. There are plenty of examples of industries where someone comes up with an idea to improve everything, exploits it for money, and then, oops, makes everything actually worse, sorry. Whether it's how we form social connections, how we explore space, or how we summon taxis, great ideas don't mean great solutions.

That doesn't mean we should stop innovating. It just means we should probably pay attention to the actual results of innovation and be wary of hype.

While I was finishing this book, Minnesota had a 60F day in the middle of December and I had to debate whether or not I wanted to change the dates that Grandfather Ghost takes place. In theory, ice should form on the lakes up north, but who knows how climate change is going to affect that. In the future of these novels, some mitigation has helped fix the problems we're seeing today, but that doesn't mean everything will be back to historical averages. Maybe things will swing the other way. Maybe not.

I want to thank my family for their support while I was writing this book. They're always here giving me inspiration and the energy to see it through. I also want to thank my editor Dave Pasquantonio. His work helped me resolve this into a novel I'm really proud of. I also want to thank SFWA and my supporters on Patreon. The support of great writer and great fans make everything I do so much easier.

-Anthony W. Eichenlaub

Old Code

Grandfather Anonymous

Grandfather Ghost

Grandfather Guardian

Colony of Edge

Of a Strange World Made

Upon Another Edge Broken

On a Forsaken Land Found

From a Barren Seed Grown

Above a Distant Sky Seen

Metal and Men

Justice in an Age of Metal and Men

Peace in an Age of Metal and Men

Honor in an Age of Metal and Men